First Black Line Edition,
Crooked Cat Books 2018

Discover us online:
www.crookedcatbooks.com

Join us on facebook:
www.facebook.com/crookedcatbooks

*Tweet a photo of yourself holding
this book to @crookedcatbooks
and something nice will happen.*

Written in loving memory of Mary Wilson
who I wish could read this novel.

# Acknowledgements

This story has been written for my dad, who has always believed in me and encouraged my writing. Dan, my lovely husband who has provided tea and confidence. Baby Victoria, who kept trying to take my laptop, and sister Dayna for all her helpful advice and laughter.

Special thanks to all the MMU class of 2013 that workshopped this novel and especially my tutor Catherine Wilcox.

Thank you to my wonderful publishers, Laurence and Steph Patterson at Crooked Cat Books, for publishing this story.

Finally thank you to David Robinson, Jacqui Doran, Kate Bendelow and Teresa Whaley for all your knowledge, help and advice during the editing process of this novel.

## About the Author

J.V. Baptie graduated from Manchester Metropolitan University in 2017 with an MA in Creative Writing. When not writing, she is also an actress and has appeared in a variety of children's shows and stage plays. You can find out more about her at **jvbaptie.com** and on Twitter **@jvbaptie**

# The Forgotten

# Prologue

*She was swimming in the sea. The tide was against her; the waves splashed off her face. Salty water filled her nostrils and mouth. She struggled to keep her head above water. Tried to swim, gasping for air. Thrashing and kicking. The water filled her lungs as she sank further. 'Help me. Help me. Please.' She tried to scream... but nothing.*

*A burst of energy. She thrashed again. Fighting with every muscle in her body. She started to move. Lights rippled in the water above. She surfaced, panting. A hand grabbed her head and pushed her back down.*

# Chapter One

## Edinburgh, 1977

She shouldn't have come. She should have just ignored his phone call but there was something in his tone of voice. Now, she stood at the conservatory door at the back of Ted's smart town house on Douglas Crescent in the West End of Edinburgh.

'My father died like this, you know.' Ted looked up at her, his blue eyes bloodshot and shiny. 'Everything keeps going wrong.' He drained the rest of his whisky. 'How can I possibly have so much and yet have nothing?' His black hair clumped to his forehead and his white shirt was wet at the shoulders.

She could see the pink of his skin underneath.

'Ted, you need to stop doing this. Your poor dad died from alcohol, so why do you need to drink all the time? This isn't how to grieve.' Helen slumped down in the wicker chair opposite him then slid the decanter beyond his reach. Sleet fell in angry lines from the sky and rattled off the conservatory roof, drowning out her words. 'I can't keep doing this.'

The glass doors were open and a puddle of water had formed on the Victorian terrazzo floor tiles. Muddy boot prints trailed from the doorway to Ted's chair.

'What happened to your lip? It looks like someone gave you a smack. I thought things were getting better.'

He flinched as he touched the cut on his top lip. 'Relax, WPC Carter. You're off the clock.' Ted made a noise halfway between a snort and a burp. He leaned back in the chair and looked her up and down. 'Don't get me started on

5

you—'

'It's Sergeant. Now, go on, how much did you lose this time, then?' Helen pointed a finger at him. 'Come on.'

'Not much. 300—'

'That's so much money. I can't believe you would just throw it away like that. What were you thinking?' Helen shook her head and looked away. 'Your inheritance won't last long if you carry on like this.'

He shrugged theatrically. 'It doesn't matter. I don't need money and you just spend all your time at work, so what's the point?'

She curled her lip and looked him up and down. 'Don't you dare start with that again, or I'll just walk straight out that door. You know, I've just been given the biggest opportunity to progress. You should be happy for me.' Helen got up with the decanter. 'Just don't do anything stupid, Ted.' He tried to protest, but she batted his hand away. 'I'll get you some coffee.' She shook her head. 'You need to sober up. How can you expect me to move in here with you when you behave like this?'

'All you care about is that job anyway.'

'That's really not fair. What's wrong with me having a career and some ambition? And I've already told you before I'm not living with another alcoholic.'

'Even when you're behind on your bills?'

'I manage,' she replied.

'You're just letting everyone down. Nobody wanted you to join the police but you only ever do what you want.'

'You're such a horrible drunk.' Tears stung her eyes. *If I was doing what I wanted I wouldn't be here with you.*

The kettle wasn't in its usual spot on the Aga. All of yesterday's dirty dishes still sat in the sink. A smashed teacup was scattered on the floor along with a cracked photo frame of Ted and his parents. Helen swept up the teacup, salvaged the picture and put it in the drawer. There was some water in the teasmade so she boiled that instead.

'For goodness' sake,' she muttered.

The holiday brochures to Brazil and Hawaii that had

caused their last argument were back on the windowsill, even though she'd slung them in the bin. Picking up the top one, she looked at the happy couple on the front cover posing on a golden beach somewhere in matching swimwear, arm in arm with snorkels in their hands like they had just climbed out of the turquoise sea behind them. Her throat began to tighten at the thought of being underwater, gasping for breath. Fear and panic constricted her throat even more as she sucked in a sharp breath.

She grabbed the pile of brochures and stuffed them back into the bottom of the bin where they couldn't mock her any more.

On the kitchen island, a brown wooden box caught her attention. She couldn't believe it. A watercolour palette, pencils and charcoal set. The things she had wanted from the art shop they visited in Glasgow. All the stuff she couldn't afford but refused to let him buy. She picked the watercolour palette up; hidden underneath that was a black leather-bound art book. She rubbed a hand over it. "Helen" was engraved in gold along the front of it. A police siren wailed in the distance, and she wondered which of her colleagues would be on shift.

# Chapter Two

A bus packed with schoolchildren pulled out in front of her. Helen trickled to a stop and rolled her window down a crack, taking in the icy November air. She liked this time of the year – the dark nights and mornings, the frost, and the good reasons to stay at home. Rows of pebble-dashed houses lined both sides of the street, some with black bags of rubbish parked outside their gates. A milk float had stopped on the corner, and the milkman was now heading up the garden path of number 5. She tapped on her steering wheel. She was late and Craven wouldn't like that. The bus driver stuck out a chubby thumb as a sign of thanks from his side cab.

Slipping the Mini into second gear, she took the left turn down a one-way road. This estate reminded Helen of one of the first cases she worked on – a string of petty robberies. A boy of about eighteen who'd do odd jobs for the elderly then rob them blind. She shook her head, remembering chasing him up the street with her little truncheon that was half the size of the ones given to her male colleagues, all the while, trying not to trip over her regulation handbag that kept slipping off her shoulder.

The fire-wrecked building was easy to spot. She watched the shaky single-decker bus accelerate away until it was a speck in the distance. The Boardwalk Picture House had been a triumph of 1930s Art Deco architecture. A once whitewashed building now grey with soot. All its windows either boarded up with chipboard or smashed over the years by kids, and what they couldn't smash they'd sprayed graffiti on. She parked behind a Rover. Her stomach churned. She pulled the key out of the ignition and slipped it into her tan leather jacket pocket. Helen screwed her eyes shut and wished that time would stop. *'In for two and out for two.'* She practised her breathing exercise and forced her eyes open. Analysing herself in the rear-view mirror, she noticed her brown eyes looked red and blotchy. Last night at Ted's she'd only managed a couple of hours sleep before she was needed on shift.

A sharp knock at the passenger-side window pulled her back to reality. She let out a gasp and turned to see the broad features of Detective Inspector Jack Craven peering in. Her cheeks burned.

'Are you coming in or what?' Craven walked around to the driver's side just as she was getting out and opened the door wide for her. He smelt sickly sweet – a combination of Old Spice and smoke.

'I did wonder when you planned on showing up.'

'Sorry, Inspector.'

'I thought you lot were meant to be good at telling the time,' Craven replied. He was wearing a brown tailored suit that had gone shiny at the cuffs. His yellow shirt was creased at the collar and looked slept in. The top two buttons were open, showing a sprinkling of salt and pepper chest hair. He didn't seem to be that much older than her – a really handsome guy but his face had been hardened by drink. Even his eyes had a tinge of yellow in them.

He made a show of looking her up and down and smiled. 'Well, at least we will have something nice to look at in the department. I didn't mean to give you a fright, pet. Caught you doing your lipstick, eh?' He looked braced to say something else but instead closed the car door and began to walk towards the crowd.

'Thank you for this opportunity, sir.'

'You don't need to thank me.' He slipped her a sideways glance. 'Well, you're not going to be here long anyway.'

'I'm planning to be,' Helen stated.

'Nah,' he snorted. 'You'll get married, have bairns and that'll be the end o' it.'

*Not this again.* 'You don't know that.' She followed him. 'I haven't heard of this place before.'

9

'Aye, is that so?' He looked her up and down again. 'Suppose you would've been too young.' Craven snorted. 'We've got a nice little one for your first job in CID.'

'So I've been told.'

'He was found by a couple of wee laddies this morning.' Craven flicked his roll-up end into a puddle and fished in his pocket for his tobacco pouch. 'You've no' got any real fags, have you?'

'I don't smoke—'

'Of course, you wouldnae.'

She shook her head. 'Sorry.'

Craven's smile faded. 'I better get you up to speed on what we've got here. It's not pretty in there. There's no wallet or I.D. on him and the body's practically still warm.'

'Could it have been a robbery? Then maybe someone dumped him in an old building? Expecting him not to be found so quickly?'

'Doubtful.' Craven shrugged then lit his roll-up. 'If you want to rob somebody, you don't torture them slowly to death. Looks like the boy suffered and someone wanted him to.'

Helen's stomach knotted at the thought and she changed the subject. 'How long's this place been shut down?' Her leather handbag thumped against her thigh. She wished she had left it in the car.

'Around five years. I think. The door was open and it looks like tramps have been dossing inside.' He stopped in his tracks and turned to face her. 'Right, let's get this out in the open before we get in there. I've no' had a WPC on one of my cases like this before.'

'I'm not.'

'Not what?'

'A WPC. It's Sergeant Carter actually, Inspector, and I can assure you that—'

'Carter… I know, Detective Inspector Richard Carter.' He shook his head. 'I know exactly who you are and I know exactly why you are here.' He pointed his finger at her. 'I don't run things like he did.' He shook his head. 'This is just a box-ticking exercise for the DCI. It makes him look modern and that'll help him get his promotion.'

Helen bit down on her lip to stop her saying what she wanted to, that she wasn't there because of her father. Even though that's what they all said, it was easy to dismiss her that way. To ignore and belittle her. She thought back to when she told her dad she wanted to be in the police and he burst out laughing, then when he realised she was serious, he couldn't hide the look of disappointment on his face and his comments about her waste of an education and how he wanted a better life for her.

'I'm not here because of my dad, sir,' she finally replied. 'If I was, life would have been a lot easier for me. I'm here to fill your staff shortage and I'll do my best for however long I'm needed.'

'Aye, right.'

'No, it is right.' She took a step closer to him and frowned, not wanting to anger her senior officer further.

He gave her a wry smile. 'Christ, I was only having a laugh, pet. Women dealing with cases like this in the CID, what's bloody next?'

'Me being here is nothing to do with anyone else. And this is not my first murder either.' Her heart pounded. 'So will we just get in there or do you want to stand out here chatting all day?' Surprising herself at her own outburst.

Craven nodded.

They walked towards the cinema. One of the double doors was open. A constable stood guard. Helen looked up at the crumbling archway. A faded sign for bingo was still on the board outside.

As they approached, the constable lifted the cordon. Other officers were moving the last of the onlookers back. A couple of teenage boys on bikes scrambled to see inside the door. She nodded in thanks. He gave her a broad smile and wink in return.

Craven shrugged. 'I just wouldn't mind but I've lost decent cops…'

Helen sighed. 'Listen, I understand that, Inspector. I'm

not trying to step on anyone's toes here.' She rubbed a hand through her brown hair which had been cut just above the nape of her neck; something that the hairdresser had called a 'wedge'. She wasn't quite used to the length of it but hoped at least that it made her look more professional.

He took one last puff as they made their way up the steps to the cinema. The metal in the heels of his boots clattered off the concrete steps. 'Oh, aye, there was one other thing; we found – a car key for a Ford.'

Helen had a quick glance around the street; a mixture of council houses and flats on both sides, plus a couple of wee shops at the top of the road. There were a few cars parked on both sides of the road, but the only Ford was one of the police cars.

He smiled. 'I did the same thing myself, love.'

She could see Detective Chief Inspector Whyte at the entrance, talking to an officer.

'A couple of boys found the body. They're being interviewed,' Craven added.

'Has Jack got you up to speed?' DCI Whyte fixed his blue eyes on her, then made a point of looking at his wristwatch. The DCI was well-known for loitering at a crime scene in case there was a media presence, so that he could get his name in the papers. His nickname in the canteen was the "failed celebrity". He was a year from retirement and she didn't know anyone who wouldn't be glad to see him go.

'Yes, he has. We're—' Whyte waved his hand to tell her to stop.

There was something about his manner that made her uneasy. The rumours hadn't helped with that. There was a faint whiff of whisky but she couldn't quite tell who it was coming from.

'Aye, well,' Craven sighed, 'we're still waiting on the lab coats to finish up in there.' He exhaled the smoke slowly through his nostrils. The sweet smell tickled at the back of her throat, which felt almost soothing.

'That wee old wifey believes she can help with enquiries.

Bobby Keaton is having a chat with her now.' DCI Whyte nodded towards an elderly woman whose Yorkshire terrier was scrambling to get back to the scene. She was talking to the uniformed sergeant, a skeletal man in his late forties.

'She looks like...' Whyte scratched his stubbly chin. 'Oh, what's her name... you know that old bird with the curlers fae the telly?'

'Ena Sharples, off *Coronation Street*?' Helen said.

'You know what, sweetheart? That's been annoying me for the past half hour. I knew you would have known that one.' He chuckled and took a few steps forward, so that he was only a few feet away from Craven.

Whyte shielded his eyes from the morning sun as he looked up at the decaying building. Some of the white frontage had fallen away leaving exposed brick. 'I used to come here years ago with the wife, until that fire a few years back. This place has been left to rot since.'

'Why didn't it reopen after the fire?' Helen asked. The steps were flecked with the white and black droppings of the pigeons nesting on the ledge above them.

'No idea, love. A lot of nice places went like that in the sixties, all replaced by modern rubbish and high-rise flats,' Whyte said as he buttoned up his coat. 'Right, Jack. I'll see you back at the station later.' He slapped Craven on the back. 'You've got it all in hand here.'

Craven tensed his shoulders. 'Aye, *sir.*'

After Whyte left, Helen followed Craven through the double doors into a wide foyer. She stopped at the entrance. They had left one of the double doors bolted shut and the other was just wide enough for them to squeeze through. The door showed no sign of damage that would suggest that anyone had broken in.

'Do you think this is the way they got in?'

Craven shrugged. 'It looks like it. The wee laddies said the door was open so they walked in. I cannae see any sign of damage. PC Rafferty used to be a locksmith; he's coming down to take a look at it.'

The rancid stench of dust, damp and smoke overpowered

13

her momentarily. The interior, for the most part, was surprisingly undamaged, considering it had been left derelict for nearly five years. The shelves behind the counter were still stacked with faded sweets and Kia-Ora squash cups. It was as though someone had just closed up one day and decided not to come back. They passed a soot-stained gold staircase and followed the red carpet through another set of double doors to the main cinema, kicking ash up as they walked.

'Inspector, we've found something we need you to see.' A young constable approached from behind and pointed up the staircase. Sweat glistened on his acne-cratered cheeks. He looked about seventeen and his uniform hung on him like he had borrowed it from his dad. 'It's over here.'

Craven nodded and took the staircase two steps at a time. Helen followed him. The officer ushered them towards a wall behind a doorway. He flinched like he was expecting a punch. Not once did he make eye contact with her.

'I'm not sure what it is,' the officer said, motioning to the wall. His Morningside accent told her he was most likely one of the new university graduates. She had tried to drop any hint of a private school accent herself.

'Right.' Craven rubbed his hands together. 'What do we have here then?' He pressed his face inches from the wall. It was one of the few areas in the corridor untouched by fire. 'Well, it looks like blood. Has the pathologist looked at it?'

'No, sir, we just found it.'

The artwork was a smudged rust-coloured finger painting – someone had drawn a circle which had two lines inside it. An inverted V shape. She tilted her head to the left as if studying a painting. The thick circle looked like it had been drawn with a fat finger or thumb, the inner markings were thinner – possibly a smaller finger or maybe even second person.

The uniformed officer stood behind them. Helen could see from the corner of her eye that he had already taken a few steps back. He was about to turn and walk away but stopped when Craven spoke.

14

'Get forensics up here now, and the photographers,' Craven told him.

The constable nodded meekly and scurried away.

'That boy will never make CID,' Craven snorted, shook his head and rubbed his chest. 'I've got a bit of heartburn,' he said, grimacing.

Helen didn't disagree. She turned her attention back to the wall. 'It's possible these markings are not blood but actually tomato sauce, oil or even paint.'

Craven shrugged.

Helen stepped back and slipped her hands into her pockets. In her experience the problem with bloodstains is that they can look like other things, it all depends on the age and the conditions the stain was exposed to. This part of the hall felt cool and dry. In an area like this a stain could last decades if not more. 'The inner markings are considerably thinner that the outer shape. Two different people could've done this.'

'Aye, hard to tell.'

'It could even be animal blood.' Helen paused for thought. 'It might have nothing to do with our victim. If vagrants have been in here, maybe an addict did this?'

'Aye.' Craven took a step back so he was in the same position as Helen. His arm brushed her shoulder. She stepped away.

'It might be some kind of cult symbol?' she added.

'Or a clock face maybe.' He pointed towards the inner markings. 'It could be a clock at twenty-five past seven, or twenty-five to five? Right,' he tapped her on the shoulder. 'I'll be back in a minute.'

# Chapter Three

Craven had to get outside and catch his breath. He stood in the alley behind the cinema and crunched on a couple of Rennies. The alley was a rough gravel path that led out to a grassy verge. He looked back at the fire door; this would have been a perfect way for someone to make their escape without being seen. At the other end of the field, soul-less modern concrete tower blocks loomed over the houses. He dragged the last puff out of his dog-end. Exhaling the smoke through his nose slowly, he flicked it to the ground, and stepped on it with his boot.

Uniform were busy searching the surrounding areas and had the unenviable job of picking through the rusted pishy steel bins.

'Fancy meeting you here.' Mike Savoy, local journalist and pain in the arse, gave a weary smile. He rubbed a hand through his thinning shoulder-length brown hair, more out of awkwardness than anything else. He had a tweed jacket on that looked new, and his pink tie hung loosely around his cheap white shirt.

Craven sneered. He was tempted to go back inside but decided to stand his ground.

'What have you got in there then?' Savoy said, cheerily.

'You could try saying that with a little less glee,' Craven shook his head. 'You've put on some weight.'

Savoy puffed out his cheeks. 'How's Liz, Inspector Craven?'

'Nothing to do with you. Looking to do a follow up, are ye? Or are you just interested in what ah have here?'

Savoy waved his pudgy hand in surrender. 'Ah'm just wondering, Jack, no story there.' He let out a chuckle and took a couple of steps closer so that he was only a few feet away from Craven.

'Do I look like an idiot? That's supposed to be funny, was it? What are you wanting, Mike, the shirt off my back as well?' Craven felt the hairs on the back of his neck bristle. The angry wind ripped through him and he felt the spittle of morning rain on his cheek.

'I was just doing my job.' Savoy took a packet of Player's Number Six from his pocket and offered one to Craven, who shook his head. Savoy shrugged and slipped them back into his pocket.

Craven rubbed his chin. 'What was our little deal – I'll scratch your back and you stab mine?'

'C'mon, Jack.' He held his hands up in mock surrender. 'It was nothing personal.'

'Right, you better get off this crime scene before I personally drag you off it, you got that?' He started for the fire door.

'You know that I can help here, right? People out here talk to me, not the police,' Savoy called out. 'Just give me something good to run with, Jack.'

Craven waved his hand dismissively and walked back into the cinema, slamming the door behind him.

# Chapter Four

'PC Macleod, you were first on the scene then?' Helen had her notebook out and her pencil braced against the page. She repeated the question. The officer nodded and mumbled, 'Aye.' through gritted teeth.

Macleod took a step back when he noticed his sergeant, Bobby Keaton, approaching. Macleod raised his voice. 'It wis all by the book. Called me in, we secured the scene and I called in the big boys.' He rubbed his bloodshot eyes. 'Ah'm ready fur ma bed. I've just come straight off the night shift.'

She nodded her understanding; it wasn't uncommon to go a full twenty-four hours straight on the job. She had done that before.

'Anyway, I heard aboot what happened to you. Ah'm surprised you're back so soon,' the officer said.

Before she could respond. Keaton pointed a finger at her.

'Before you ask, sweetheart, I've already got all my officers out knocking on doors and searching the scene. This is no' my first day on the job and I was in CID.'

It was common knowledge around the station that he'd been in CID and a drinking problem had put him back into uniform. It was another common story she had heard a million times over. The bags that sagged under his yellowed eyes told her it was something he had not overcome.

'Leave it to the experts, old Bobby Keaton kens what he's doing,' Craven said as he came in through the fire exit. 'Bloody press are out there already. Someone is calling them. I cannae go to the toilet without Savoy trying to stand over ma shoulder. I cannae stand that idiot.'

Keaton shrugged. 'I had expected him early to be honest with you, pal. He's a shark, always around when there's blood.' He took a gulp from his cup.

'Aye, never a quiet moment in CID, Bobby, you'll ken that better than anyone else. Shite pay, while all the rot you arrest make their way to the bloody Costa del Sol. I cannae even afford a decent packet of fags.' Craven shrugged.

Keaton nodded towards Helen. 'CID short-staffed at the moment?'

'Aye, you ken the same old story; good coppers are dropping like flies or being bumped back into uniform,' Craven replied.

Helen rolled her eyes, deciding that she'd heard enough. She pulled one of the battered doors open. 'Well, if we're done sharing our heartfelt stories can we get back to work?'

Keaton pointed to the door. 'He's doon there slumped in one of the seats.' He slipped a glance at Craven to get approval, then added to Helen, 'You might be better staying out here, love. MacLeod can talk you through the crime scene a wee bit more.' He waved his radio towards the entrance. 'Or go outside.'

'Thanks for the advice but it's not my first day on the job either. Shall we?'

'Ladies first.' Craven motioned to the door. 'Catch you back at the station, Bobby.'

'Aye.' Keaton nodded.

'And, Bobby, stick a few more officers on the door, will you? Keep them sightseers at bay. We'll be fighting them back with sticks shortly.'

Keaton smiled. 'Morbid bastards, the lot of them.'

\*\*\*

The wet metallic smell of blood and death hit her. It brought her back to her training days when all new recruits were brought down to the morgue and forced to face it. They had to make sure you could handle it. You learned to put on a brave face or you wouldn't be in the job for long. It wasn't the sight of death that would cause you to bring up everything you had eaten, it was the smell. It never left you no matter how hard you tried to scrub it away afterwards. Helen swallowed, she could taste it on her tongue.

Helen stood behind the top row of red velvet chairs. Even from up here the smell of rotten eggs mixed with old cigarette smoke hung in the air. She looked down onto the screen. The body was still in situ, in a chair in the front row. Only the top of his head was visible. The click of the photographer's camera capturing the scene echoed throughout the theatre. The room was illuminated by the thick white glow of the lamps, making the scene look oddly inviting, like a stage play rather than an actual crime scene.

Craven tapped her on the shoulder as he stomped past her. He thumped down a couple of steps then stopped. 'You staying up there all day, or what?' He waved a hand in the air, signalling for her to follow.

'Lead the way.'

As they approached, the smell of shit and piss stung her nostrils. Helen put her jacket sleeve to her nose and sniffed the Charlie perfume she had sprayed on it earlier. It was quite common for the bowels to empty after death. One of the reasons for wearing gloves when examining a body.

The pathologist was in the process of closing his scuffed leather medical case. He looked up from it, his wide-rim spectacles slipping down the bridge of his nose. She'd been to his training class on blood analysis. Alex Winston... was that his name?

'Good morning, Inspector Craven,' he chuckled. 'Oh, they like to keep us both busy, don't they?' Winston's leathery face didn't look that different a colour from the grey corpse in front of them. He spoke with a Sandhurst accent that sounded fake to Helen's ear.

'Always,' Craven rubbed his hands together. 'Right, gie me all the answers then.'

Detective Constable Terry McKinley, another new young recruit into CID, was standing as far away from the scene as he could, a white handkerchief covering his mouth. Two other constables were brushing for fingerprints. They looked more relaxed than everyone else in the room put together. PCs were the ones who were most used to death; they were the ones called out first, nine times out of ten. To them, this was just a normal day on the job.

'Photographers and fingerprints are almost finished in here, sir.' McKinley's voice was muffled through the handkerchief. Craven ripped the fabric from his face, crushed it into a ball and shoved it into the palm of McKinley's hand. His blond fringe flopped in front of his eyes.

'Put that stupid handkerchief away, you look like a bloody fairy.'

'Sorry, Inspector.' McKinley crumpled the fabric into his trouser pocket. His face flushed red and he looked down to the ground.

Craven shook his head. 'The DCI must bloody hate me.' He fixed his eyes on the corpse slumped in the seat then fished in his pocket for his tobacco pouch.

'You know the rules.' Winston shook his head. 'No smoking on my crime scene.'

Craven slipped the packet back in his pocket. 'Nae bother, Alex. How are you keeping anyway? Thought they'd be replacing you.'

Winston gripped the armrest of an empty seat and pulled himself up from his kneeling position; his face went red. Winston looked close to retiring, his stomach spilling over the tight belt that held up his trousers. His bald head reflected the lights above them. He had wispy tufts of grey hair at the sides.

'I could certainly say the same to you, or are your colleagues just getting younger and younger these days?' Winston chuckled. 'Who is this lovely little lady? Aren't you going to introduce me?'

'Helen Carter.' Helen held out her hand.

Winston cupped both hands around hers and maintained eye contact with her. They felt warm and damp.

Craven put his hands on his hips. 'Enough of the pleasantries, what can you tell us?' Winston looked like he was about to say something but Craven carried on. 'I want the short version. Ah'm bloody gasping for a fag.'

She wriggled her hand free. He wiped his hand on his shirt afterwards. He either winked or his eye twitched, Helen wasn't sure.

'Okay, short answer? Your victim died of blunt force trauma to the back of the head,' Winston replied to Craven.

Helen stepped forward past Craven. It was hard to tell the age of the victim but from his fashionable clothing and hairstyle, she would guess he was young, maybe mid-twenties or early thirties. What little she could see of his auburn layered hair was matted with blood. His green velvet shirt was ripped open and torn at the collar. A purple cravat hung loosely around his neck and the sleeves of his shirt had been rolled up. Stab marks peppered both arms and he had been tied to the chair with thick rope tied around his wrists. Judging from the rate of decomposition, he had not been dead long. His eyes were open, the whites of them were pink. It looked like he was staring off into the distance.

'Rigor is present,' Winston added as if he knew what she was thinking.

Helen nodded. The victim's face was swollen and bruised. The left side of his head had caved in. His lip was cut, and fingers bent at awkward angles. One of his shoes was off and had been placed beside his foot. They were polished, no scuff marks. His fingernails were clean and filed short to the finger. Her stomach tightened. She had never seen anything like this before.

'This lady's not squeamish, is she?' Winston tapped her on the arm. She ignored the comment and avoided his gaze. She thought back to what she had learned in American FBI forensics journals about blood splatter and how to tell if a body was moved after death or if the person died where they were found.

'The victim wasn't dumped here by the looks of things,' Helen finally said.

Winston arched an eyebrow. 'That's right.' He pointed a chubby finger at the pool of blood on the floor. 'If the victim was dumped as you so bluntly put it, my dear, the blood would trail from the stairs instead.'

'What about the murder weapon?' Helen interjected.

'Murder weapons,' Winston corrected her.

'Well, there's not been anything found in the bins outside or in the building, uniform are still out looking. From his clothes, I would say he was on his way to work. You dinnae wear a smart suit and tie for no reason,' Craven replied.

'Or he was on a night out,' Helen countered.

'Maybe.' Winston took a step back from the victim as if examining an artist's canvas. 'There's a lot to go through with this one. The circular fracture would suggest—'

'A hammer or a pipe,' Helen interrupted.

'I don't think I have met an officer so eager to earn their stripes.'

'What are those marks on his neck?' Helen asked, undeterred.

'It looks like he was strangled with some of the rope. See how his face is swollen and his eyes have haemorrhaged? You can see some of the braid pattern here.' He pointed to the neck.

'What about the marks up his arm?' Craven rubbed his stubble.

Winston shrugged. 'The wounds up his arm are not defensive. Those happened after he was tied to the chair. I think they're from a diamond head screwdriver, based on the patterns.'

Helen exhaled a breath. 'There's a lot of rage there.'

'Aye,' Craven replied.

Winston added, 'Obviously the *crème de la crème* is the head injury. That's what did it.'

'Whoever did this must have brought the murder weapon with them. He had no wallet on him? No jewellery?' Helen pointed to the victim's finger. 'There are indentation marks around his right index finger. It looks like he was wearing a ring.'

Winston nodded.

'Just get this body to the morgue and get me the results

ASAP,' Craven interjected.

'There's one other thing.' Winston handed Helen a card wrapped in an evidence bag. 'That was found under the chair.'

Helen turned it over in her hand; a business card for George Stanley, Private Investigator. She saw writing in smudged pencil on the back: "8pm Thursday."

'George Stanley?' Craven snatched the card from her hand.

'Does that name mean something to you?'

'Aye, it does.'

# Chapter Five

George Stanley fantasised about the different ways he would make Clint pay. He had been standing at a bus stop on the Royal Mile, watching the shop the past half hour. Tourists, clutching cheap tartan scarfs and tins of shortbread, poured in and out of the tat traps that spiralled all the way up to Edinburgh Castle.

Plenty of locals still lived in the old flats around them – although you could hardly tell. A group of Yanks brushed past him with leather wallets bulging out from the back of their jeans and Polaroid cameras draped around their necks. They pointed and snapped the cameras at a tobacconist shop. *Why the fuck do you want a picture of that? No' got one of them at hame, no?* Even the murky clouds that hung heavy in the sky didn't seem to deter anyone. A lone piper in front of Parliament Square blasted out *Cock of the North* to a group of overexcited women. *Sad bastards.*

A rag and bone man's horse and cart clattered past. Stanley took a sharp drag of his cigarette and instantly regretted it upon smelling the horse's stench of dust and manure. He crossed the road behind the 21 bus and flicked his cigarette into the gutter.

He followed a couple of teenage girls as they headed into the department store. The skinny blonde one wore a red knitted cardigan with big pockets. She had a beaded bag draped over her shoulder. The other girl had her hair scraped back tightly into a pony tail and had a tight leather mini skirt on. She gripped two brown paper carrier bags tightly. The girls stopped abruptly to let him past, the blonde grinning at him. He smiled back, knowing exactly what they were up to. Any other time he might have stopped them, but today he just kept walking. The girls were heading over to the hats and handbags section.

Wendell Clint did not bother to look up from the folder he was flicking through. Stanley slapped his case file onto the glass counter and began to empty its contents, making a point of thumping each individual sheet of paper out onto the glass. The noise caused Clint to lose grip of his till receipts and they fell down onto the red carpet.

'What are you doing here?'

Stanley ignored his question.

Clint pressed his brow-lined glasses back up. He stared at Stanley. Stanley flicked the invoice onto the counter. He watched the spark of recognition flare in Clint's eyes, and he then watched as the plastic smile spread on his thin features.

'What is the meaning of this? I thought I'd told that bloody secretary of yours that—'

'Oh, I heard what you told the secretary, every single fucking word, but now I'm going to talk you through the invoices. See, I don't think you quite understand the meaning of paying for services rendered, Mr Clint, so I'll explain it to you.'

Clint shook his head but Stanley pressed further, squashing the urge that he had of wiping that ever-expanding smirk off Clint's face. He would have done that in the old days. Make him pay one way or the other. Smash his teeth straight down that little throat.

'Now you see this wee bit here?' Stanley tapped the invoice and Clint stepped backwards.

'That's my hotel bill for following your wife about as requested by you. Hotels in Glasgow, Aberdeen and then in Newcastle. Three nights in five-star accommodations, that's thirty pounds. Then there's my petrol. Then there's film.' Stanley whipped the black and white photographs of Clint's wife and boyfriend from the back of the file and flicked them like Frisbees. They landed on the floor behind the counter. 'Not to mention my hourly rate of ten pounds, all of which you had agreed to.'

Clint lowered his voice, checking no other customers

were within earshot and lowered his voice He stepped forward placing both hands on the counter so that he was now inches from Stanley's face. 'I am divorcing my wife and I suggest that you try your bullyboy tactics on her to get your money back.' He hissed. 'She has spent enough of my money on her boyfriends.' Clint flicked another glance around the store before continuing. 'No one will get as much as a tanner out of me for her.'

Stanley dug his nails into his palm. 'If that's the way you want to play it, Clint.' He gathered up what was left of the case file and slipped it back into his pocket.

'Is that a threat?'

'Aye.' Stanley's eyes narrowed.

They both heard the door open. Relief washed over Clint's face.

'I'm going to get ma money from you; however you want to play it.' Stanley turned and walked away. A bead of sweat trickled down his neck.

'Mr Stanley, I suggest if you do want your money you speak to my solicitor. If you can afford the legal cost, that is?'

Stanley kept on walking. He could see the two girls were also on their way out of the store; both with crocodile skin handbags on each shoulder. The blonde one was also wearing a white wet-look mac now over her cardigan. He quickened his pace, so that he was now behind the girls and, for the first time in the day, he felt a smile tug his lips and he made an over-exaggerated motion to open the door.

'Let me get that for you, ladies.' He pulled the door open wide. They both looked at each other then back at Stanley before the blonde one nodded her thanks. They made a quick getaway left, down towards Waverley Bridge. He caught them glancing over their shoulders a few times before they disappeared out of sight.

# Chapter Six

'This should be left to uniform, Helen. Craven told us to go back to the station.' McKinley followed her, his hands in his pockets. The wind whipped his unruly hair back and forth. He looked about twenty and still had some acne scarring around his chin.

'Well, feel free to head back to the station anytime. I'm not going stop you.' Helen turned to McKinley but kept a steady pace down the road, sighing once they were out of sight of the police vans. 'I just want to try the key in a few cars. We'll be a couple of minutes at most.'

He waved his hands in the air. 'This is a long shot, you know. We're wasting our time. Jack will go ballistic once we get back to the station.'

'Don't tell me you're scared of Jack, are you?'

'Scared of Jack? You're new, Helen, so I'll let that slide. You're not even close to seeing the real him yet.'

Helen glanced at him but he immediately looked away. She wanted to ask what he meant by that but decided she would leave it. Jack had a reputation for being rough. She had learned that much in the canteen, but then didn't everyone have a story? They liked to talk down the station. She had learned not to put stock in it until she had seen for herself. She decided it was best to change the subject.

'What made you join traffic?'

'I've always liked cars as far back as I remember – or obsessed as my mum would say. That's why I joined the police force. What's better than getting to drive flash cars and chase bad guys?'

Helen chuckled. 'You make out like we're in *The Sweeney*.'

'Got to find excitement somewhere, I suppose.'

'Sure, so tell me then – why are you not in traffic anymore?'

McKinley bit his lip and looked up at the sky. 'I always wanted to be in CID but I didn't expect to see someone's head caved in like that just a few weeks into the job.' He shrugged and quickened his pace.

'Traffic's just as bad,' Helen replied.

'How many cars are you going to try that key in?' He stopped a couple of feet behind her.

So far she had tested the key in five different Fords with no luck. 'There's plenty of side streets he could have parked in.' Helen slipped the keys back into her jacket pocket. Her radio thumped against her hip with each step. She turned left onto Moncrieff Drive. So far, the only Ford she had seen was the Anglia that had just ripped past them.

Concrete flats with steel balconies took up both sides of the street, broken up only by a patch of grass with a makeshift sign stating "No ball games" and a newsagent that looked closed. Two teenage girls on a balcony on the top floor sat hunched over a magazine, with the Bay City Rollers' *Saturday* spilling out of the wireless beside them.

McKinley broke into a jog and caught up with her. He had his hands in the pockets of his cords as his pale orange shirt whipped back and forth with the wind.

Helen slipped him a glance. 'Did you forget your jacket this morning, Constable?'

'Aye, it's draped over ma chair back in that bloody station. Jack had me out of there like my arse was on fire this morning.' He flicked a strand of hair out of his eyes.

From what Helen had been told about McKinley, he had joined the police a young recruit at eighteen before he managed to make the jump to CID as an aide, after the amalgamation of the forces. A promising young prospect, if not still a little green. She looked up at his six-foot frame. He offered a faint smile before his gaze fell down to the pavement.

'Will you be coming to the pub later on?

'With all this on?' Helen put her hands into her pockets

29

for warmth.

'There's always going to be something on.'

'Well, maybe,' she muttered.

'You'll enjoy it once you get there, Helen. You know, our victim could have walked to the cinema?'

'Yes, I suppose he could have done.' She scanned the street; a Vauxhall, Mini and Rover. The sound of a dog barking in one of the flats echoed in the street, which then silenced as they walked behind a Leyland van.

'It's also possible he got dropped off at the pictures, or he could have got a taxi... a bus....'

'We don't know anything yet.' Helen shrugged, then looking left she crossed the road, stopping abruptly. She tapped McKinley on the arm at the sight of a rusty canary-yellow Ford Escort. It was parked in front of a semi, the front wheel mounted on the pavement. She fished in her pockets for the keys.

'Well, I thought I was past all this but the licence plate looks fine and no obvious sign of tampering.' He waved a gangly hand in the direction of the car.

'How do you know?' Helen slotted the key into the cylinder. Rust bubbled along the side panel and underside of the bonnet.

'Well, they look secure and I can't see any marks on the plate to show that someone has tried to change any of the letters.' He had both hands in his trouser pockets now and he stamped on the spot a few times, trying to put some warmth back into his body.

Anticipation surged through Helen like electricity. She turned the key one click to the left and the lock gave way without a fight. She bit her lip, her hand braced on the rust-speckled silver door handle. She could see the reflection of McKinley in the driver's side window. He had stopped stamping his feet and was now watching her. She pulled on the driver's side door, her relief visible when it opened with a groan.

McKinley chuckled. 'Now that we've found the car, it seems like you dinnae know what to do next.' McKinley walked past her and around to the bonnet. He had a small silver pocket torch and a mirror in his hand. Helen looked him up and down. He blushed and waved the torch at her.

'Old habits die hard I guess. Now, are you going to help me here? Or am I going to do it all myself?'

'It's just... well, it's not the type of vehicle that I would have imagined him to drive – you know from the clothes.'

He angled his slender frame to look under the car, pausing briefly before he spoke. 'Sometimes you can never tell.' McKinley placed his hand on the bumper to stand up, the suspension creaking under his weight. 'A car's just a thing to get you from A to B.' He brushed some dirt from his cords. 'Personally, I've never seen the point in getting one anyway, well, not on my salary, and I was always driving when I was in traffic.' He moved around to the passenger's side rubbing his hands along the metal work as he did so. 'It's no' a bad little runner though.'

Helen shrugged and opened the door wide. She checked under the seat and pedals, then the side panel, uncovering a few discarded fag packets and betting slips which she threw onto the back seat. The Escort smelt of sweat, stale lager and cigarettes. She tried to avoid breathing through her nose and left the door open as wide as possible. A schoolboy shot past on a BMX, narrowly missing clipping her and the door by inches. Sitting in the driver's seat, she pulled the door shut. It was then her eyes fell down to the seat and its adjustment. The back of the chair had been adjusted so that it was poker straight. The chair, Helen guessed, was about two feet from the pedals, while the passenger seat was pushed as far back as it would go, touching the back seat.

'Pass me them then.' McKinley clicked his fingers and then held his hand out.

'Pass what?' Helen said, slipping her hand into the driver's door cubby. Empty apart from some cigarette ash which she brushed off her fingers.

He rolled his eyes. 'The keys. I'll go check inside the boot.'

Helen chucked them and McKinley caught them with one

hand before making his way around the back. She heard the clunk of the boot opening.

'Anything, Terry?'

McKinley didn't respond. Helen twisted her body to see around to the back.

'Nope,' he eventually said. 'Just a few bits of rubbish, fag packets mostly and a couple of empty cans of Tartan.' She heard the cans clunk together as McKinley pushed them aside.

She slipped down the sun visor and struck gold.

Insurance papers wedged into a slit cut into the shade.

'Terry, how tall would you say our victim was?'

'Emm,' McKinley scratched his mop of hair. 'I would say my height or maybe just a wee bit taller. Well, he liked his fags… eh cigarettes, I mean.' McKinley nodded to the crumpled packets and leaned in through the passenger's side door. He crinkled his forehead. 'That seat would fit somebody about your height, Helen. Maybe someone dropped him off?'

Helen pulled out her radio. 'We better get photographers and fingerprints.'

# Chapter Seven

George Stanley should have known. The van had been parked opposite, this morning. Why didn't he take a look at the driver? There wasn't normally anyone parked there. None of the neighbours had a van and it hadn't been there when he'd got home. He hadn't paid much attention until it pulled out behind him and closed in on him at the traffic lights. The front bumper inches from his rear. A medium-sized van with an almost car-like square front. It looked like one of those Leyland Sherpas. Adrenaline shot through him.

Since the traffic lights, it had been behind him all the way down every random side street and sharp turning. Stanley pressed on the brake. If he could get some distance he might be able to see who was following him.

Whoever it was stuck close to his bumper as they emerged onto the Corstorphine Road, the Leyland going through a red light to keep up with him. Amateur. When Stanley pulled into the right-hand lane, a few seconds later, it did so too. He gripped the steering wheel so tightly his hands ached.

He slammed on the brake. The battered blue Leyland swerved, nearly rear-ending him. The van pulled back and he finally got a look at the driver, but not a good one. Male and big. Stanley could see the figure dwarfed the window but the headlights were dazzling. Stanley blinked spots away from his eyes.

The traffic was starting to build as he passed Edinburgh Zoo. He turned right down Pinkhill and flicked his cigarette butt out of the window. His heart thumped in his ears.

The Sherpa van turned with him. The number plate was cracked but he got some of it.

This was going to be it. 'I'm no' in the fucking mood.'

Stanley stopped the car on a wide stretch of road. The hairs on the back of his neck stood on end. The steering wheel shook. Engine roaring, the van sped past leaving a trail of black exhaust smoke behind and disappeared out of sight.

When he was sure the van wasn't going to double back, he reached a shaky hand into the glove box, taking out a half-bottle of whisky and bottle of old aspirin, downing a couple. The whisky stung his throat and moved down into his stomach. He had one last swig to get rid of the shakes. Sighing, he put the bottle back in the glove box and started the engine.

A few minutes later he was parking up at the office, an old boarding house style building. It had been converted into offices sometime in the late sixties. The floor above theirs had been empty since last Christmas, although the golden lettering for Chartered Accountants was still emblazoned along each darkened window. The name of the firm had been scratched off. He looked around the street for the van just in case. Bile rose in his throat and his heart was still pounding.

He parked beside an Austin Princess that had seen better days and slipped the piece of paper with the licence plate number into his pocket. From this angle, he had a perfect view of the office. The rusted bars on the back window made it look like a prison. He stopped short of the front door and could hear the faint sound of music. That meant that Maud was in this morning.

'Maud?' She was flicking through the steel filing cabinet. 'Maud!' Stanley shouted over the disco record that was crackling away on the turntable. He lifted the needle and the record stopped with an abrupt scratch. Maud screamed and dropped a file onto the floor, the pages scattering out all over the lino. She tucked a stray strand of hair behind her ear. and bent down to pick them up.

'Sorry.' He made a move to pick them up for her.

She let him and eyed him warily as she smoothed a crease from her azure blue dress.

'Why on Earth do you have to play that music so loud?'

He bundled the pages back in.

She shrugged her shoulders. 'It helps take my mind off things.'

'I'm sorry.' He made a half attempt at touching her arm.

'Don't.' Maud stepped back out of his reach. 'It's fine.' She took the folder from him. 'Anyway, I wasn't expecting you in the office. I always put on music when I'm alone. Makes the time go quicker.'

'Suppose so…'

'Well, from the look on your face, you didn't get the money then?' Maud peered over her half-moon glasses. 'I told you it was a waste of time.' She put her hands on her hips. The frilly sleeves of her dress made her arms look double their size. 'You should have heard the way he spoke to me on the telephone, by the way. The bloody nerve! Stupid schoolgirl, he called me. I hope his stinking shop goes bust or burns to the ground.'

Stanley made a clicking sound with his tongue. 'Well, you never know, you might get your wish. If he doesn't give me ma money.'

Her face softened. 'I'm sorry, George. I don't mean…' She paused searching for the right words.

'No, it was a waste of time. He knows we don't have the money to take him to court. But if he thinks I'm going to forget about that money.' He shook his head. 'I'm no' finished with him. I'll get what I'm owed.' Stanley poured himself a mug of coffee from the tea tray on top of the cabinets. The sugar bowl was empty. He took a gulp then grimaced.

'Sorry, haven't boiled the kettle yet, that's yesterday's.'

'Could you no' have told me that before?' He placed the mug on his desk.

'I forgot. I've been distracted, dealing with all this.' She motioned towards her desk. 'There's at least a week's work here and the final demand for the telephone bill's come in this morning.' She moved around to her desk and picked up a note. 'There's a woman that wants to talk about a case. I was going to go. It's a matrimonial one.' She looked up at the clock. 'It shouldn't take long.'

'Are you going to the hospital tonight?'

She nodded, blinking hard. Her bright blue eyes were shiny.

Stanley perched on the edge of his desk. 'Chuck me the case and I'll sort it. Matrimonial is my favourite,' he said, the hint of sarcasm creeping into his voice.

'I have time before visiting hours.'

Stanley smiled and shook his head. 'Don't be silly, give it here and do me a favour will you?'

'What?'

'Just go and put that kettle on.'

# Chapter Eight

This didn't look good. George Stanley had the address in Cousland marked on his a-z. It had taken him an hour of wrong turns and farm roads to get here. He was now driving along a road no bigger than an alleyway with brick walls on both sides. The house was just at the bottom of the road and he was able to drive straight up to it. The iron gate that would have kept away unwanted guests lay rotting in rusty pools of rainwater.

The cottage had an adjoining outhouse. The windows were smashed, and the timber around them had rotted. The house was empty and it looked as though it had been like that for a long time. Taking out a Mayfair, he placed it to his lips and lit it, taking in a deep tarry drag. If someone was in the house, they would have heard him drive up. He got out of the car. Slates that had fallen from the roof crunched underfoot. The front door was ajar and a candle flickered in the upstairs room window.

'Hello?' He stubbed out the cigarette on the oak-panelled door and stepped inside. The smell of wet rot hit him as he stood in the hallway. He couldn't make out much except for four closed doors and the distant echo of nesting birds in the roof. Squeaks and frenzied scurrying came from a room next to him. He looked back outside to his car and started towards it. A crash from upstairs stopped him.

'Hello...?' He stepped forward. The floorboards groaned under his weight.

Silence.

Stanley headed upstairs towards the noise. Flickering light leaked from under the door. He placed a hand on the doorknob. He couldn't hear anything in the room.

He twisted the knob round slowly. The door creaked as

he pushed it open. He swallowed hard. The air felt dry and the dying smell of tobacco smoke swirled around him. The candle that he had seen from outside glimmered faintly on the windowsill. There were two more candles down on the floor, and an open toolbox. A solitary chair sat in the middle of the room.

It happened fast. A smash from behind. A crack of something solid against his skull. His vision blurred. Stanley threw an elbow backwards. It hit something hard – someone's face. The assailant grabbed his arm. A screwdriver came towards his abdomen. Stanley managed to grab it and twist it. A man gasped behind him. The screwdriver dropped to the floor. Another smash to Stanley's head. A ping echoed in his skull. Stars engulfed his vision. He collapsed. Footsteps moved away. Darkness.

# Chapter Nine

Helen drove them both back to the station. They had driven most of the way without speaking mainly listening to the radio. Helen decided to be the one to start the conversation and chatted about family, friends and lack of weekend plans. ABBA's *The Name of the Game* blasted out of some station they had tuned into. Helen turned left. Her stomach grumbled. She couldn't remember the last time she had eaten anything and she had to drive round the car park to find a place to park, finally reversing into a tight space in between two unmarked pool cars before wrenching up the handbrake.

McKinley made a quick escape to the newsagent for some cigarettes, newspapers and chocolate. Helen opted to head straight inside, hoping that the canteen would still be open. She fished in her bag for coins; if it wasn't open at least she had enough money to raid the vending machine for a couple of sweets and a packet of crisps.

Fettes Police Station was a five-story modern flat-roofed concrete square that acted as the headquarters for Lothian and Borders. This ugly lump was purpose-built a few years ago, after the amalgamation of Edinburgh City Police into Lothian and Borders. CID was on the third floor, and on a sunny day, she could see right out to Arthur's Seat. Directly across the road was the high school where she had spent many afternoons presenting the road safety campaign to a load of spotty-faced, bored teenagers.

As she pushed open the glass door to the station, a funny smell hit her. She couldn't quite put her finger on it but it was in all of the rooms – a mixture of bleach and tobacco smoke. A smell that over time, she hoped she would become accustomed to.

A row of red plastic chairs were bolted to the walls in the waiting area; though they were empty at the moment it would be a different story on Saturday night. Curled posters telling people to "clunk click every trip" or to watch their valuables had been slapped on nearly every free space on the wall. The Staff Sergeant looked up at her then back down to his reports. She headed through the double doors and down the stairs towards the canteen.

The breakfast rush was over. Now it was the lunch menu and there was never much to choose from. It was Friday, and Fridays meant gammon and pineapple rings, stewing under heat lamps. They would probably sit there all day. To the left of them, a metal pan full of thick white chips, then another pan full of peas soaking in water. Pausing briefly, Helen moved along to the sandwich counter; she grabbed the most decent-looking packet of canteen-standard cheese sandwiches from the shelf. She would wash them down with a quick coffee and pot of yoghurt.

The canteen very much felt like high school all over again with an established hierarchy. Awkwardness she would go out her way to avoid. For many of the cops though, coming down to the canteen would be the only time they got a cooked meal.

Her stomach rumbled and she took a bite of her sandwich as she made her way out of the canteen. The sandwich was soggy from the tomatoes, and the cheese resembled orange plastic and tasted like it. She chewed on it as she made her way back up the three flights of stairs to the CID suite.

DC Smith popped his head around the door with an air of exasperation. 'The DCI wants us all through next door for a briefing.'

Helen shoved the remnants of her sandwich in the bin and stood up, wiping the crumbs from her blouse. She felt for her notebook – it was already in her pocket. DC Randall muttered something under his breath and was the first out the room, a few other officers quickly behind him. As she got to the door, it slammed shut with a thud inches from her face and she was left alone in the CID suite. *What the hell is wrong with me?* Conversation and laughter leaked through from next door. She looked back at her desk; she could keep going through the reports. *No.* She opened the door. *This will pass.* She couldn't let them win.

Most of the officers in CID assigned to the picture house case were already in the room. Thankfully, Whyte wasn't and she was surprised to see that McKinley was still missing. Craven looked over a few times as he took a drag on his roll-up. He had a manila folder in front of him and he brushed away the ash that had collected on top of it.

She took an empty seat next to another sergeant with whom she had chatted to in the pub a couple of times before. He nodded his hello then went back to his conversation about football. Helen looked down at her notebook and re-read what she had written earlier. Tiring of that, she took in a deep breath of the smoky air. It calmed her nerves – that was now becoming a habit.

The briefing room was a cramped windowless space with a large circular table and film projector at the front. Plastic chairs had been stacked up against every available gap the wall. The board still had papers and photographs pinned up from another crime, a spate of house burglaries. None she had worked on.

The station still had that new feeling with furniture and boxes stacked up in places. A few of the rooms were still shut off and were in the process of being painted.

DCI Whyte entered the room and the sea of voices died away in an instant. A few of the younger constables looked down at their notepads. Whyte had a half bottle of North Port in his hand. He held it up. 'This wee beauty gets opened when this case gets closed.' He thumped it down onto the table. The audience cheered with approval. He loosened his tie and smiled.

Whyte was wearing an expensive-looking suit but his shirt had a damp coffee stain at the bottom. He held up his hand for silence.

'Right lads, got your listening caps on?' He mopped a bead of sweat from his brow before he continued. Under the strip light, Helen could see the spider veins that spread across his cheeks. 'Uniform so far hasn't picked up anything from the surrounding houses.' Whyte shakily flicked through a couple of pages in his notebook.

'Right, DC Bell and Randall.'

Helen followed his gaze. She'd be surprised if he actually knew any of their first names. 'I want you to double back, speak to these people. Friday morning at school time? Someone saw something. They're just no' talking to us. If you still struggle take Carter with you.' He waved a hand in her direction. 'She'll be good at all the touchy-feely stuff.'

'Aye, sir,' they both said in unison.

Helen bit down on her lip hard then rubbed her tongue over the indentations. Most of the officers in the room had children waiting for them at home. Yet she was meant to be the touchy-feely one.

Bell then muttered something inaudible under his breath and scribbled onto a piece of paper. Bell's trousers were up to his waist and his shirt too tight. The buttons down it appeared to be struggling to contain his muscular frame. He looked like he had just walked straight off the set of *The Incredible Hulk* and had the same black spiky hair as the character of the title too.

Craven stood up before speaking. 'DCI, we're still waiting on forensics to come back to us with formal identification and so far we've not recovered the murder weapon.'

'It's very strange.' Helen added. 'We need to think about why he was he killed like that.'

Randall laughed. 'I dunno darling. This is not an episode of Miss Marple. You should be thinking about who killed him.'

Craven pursed his lips as though he were about to say something but he refrained.

'Right,' Helen took a deep breath to steady herself before continuing. 'If we want to find the killer then it's the question we need to ask.' She looked around the table. 'Our victim was tortured to death slowly. The murder was messy but they tidied up after themselves. There's no murder weapon. There's not a lot of blood and it's all confined to the chair where he died.'

'What's your point?' Craven looked bored.

'I've made a profile of—'

Randall spoke over her. 'The symbol on the wall also might be a message to us.' He had the marking drawn on his notebook in front of him. 'Mind you, I've no' seen anything like this before in all my twenty-five years.' He traced the shape with his pencil.

'This was planned. I think our attacker or attackers know the victim and he wasn't just picked out at random,' Helen replied.

'I agree,' Craven stated. 'He'd have to know the person to walk into an old picture house like that.'

'I think we're also looking for someone local to the area.' In her experience, this kind of murderer felt comfortable killing close to home. She thought back to the FBI profiling she had studied at university. 'The frenzied attack could be an indication of a schizophrenic, possibly.' She pushed the thoughts from her mind. 'The Ford Escort driver's seat was adjusted for someone smaller than our victim.'

DCI Whyte looked confused.

Craven explained. 'I asked Helen to go and look for a Ford car in the area of the picture house to see if we could find one that would fit the key recovered at the scene.' He looked around the room. 'The key fitted an Escort and I've asked McKinley to check the PNC.'

'There were insurance papers in the car also, sir,' Helen said to Craven.

'Great, Jack,' Whyte replied. 'Carter, I want you to gather a list of everyone who worked at the pictures and get that to Jack ASAP then he can commence the interviews.'

The door opened and a pink-cheeked McKinley popped his head round.

'Are you going to come in or what?' Craven sighed.

'Sorry,' McKinley mumbled. 'I've run the car through

the PNC. It's not been reported stolen.' He looked as though he had jogged the three flights of stairs up to the incident room and was still struggling to catch his breath. He held out the paper. 'The registered owner is a George Parson, sir. I have the address for him here.' McKinley looked back down at the piece of paper he was clutching, 'He owns a bed and breakfast. His age and body type are a rough fit for our victim.'

Craven snatched the paper. 'I'll speak to him before I speak to George Stanley.'

'Last but not least,' Whyte added. 'I'll catch you all at the pub the night for old Jack the lad's birthday. He'll be paying.'

Craven looked around the room laughing. 'Aye, that'll be bloody right.'

That would be the day seeing him pay for anything without a Green Shield Stamp book in his hand. He even had a tin on his desk that people put their unwanted stamps into, not forgetting the one he had going in the pool for her leaving date.

\*\*\*

Some of the sniggering as she walked up the corridor should have given it away. The office was sweltering, every window had been cracked open. Fans sat humming on the corner of most of the desks but all they seemed to do was circulate the warm, smoky air.

Randall, one of the biggest culprits, had a fag dangling precariously from his lips while he battered a typewriter. A bead of sweat dripped from his temple.

Helen noticed her desk straight away. She was going to bite, then thought better of it. Stacks of papers and files had been dropped onto it and piled on top of the things that she was working on. Infuriatingly, the field police manual given to her by her father was somewhere underneath all that rubbish. She could have punched Craven; just walked up and stuck one right on him. He wouldn't have expected that.

Helen fished through the pile for her Dad's book. She thought back to the conversation she'd had with her father when she told him that she wanted to join the police. The look of disappointment on his face was still fresh in her mind. He had tried to hide it but he was never very good at that. He never said much about it afterwards and helped her with her training before his accident. It was a look she used to see all too often, now it was too late to make him proud of her.

She draped her jacket over her chair and pushed the papers back so that she had enough room to put her handbag on her desk. Stacked up behind her typewriter was an old calendar of nude women and yellowing copies of page 3 of *The Sun.* She grabbed them and threw them into the wastepaper basket. If the others thought that this would bother her, or even worse that she would be sorting out his filing, they were mistaken.

She sat down in her chair and opened her desk drawer. He must have emptied the entire canteen's supply of Marathon bars. She bit her lip while pulling a half-eaten one out and dropping it into the wastepaper basket; it landed with a thump. She then grabbed a handful of empty wrappers; there must have been about a hundred of them, crumpled and sticky. Some were so old that the wrappers had faded.

'For a woman, you're no' very tidy, are you?' Craven said taking a bite out of a Marathon bar. He was enjoying this. He put his mug down on her desk. 'Black, two sugars, sweetheart.'

'Sir, I'm gathering the address of everyone who worked at the picture house.' She sat back in her chair. 'I also had some files from the main index here of known criminals fitting our victim's descriptions.' She let out an exasperated sigh. 'Well, somewhere under this pile.'

'When I tell someone in this station to do something, they get it bloody done, and you being a woman makes no difference.' Craven shook his head and went back through to his office, leaving his cup behind.

The Inspector's office was a glass partition to the side of the main CID suite with mahogany-coloured frames and door. Most days the blinds would be drawn but today they were pulled up. There weren't many other officers in the office. Most were out on door-to-door enquiries.

Sally, a bottle-blonde typist from the floor below, was perched on the corner of the oak-stained desk. Craven had left the door open. A gold-framed photo of his wife and two children sat on his desk. It seemed to face out into the office rather than at him. Sally sat cross-legged, flicking her hair in his direction. They were having a good joke about something Helen couldn't hear. As far as Helen was aware, Sally was Terry McKinley's girlfriend and he even helped her get the job downstairs.

Helen could feel Craven's stare. He gave an exaggerated laugh, then patted Sally on the knee. Helen shook her head as she headed for the kettle – it was already boiled. She topped up the coffee already in the cup with hot water. She put the mug on his desk.

Helen just got back to her own desk as the phone rang.

'Is Jack there?' It was a woman's voice.

'He's in his office. Who is this?'

'Liz.' She cleared her throat. 'I'm a friend of Jack's.'

Helen looked over to Craven. He appeared to be deep in conversation with Sally. 'He's very busy with one of the typists. They've been in his office for quite a while. Do you want me to—?'

'No, no,' Liz bristled. 'I'll speak to him later.'

Helen hung up the phone and started to tidy her desk. She felt a twinge in her stomach when Craven emerged from his office a couple of minutes later.

'Right' Craven slipped on his jacket. 'Carter, you're with me.'

# Chapter Ten

'This looks alright doesn't it?' Craven said as he parked in front of Parson's Bed and Breakfast, a detached Edwardian house with a conservatory on the side.

'Suppose so,' Helen mustered, as she unclipped her seatbelt. The sign outside the door boasted that the hotel was within short reach of Princes Street. Colour TV, lounge, H&C in all bedrooms, central heating, and all under the personal supervision of Mr and Mrs Jim Parson.

Craven nodded to the sign and lit his roll-up. 'Not fancy a wee night here, then?'

Helen ignored him.

Another sign propped up in the front window said, "No Vacancies".

Helen's stomach gave a rumble. It had been hours since the sandwich from the canteen. She swallowed hard; her throat was dry and a headache swirled behind her eyes. Craven must have heard her stomach because he looked at her.

'Once this is over we'll get something to eat.'

Helen nodded. She rubbed her temples, trying to ease the headache. 'That's a good idea,' she said, eventually.

'Aye.' He nodded and opened his car door. 'Best to get this over with quick then.'

The aroma of fish and chips wafted in from the restaurant. Various scenic watercolours of Edinburgh lined the hallway on both sides. They had to walk past the restaurant to get to the reception. Smart, she thought. Helen tried to avoid looking at the menu. The special of the day was cod and chips with mushy peas. Pudding was strawberry trifle. She could really go for some of that with lots of cream. A teenage girl with pinned blonde hair looked up and offered a big smile as they approached.

'Are you both here for the evening meal?' She moved around from behind the desk and picked up two menus.

'Unfortunately, no.' Craven presented his warrant card. 'I'm Inspector Craven and this is Sergeant Carter. We are looking to speak to Mrs Parson. Is she around?'

The girl stopped and stared at them. She gripped the menus and looked them both up and down. 'And why do you want to speak to my mum?'

'We just need to have a quiet word with her. Can you go and get her?' Craven walked past the girl and looked in the reception cubby then shook his head at Helen.

Helen smiled. 'We think she may be able to help us with our enquiries.'

The girl nodded but didn't say anything. She took a step back, then shouted, 'Mum!' Getting no response, she sighed. 'She's probably watching the telly.' The girl started down the hall. 'Follow me.' They went through to an outhouse building.

'That lassie is a teenager, I thought Jim Parson was in his thirties?' Craven whispered to Helen.

Helen shrugged, checking that the girl hadn't heard him.

'Mum.' She knocked on the door. The girl waited a few seconds then opened it.

'This is our flat, really,' she said, as they followed her through. The smell in this part of the building was different. Coffee, and it was colder in here too.

A jazz record crackled on the turntable. Helen slipped a glance at Craven. A small smile tugged the corners of his mouth.

Mrs Parson was sitting cross-legged on a green and orange floral print armchair in front of the window. She was reading a book under an ornate Victorian-looking lamp. The woman, in her late fifties looked up from her book, her lips pursed. She had shoulder-length wavy silver hair, pinned back from her face with a golden hair comb and was wearing a lacy blouse and pink scarf that matched her lipstick. Helen thought she would have been very pretty in her younger years.

'Mum, these two police officers are here to see you.'

'Police?' She stood and flipped the needle up on the record player. Mrs Parson crossed her skinny arms and did not sit back down. 'It's about bloody time!'

Craven motioned to the three-seater sofa opposite. 'You don't mind if we sit here do you, love?' He sat down.

'Please, Mrs Parson, take a seat,' Helen said.

'I take it you've found it then?'

'Found what?' Helen asked.

'For goodness' sake.' An exasperated sigh escaped her. 'The car?'

Helen looked at Craven.

'Take a seat, Mrs Parson.' Craven waited until she had sat down before continuing. He took out his notebook and read from it. 'Aye, we want to ask you about a car. Does your husband own a Ford Escort, Index Mark EXY 77B?'

'Yes, we got it a couple of years back. I'm not sure why you're asking this all now though?'

Craven looked at the girl. 'Perhaps you should go back to reception.'

'Julie, go back out front and cover the desk.' Mrs Parson waved towards the door, her gaze not leaving Craven's. The girl padded out of the room without a word.

Helen took a deep breath before speaking again, not quite sure of the right words to use. 'I'm very sorry to inform you that we found a deceased male in the early hours of this morning and your husband's car keys were in his pocket. The car was found very close to the scene.'

She removed her glasses. 'I don't understand. Someone took the car then died? That's horrible.' She shook her head. 'I've always said that car was a death trap.' Helen thought she could see the hint of sadness in the woman's blue eyes.

'The person we've found is the same age as your husband.'

'My husband? No, he's in the kitchen.'

'In the kitchen?' Helen looked at Craven.

She called for her husband, 'Jim! ' By the third attempt, she looked livid.

The door opened and a man with a receding hairline in his early thirties poked his head round. 'Yes, love?'

Craven made a face to Helen.

'Ah, for God's sake, Jim! I've been shouting on you.'

'Sorry, darling.' His eyes opened wide when he saw Helen and Craven on the sofa. He hobbled into the room. The chef's outfit he was wearing hung awkwardly around his neck.

'Mr Parson, we need to ask you a few questions about your car,' Helen said.

He looked down at the table. 'Okay, what about my car?'

'They've found a dead body and he had your keys!' Mrs Parson chimed in.

'Dead?' He paused 'How?' He didn't look up. In fact, he looked everywhere else, except at her.

'Did you know your car was missing?' Helen looked over to Mrs Parson. 'Your wife seems to be under the impression that—'

'Yes,' he interrupted. 'I was going to go to the police station this evening to report it stolen.' He looked over to his wife. 'I didn't want to worry you. It was stupid of me, I just…' A bead of sweat ran down his temple.

'I thought you said you called the police,' Mrs Parson sighed.

'I was hoping the car would turn back up.' He looked at his wife. 'I was just so distracted with the wedding.'

'When was it stolen then?' Craven took out his notebook.

'From outside here, on Wednesday night.'

'Now, you say you were hoping it would show back up. Have you got any idea who would take your car?'

'No.' He tilted his head to the left. 'No, I can't think why anyone would steal my car. I mean it's not exactly new.'

'So, you would have had plenty of time to call the police then,' Craven replied.

'I guess so…' Mr Parson rubbed his throat. 'I was going to…'

Helen looked at Craven. He was glaring at Mr Parson.

'Where were you on Thursday night?' Helen asked.

He made a clicking sound with his tongue. 'We were away at a wedding in Newcastle and we didn't get back until first thing this morning.'

'Any witnesses?' Craven turned the page of his notebook.

'Well, everyone at the wedding would have seen us and we stayed over in the wedding hotel afterwards,' Mrs Parson replied and fished in her handbag. 'The hotel reservation is in here, somewhere...' She produced a reservation card and handed it to Helen.

'Thank you.' Helen took the card.

'I'm really sorry, but if that's everything, I need to get back to the kitchen.'

'Now,' Craven smiled. 'As you are going down to the police station to report the car stolen. You can speak to one of my officers about it this afternoon. I'll let them know to expect you. We'll have some more questions for you then.'

\*\*\*

'Safe to say he's hiding something,' Helen said when they were back in the car. 'And we have no idea who our victim is.'

'Aye.' Craven turned the ignition and grinned. 'He must've been at least half her age. Only one reason he'd be interested in an old bird like that.'

'Maybe he loves her. Age doesn't have to mean everything.'

'Aye, your boyfriend's old, isn't he?'

'I wouldn't say he's old. Who told you that?'

'He's a solicitor, isn't he? I heard he had to take time off as he kept coming in stinking of drink.' Craven shrugged. 'Everyone gossips in that station. Do you not want a man your own age, naw?'

'That's none of your business.' Helen bit her lip then changed the subject. 'Parson was panicking. We'll get more from him, asking him questions without the wife.'

'Aye, that's what I was thinking,' Craven said, slipping the car into first. The tyres squealed as they turned onto the street.

He looked at his watch. 'I need to drop something off somewhere. It'll be quick.'

# Chapter Eleven

Did blood have a boiling point? Because he was sure that he had actually felt his boiling inside him. Craven could have murdered someone given half the chance. That was a lie. 'Someone' was too vague; it wasn't just anyone, but Dr Nairn. Dr Milton Nairn, late forties, thinning grey hair, beady dull grey tap-water eyes and a nose big enough to plant a punch on. Yes, that would be nice, to plant a big knockout blow. Craven continued to smile through gritted teeth. The man was skinny, far too skinny. A little vulture who now had his bony claws firmly entrenched in his family.

To be fair, Nairn had let him in without much bother. A few protests of 'We're busy – could you come back tomorrow?' And, 'I can give the gifts to the twins for you.' *Aye, that would be bloody right*, was his response to them all. After a few uneasy minutes at the door, he was eventually let in and led through into the front room. Balloons and paper decorations festooned the walls.

'You can relax, pal. Ah'm only here to enjoy the party,' Craven said to him.

The front room brought back all the memories of when he used to live here. The fireplace, wallpaper, curtains and even the knick-knacks on the mantelpiece. Nothing out of its place and nothing much had changed, since the day he walked out. He could still smell the faint whiff of the lavender candles she insisted on burning everywhere.

Nairn cut into his thoughts. 'Oh, I am relaxed, Jack. You see, I just don't think that Liz… well….'

'You go put your pinny back on and I'll wait here. I'll handle Liz. I did it for five years, remember?'

A group of women he didn't recognise stood by the bay

window clutching wine glasses.

'Alright, ladies?' He waved over at them, a couple of them erupting in smiles. Only one of the women fixed him with an icy stare. He was happy with that.

He hadn't been invited to the birthday party, most likely his ex-wife's idea, but he had turned up anyway. He couldn't give a toss about her, but the twins he would do his best to have some say in. He would be damned if they turned out like her or the little vulture. He slipped a glance towards the doorway. She was probably in the kitchen; he could hear voices from there. He was tempted to go in. She was never there when he was married to her. Nairn continued to make uncomfortable conversation. The children giggled through mouthfuls of sausage rolls on colourful party plates.

'We've been thinking about holidays.'

Craven hated the way the man insisted on making useless conversation. He ignored him but Nairn carried on with it, regardless.

'Skiing, Jack, it's all the rage.'

'What's all the rage?' He looked around the room not making eye contact with Milton.

'Skiing. Skiing is all the rage. It's where I'm taking everyone this year. I suppose that's hard on a policeman's salary? Not much money to really do anything, I suppose.' He bounced on the spot as he spoke and had his hands in his pockets. 'We've been doing a lot of foreign holidays. It's important for health to get the sun, I always say. Good for the wellbeing of the mind, also.'

Craven shrugged, 'Never really had an interest, pal.' He took out a cigarette and placed it to his lips.

'You should try it then, a nice package holiday. You will be able to get a cheap one somewhere. Get you away for a couple of weeks. We're never off an aeroplane, and I'm brown all year now with the sun. I just can't get enough of it.' Nairn motioned his head to the children. 'Emm, Jack we don't like smoking in front of the youngsters.'

Before Craven could answer, a roar of laughter erupted

from the children as the music stopped and a little blonde girl with bunches in her hair opened the parcel. He was behind with the times, and it took him a while to eventually recognise the music. The Bay City Rollers that all the kids seemed to be into these days.

'You should probably try to stop.' Nairn scratched his ear and then pointed to the cigarette. 'I have seen a lot of policemen over the years. I wouldn't exactly say that it's a profession with longevity.'

'I'll think about it. Now, where's Liz then?'

The vulture's face tightened and he made a circle with his mouth. He looked as though he was searching for words when Craven put a hand up in motion to surrender.

'You can go easy. I'm only here to give the wee ones their presents and to wish them a happy birthday.'

'Oh, I don't mean anything by it, Jack. It's just... well, we had thought it best that—'

Craven didn't bother to let him finish. 'I'll go outside for a fag. I take it that's where Liz smokes hers?'

'I'll see you when you are back. Perhaps we can have a small glass of something? If you have time that is. I bet you'll want to head away and get back to whatever you're working on.'

Outside Craven felt his heart race. He drew on his cigarette in sharp drags, finishing one then taking the last from the packet before throwing the empty box into the pond. It landed with a ripple and stayed on the surface. He exhaled the smoke and leaned back against the damp wall. He moved away, then paced down the path. His cigarette had become damp but he liked the smell, it was calming. Soothing.

They had both bought this house, just about ten miles from Edinburgh, ten years ago. One thing led to another and he moved out back to his flat a little under two years later. A Georgian manse building that wasn't quite his style but the one the wife had wanted. He flicked the butt of his cigarette onto the garden path. He had learned the hard way that she always got what she wanted.

He went back inside the house. The birthday party was in the front room and he could hear squeals of laughter at the game of pass the parcel that ensued. Annabel and little Jack were sitting at the top of the table. Both had grown and both had been equally unimpressed to see him. He had the presents for them. A Meccano set for little Jack and a Holly Hobbie doll for Annabel, carefully wrapped by one of the girls from the typing pool down at the station.

Nairn had noticed them right away, and offered him his bony hand. 'What's this?' The corner of his lips twitched into a sneer. 'Shall I give them to the children? They already have a lot maybe we could use these for pass the....'

'Fuck off, Nairn,' Jack whispered with a smile. 'I'll give them to my own bloody children.' The vulture backed off, his hands back in his pockets, as he rocked back and forth on his feet. It seemed an eternity before Liz made an appearance. He wanted another smoke and a drink of something strong. Right now he really didn't care in which order.

Liz came in with a silver platter of sandwiches in one hand and in the other – a tray with a cheese and pineapple hedgehog. She placed the sandwiches on the table. They were perfectly cut into little triangles and she had a paper party hat on her head. She looked older than when he had last seen her. Streaks of grey now apparent in her wavy blonde hair, she wore a pink frilly hippie-looking dress which he was sure he had bought her a few years back.

'Jack, I didn't expect you here.' She glanced around the room as she spoke making sure that none of her had friends noticed. She pulled him aside. 'You should have brought your girlfriend inside instead of leaving here to wait in the car.'

He smirked.

'God, you look terrible. You're starting to look like an old man.'

'Thanks, Liz, and here was me about to pay you a compliment.'

'I saw your car from the kitchen window and I can see

her in the passenger's seat. I did try and call you earlier but you were too busy with some typist.'

'Was I?' Craven snorted. 'C'mon, love. I didn't want to miss giving the twins their birthday presents.'

'Oh, no. Don't 'come on, love' me.' She shrugged and looked down to the ground. 'Well, that's never ever stopped you before. I wouldn't be half-surprised if they didn't even remember who you are.'

'Aye, well, you did you best to make that happen didn't you?'

The little vulture stepped in. 'Listen, Jack, we don't mind you being here at all. We are very happy with you being here actually.'

Craven shook his head. When the music stopped and the game was over, Annabel and Jack ran over, both smiling, their cheeks smeared with ice cream.

'We've been having a great time, Dad!' His son had a sheriff's outfit on and he pointed his plastic gun at Craven then shouted, 'Bang, bang!'

Craven put his hands up in surrender. 'Wow, you got me, son! Did you get this for your birthday?' The boy nodded but didn't say anything.

'Yes, Milton, got it. You love it, don't you?' Liz smiled, all the while giving Craven the filthiest look she could muster.

'He's got us horses too.' Annabel chimed in.

'Horses?' Craven looked away. He patted his son on the head. 'Well, I can see why your mum married him, then.'

'We're in a play on Friday, Dad.'

'A play? Really?'

Both kids looked at their Mum. 'Can Dad come, please?'

Liz shook her head. 'Your dad's busy…'

'No, it's alright, I have that evening off.'

'Are these for us, Dad?'

Craven nodded. Both of them took the parcels and gave him a hug. Liz ushered them away. 'Shall we go and see what Dad has got you?' They both nodded and went back to the table.

Craven left not long after this. Nairn offered a drink and as much as he wanted one he refused. He watched a few more games of pass the parcel and disappeared before the birthday cake, jelly and ice cream.

# Chapter Twelve

The White Cockade – the pub they all used for any after-shift drinking – was on Rose Street, a narrow thoroughfare behind Princes Street which always seemed to be busy with cars and delivery vans. A couple of modern wine bars had appeared on the street since the last time she'd visited.

A battered board on the window, advertising cheap whisky and to "Book your function now before Christmas" was almost too faded to read. Helen pulled up the collar on her duffle coat and watched the breath escape from her mouth like a plume of smoke. She fished in her bag for her pocket mirror – makeup was minimal, no blusher needed as her cheeks were bright red from the Firth of Forth wind that whipped along the street. She rubbed away the mascara that had already begun to collect under her eyes. Condensation crept down the windows and the chalkboard that advertised the specials hung loosely on the wall.

Her heart raced. She took another deep breath and then exhaled slowly.

*Fuck it.* She followed a couple of uniforms she recognised into the pub. Smiling, they held the door open for her. The bar was rammed with people and it reeked of stale lager and cigarette smoke. McKinley was waving at her from a table in the corner. Craven looked her up and down and went back to his drink, draining the remnants of his pint. Helen took the spare seat next to Bob Keaton, who was nursing a full glass of what looked like fresh orange juice. He had an uneaten scotch pie on a paper napkin in front of him.

'Hiya, have you all been here long?' Helen sat down, blood rushing to her cheeks.

'Not long, Helen. You know Sally, right?' McKinley

motioned to Sally and they both nodded to each other. Helen had a quick look around; some of the other officers from CID were playing darts.

'Right, what are you all having?' Craven heaved himself up; narrowly missing the other empty glasses in front of him. He rubbed his hands together. 'Ah'm gonnae get pished the night.'

'Same again, Inspector,' Sally said as she twirled a lock of her blonde hair.

'Helen?'

'Thanks, I'll take a Blue Nun then, Jack.'

'Now…' He pointed at them. 'Before you all start to think ah'm changing my ways, this is the only round ah'm buying.'

Keaton made his excuses and headed to the toilets, taking his drink away with him.

'He's so much nicer with a drink in him, isn't he?' Sally pressed on her lipstick with a napkin then frowned.

'Who is?' Helen asked.

'The Inspector.' Sally pulled out a pocket mirror from her fur-lined handbag and examined her makeup; with a look of approval, she applied another coating of cherry-coloured lipstick then slipped it back into her purse. 'Just come straight from work, did you, Helen? I think that's brave.' She looked to McKinley for approval. 'I couldn't go out without makeup on and a nice dress.' Sally smiled and adjusted her matching low-cut cocktail dress that looked at least a size too small.

'Eh, no actually – but I didn't think a drink in this place warrants anything more than a bit of mascara.' Helen motioned to the sparkly turtleneck top she was wearing. 'I don't wear this on shift though.'

McKinley suppressed a smile.

'I'm only staying for one anyway.'

Sally let out a chuckle and flicked one of her peroxide curls. 'I think I win.' She gave McKinley's arm a squeeze and he blushed.

'Win what?'

'We had a bet on when you would say you were only staying for one.

'Ah,' Helen mustered.

'Nothing bad like, we were just having a laugh.' McKinley shifted awkwardly in his seat. 'I'll not be staying long either. I'm knackered.'

Helen nodded. She noticed Sally slip another glance towards Craven at the bar. When Craven turned towards the table, Sally bit her bottom lip and turned away.

'So, Sally, how long have you two been seeing each other?'

Sally looked at Helen wide-eyed. 'What?'

'You and Terry, I mean.'

'Oh, right…well, about six months,' she replied, crossing her legs.

'I got her the typist's job in CID,' McKinley replied.

Sally took a sip of the pink cocktail she was drinking then spoke. 'I was in London before that. I came back home when money got tight. I knew Terry from school.'

'London? That must have been—'

'Oh it was, I did three years of stage school and I was a dancer also.' Sally leaned forward. 'Ballet. I wanted to be a part of Pan's People.' She shrugged and took another sip of her drink. 'Then it all kind of fell through.' She looked over to Craven and Helen did the same. Craven was wearing a wide-collared orange shirt and skin-tight brown trousers and was freshly shaven.

'I didn't know Pan's People did ballet?'

Sally shrugged her shoulders. 'This is all just temporary though. I'm doing an evening theatre course. I want to be an actress.'

'I did some theatre stuff,' Helen replied, finally finding something to talk about.

'Really? What things?'

'Amateur productions.' Helen thought for a moment. 'The last one I did was *An Inspector Calls*.'

Sally's mouth tightened. 'I'm only into doing acting for a job. You know, like… proper stuff.'

McKinley leaned over towards Helen so he could whisper in her ear. She caught his hot whisky-breath and grimaced.

'Jack did alright for himself, you know.' He tapped her on the arm. 'His wife, or as I should say ex-wife…'

'How much have you had to drink?'

'Only a couple.' He slurred his words. 'He married up in the world you know, but his wife caught on.'

'What are you talking—?'

'Elizabeth Anderson, heard of her?'

Helen watched Craven. He was putting the drinks onto a circular tin tray and cracking a joke with one of the guys at the bar.

'Is that name meant to mean something?'

'Her parents owned a string of shops across Scotland and had made their millions fae it.'

'You mean to tell me that the man who collects Green Shield Stamps like a religion and smokes rollups…' Before she could finish McKinley pulled away as Craven approached.

'I've just been telling Helen I was nearly in Pan's People.' Sally smirked.

'Pan's People's no' what I call dancing, sweetheart.' Craven winked at Helen and put the drinks on the table. He slid the glass towards Sally. Her hand brushed his. He pulled away.

'Thanks.' Sally leaned forward, her dress slipping down her chest. 'I'm really thirsty this evening, Inspector.'

Helen cleared her throat and picked her glass of wine off the tray. Craven drained most of his pint in one go and was avoiding Sally's eye contact. He stared at Helen.

\*\*\*

Helen started the engine. She was meant to head to Ted's but decided to have a drive around town to clear her head. She reached into the dashboard cubby and pulled out a mint. She didn't want Ted to smell the wine – even though she'd only had a couple of mouthfuls. Ted's dad died, suddenly, in his mid-fifties. Ted drinking had gradually got worse since then. Instead of taking a right turn after Dean Bridge, she took a left. The car rattled along the cobbles before she got to some smooth road and drove past the massive brutalist St James shopping centre. It must be one of the ugliest concrete lumps in Edinburgh but the shops were good. Last summer she'd taken her mum for scones and tea in one of the posh hotels before going shopping there.

Helen was about to head towards Ted's house when she saw familiar blue flashing lights near the bottom of Arthur's Seat. She should have carried on but something in the back of her mind told her to stop and have a look. She flicked the radio off and pulled in behind the police car. One of the officers rattled on the window and waved her on. She shook her head, pulled out the warrant card and wound down the window.

He leaned in. 'Sorry, love, thought you were just trying to be nosey.' His nose was running and his cheeks were red from the wind, his breath came out as vapour.

'What have you got here?'

He took his hat off and scratched his mop of brown hair. 'Male found heid down. I didnae know you lot were getting called in.'

She looked up at the ancient brown and green volcano that loomed over Edinburgh.

He pre-empted her question and shook his head. 'It doesnae look like he jumped or fell.'

'I'll take a look.' Helen grabbed her handbag from the passenger's seat and climbed out of the car. 'Where is he?' She wrapped her jacket tightly around herself and slipped on her woolly gloves.

'Just down that verge.' The uniformed officer pointed. 'I can take you down if you want? He was found by a dog walker. It looks like he might have been there all day and maybe the night before, and it wis freezing last night.'

'Thanks, but I'll find my way,' Helen replied and

headed down the gravel path with her hands in her pockets to keep some warmth. The unsteady light from a torch told her it was not far away.

As she approached, another uniformed constable with close-cropped ginger hair looked up and frowned.

She held up her warrant card.

'I didn't expect CID.' He had disposable surgical gloves on and was in the process of examining the body.

He swallowed and looked like he'd eaten something bad. 'He bloody stinks. His clothes are filthy.'

From the state of him he was most likely a vagrant, wearing a ragged, baggy, knitted green jumper and brown trousers. The jumper looked stretched at the cuffs and was made of thin material. She couldn't see a shirt underneath it. Muddy tatty white plimsolls on his feet. No socks.

It was the job of the officer to make sure there were no obvious bruises or injuries that would make his death suspicious and to make sure above all that he was actually dead. Helen thought back to a death only recently when the person still had a faint pulse but was nearly sent to the mortuary.

She didn't envy the miserable-looking officer. His jaw was clenched and he held his hands out away from his own body. His fingers were spread apart like he was going to play piano.

'I was just passing and thought I'd take a look.' Helen crouched down beside the man who was lying on his stomach. Most of his hair was grey and patchy. An old scar trailed the back of his liver-spotted skull. The stench of old body odour and a smell she could only describe as rotting cabbage hit her, the icy wind doing little to sweep it away.

'I'm knee-deep in puddle water and mud, so be careful,' the officer added. He moved the corpse onto its side and a low groan escaped from the jutting mouth.

It was strange the first time she'd heard those noises but it was just the gas trapped in the dead body.

'Thanks.' Helen looked down.

The officer's trouser-ends were soaking and the knees had grass stains. He rolled up a soggy cuff and shook his head.

'Suspicious?' Helen asked.

He sucked in breath. 'Nothing to say so at the moment. It looks like he drowned in the puddle but I can't say for certain. I can't see any sign of trauma either. I'll go with him in the ambulance.'

Drowning was most likely accidental. Helen's heart sped up and her throat tightened. Thoughts of drowning flooded her mind. She looked away from the puddle then pulled out her pocket torch and shone it down on the man. He looked in his late sixties. His cheek bones protruded. Mouth wide-open revealing bare gums. Eyes shut.

'What about I.D.?' Helen stifled a cough. The vagrant's trousers had no pockets. They looked homemade, maybe out of some kind of sack material.

'Nothing on him.'

'How long do you think he's been down here?' Helen looked around; there were a couple of empty cans of Tennent's just a few feet away.

'Not that long. I think we're looking at a day at most, maybe even a few hours but I'm not an expert.'

When she got back to the Mini it had just gone past ten. She slumped into the chair and put her head in her hands. After a while, she decided to drive straight home.

# Chapter Thirteen

When Stanley came around, the bedroom window was open. Rainwater dripped in a rhythm – tap, tap, tap. It sounded soothing until the pain in his skull returned, and he remembered where he was. Pigeons fluttered on the window-ledge outside. The smell of dust and damp hung in the air. Stanley forced himself upright, moving woozily to his feet. He staggered along the corridor and down the stairs where the handrail felt loose as he leant on it. The front door was still ajar, and relief warmed him when he could see his car outside.

'Shit,' Stanley murmured when he saw the state of the car. He had the overwhelming urge to be sick and burped a few times as he staggered out. The cold air felt soothing on his burning cheeks.

He perched on the front wing of his car. He wasn't sure for how long. He regulated his breath to try and slow his racing heart. The brick used on the windscreen had been left on the bonnet.

'Bastards.' Stanley picked it up and hurled it onto the grass verge. 'Bloody bastards!'

He could handle being knocked about easily enough. In his line of work, that came with the territory. A few different scenarios had run through his mind. Maybe he had disturbed a tramp who was dossing, had got scared and ran. The damage to the Victor... now that was personal.

He fished in his pocket for his handkerchief then held it to his head until the bleeding had eased off. He must have hit the corner of his head when he had fallen. Wincing, he touched the gash; a nasty welt had formed above his eye. He peered into the wing mirror. *I'll probably need stitches,* he thought, spitting some blood onto the gravel. He felt his teeth. At least they were intact. *Thank goodness for small mercies.* The back of his skull ached where he had been hit. He couldn't work out what the hell had hit him but that half-brick looked a likely suspect. That was when he noticed it. A necklace with two intertwined hearts was lying on the gravel.

He picked it up with his handkerchief and slipped it into his pocket, making sure not to touch it. The clasp was broken on it like someone had pulled it off.

He opened the driver's side door of the Victor by wrapping his hand in his jacket. He had brushed off most of the glass. Before that, he had spent about half an hour sorting the windscreen so he could drive home, before realising all the tyres had been slashed, and that the blade which had done the damage still protruding from the back left one.

There was a working payphone just a five-minute walk down the road. It stank of piss and the glass panels for the door were smashed, but it still worked. He exhaled deeply then dialled the number. He had managed to call the tow in as a favour from the garage. Blake, the mechanic, had taken one look at his face but had known better than to ask what had happened.

# Chapter Fourteen

Helen groaned. The sharp trill of the telephone pounded through her head. She rubbed the sleep from her eyes. The paperback she'd been reading fell onto the floor with a thump. It took her a couple of seconds to work out what the noise was, or even where it was coming from. She leaned over the sofa and picked up the receiver from the side table, as her foot hit something. 'Damn!' She'd kicked over her tea. She had to stop doing this. She couldn't remember the last time she had actually fallen asleep in her own bed. The Frankie Miller record she'd fallen asleep listening to left the sound of static as it spun on the turntable. She tried to read the clock but her eyes wouldn't focus. What had possessed her to get that Art Deco clock? It had white hands with a white faceplate. It looked nice, but even in broad daylight, she couldn't tell the time from it.

'Hello,' she mustered. Her throat felt tight and dry.

'Helen, it's me…'

She sat up. 'Ted, is everything alright?'

'I'm sorry, it's late. I hope I didn't wake you.'

'No, just dozing – what time is it?' She rubbed the wet patch of tea with her foot. It soaked into her sock.

'I thought you were coming to stay at mine tonight?'

'I was going to.' She rubbed the sleep from her eyes. 'I got caught up with work…'

'I really wanted to see you tonight, sweetheart. My mum was asking about our plans this weekend – she really wants to see you again.' He let out a half-hearted laugh. 'She keeps asking after you.'

'That's very sweet.'

'Do you fancy me taking the car and going for a nice drive afterwards, maybe stay at a really good bed and breakfast?'

'Oh.' She flicked a stray strand of hair from her face. 'I'd really like to but…'

'I won't be drinking. That's all over and done with.'

'It's not that. I'm glad but—'

'I would've phoned you earlier but I just got home. My bloody train was three hours late. British Rail…'

'I have to work.'

'I thought you were off this weekend.'

'I was, but I was at this horrible—'

'Oh God, I hate you having that job. It's so dangerous. You should be using your psychology degree-maybe even open up a practice or something.'

'It's not that bad—'

'No, no, no!' He interrupted her again. 'Not that bad? Only a few months ago some thug nearly broke your arm.'

'I know but… Ted, you wouldn't have met me if I didn't work in the police, remember?'

'Yes,' he sighed. 'I know, but it's different now. I have enough money. You can move into the house with me. You don't need to do this. I know I've been pushing you away but I stopped. I know what I did a few days ago was bad but I *won't* be gambling again.'

'I'm in the middle of a big case. We've all been doing double shifts and I would come down after work, but I don't know what time they will need me until, and they might need me to go in tomorrow.'

He snorted. His voice was more collected now, detached. It was in the same tone that he used to brief his clients.

'I'm so sorry, Ted. There was a murder this morning and another—'

'There's always a case, or there will be a case.' She heard him take a deep breath. 'Look, I'll maybe speak to you later; I've got plans to cancel now and new plans to make. Why don't I come and stay with you?'

She looked around the room. To the peeling wallpaper around the fireplace. To the oak-coloured cladding with the damp stains, and up to the missing poly tile on the ceiling.

'Maybe,' she said finally. Most of her things were still in battered cardboard boxes. The smoke-stained curtains from the last tenant still hung at the windows. 'Ted, I'm really sorry. I'll make it up to you, I promise.'

'I'm going to go. I'll phone you tomorrow.'

The line went dead.

*** 

Helen's mind raced as she climbed the stairs to CID. She thought about the drawing on the wall of the picture house, the battered body and the old man in the park.

'You had a good night, didn't you?' Helen asked a red-eyed McKinley when she arrived at CID. She draped her jacket over her chair. She would talk to Craven about the body in the park when he got in.

'Aye, I stayed at Sally's last night, didn't sleep much.'

'Really.'

'Aye, we were…We were just talking.' McKinley bowed his head and his face reddened.

'You don't need to explain anything to me, Terry, but maybe go and get yourself a cup of coffee.'

'I will shortly.' McKinley rubbed his forehead; he was still in the same crumpled clothes from yesterday. Foam cups and chocolate bar wrappers were scattered about his desk. He pushed them into the wastepaper basket.

'Seriously, you look rough. Go get yourself a cup of coffee and splash your face with some water,' Helen said, sitting down at her desk.

Helen had made her excuses and left early last night left. Terry and Sally hadn't noticed. As much as she tried she just never got the whole "nights out in the pub" mentality of drinking until you dropped, coming into work the next day stinking of fag smoke and smelling like a brewery. She could understand when a case was finished but this one had barely begun.

McKinley stretched his neck as he looked up from his desk. Dark patches of sweat pooled under his armpits.

70

She heard Craven in his office coughing his lungs up. It seemed to be something he did in the morning regularly. The coughing stopped and he appeared in the doorway. Almost as if he had read her mind. Craven laughed. Only it wasn't in amusement.

He shook his head. 'Cannae handle your drink, son. Should have gone to your bed on time wi' a cup of your mum's hot chocolate.' Craven looked around the room like a comedian looking for audience approval. She looked away.

McKinley stiffened in his seat and mumbled. 'Aye, sorry, Inspector.' He stifled a yawn.

Craven slapped his hands on McKinley's desk and leaned in so that he was inches from the man's face. A deer caught in Jack Craven's headlights.

'Have you gone through all the missing person reports?' Craven snapped.

'Yes, there was no one fitting our victim's description.'

'What about a list of everyone who worked in the cinema?' He snatched the paper from McKinley's hand.

McKinley rubbed spittle from his cheek. 'It's been hard. I only got a few of the recent names. A lot of the records were destroyed in the fire,'

Craven flicked the paper back onto the desk and McKinley shook his head meekly.

'So you're telling me that since this morning we still don't even have a wee clue as to who our victim is?' He emphasised the 'wee' with his thumb and index finger and rolled his eyes. 'So someone battered a person to death and not one person saw anything out of the ordinary? Just a typical day, eh?'

'Inspector,' Helen said, 'we're still waiting on his fingerprints coming back. We might know more then.' She held up the newspaper. 'Someone might come forward from the information printed in this.' The *Evening News* had run with the headline: 'Suspicious Murder in Old Picture House.'

The telephone rang in Craven's office.

Helen took a quick scan of the spread. The front page and the following two pages had been dedicated to yesterday's crime, complete with black and white images of the front door marked off with police rope and a uniformed officer standing at the entrance. The last page was dedicated to how the cinema used to be in its heyday, leading up to its closure in 1972.

*Nothing new there.* Helen stifled a yawn and her eyes watered. She took a final gulp of coffee then chucked the foam cup into the wastepaper basket under her desk. Pleased that she had managed to get it in there despite throwing it from an awkward angle, she picked up the phone to speak with Ted, half-dialling the number, when Craven came over and hung up the call. 'I want you down the morgue with me.'

# Chapter Fifteen

'I've got some somewhere.' Craven leant over Helen and rummaged through the glove box. Marathon bar wrappers and empty Lucozade bottles spilled onto the floor.

'What exactly are you looking for, Jack?' Helen picked a sticky bottle from her lap and shoved it into the door slot.

'Ah, found them!'

Craven waved the half-empty roll of Polo mints at her. 'The mint with the hole!' He popped one in his mouth and offered one to Helen before slipping them into his pocket. 'Eating mints will help with that bloody smell in there, sweetheart. I would.' He rubbed a hand across his stubbly chin and glanced up at the building then back at her, before saying, 'They'll no teach you any of this at university.'

Helen shook her head. 'Well, I studied psychology at university so going to the morgue wasn't really a prerequisite for that. I've been in the morgue before though.'

'Your parents must be really happy with that then.'

'Happy with what?'

'Waste of an education to end up in the police, eh?' He popped another mint in his mouth.

'Jack, my parents are completely supportive with me doing whatever makes me happy and I think understanding psychology is an important aspect of being a police officer.' Helen turned to face him slightly in her chair. 'I can understand the way people think, their motives for thinking that way…' Helen trailed off when she noticed Craven roll his eyes. When he stopped, she continued. 'Listen I have a better understanding of what someone is likely to do and in working out their motives. I also studied modern techniques like criminal profiling.'

He scrunched his face up. 'Criminal what? Load of bloody rubbish—'

'It's essentially creating a profile of the suspect based on the nature of the crime and the way it was carried out.' She could see he wasn't interested but carried on anyway. 'That way you can build up a picture of the characteristics the suspect most likely has.'

'Bollocks. There's nothing better than working your way up the ranks, gaining experience as a copper. University can't teach you what that can.' He crunched on a mint as he spoke. 'Classrooms are not where you learn about criminals, darling.'

She let out a laugh and shook her head. 'Besides going to university teaches you how to be independent, it's not all just about the course.'

Craven shrugged. 'Nah, you dinnae fork out loads of money at a posh school just to end up being paid peanuts as a WPC.' He sucked on the mint then shook his head. 'I would go mad if my bairns thought about doing that, like.'

Helen bit her lip before responding. 'We will just have to disagree on that then, Jack. I've done well in the police. I love what I do and I'll continue to do so.' She folded her arms. 'I love my job.' She unfolded them in case he read into her defensiveness.

They both sat in silence. Craven crunched the mint but the faint linger of cigarette smoke still hung in the air. He then took another one from the packet. Helen clenched her fist. She wanted to tell him to go in, just to get it over with, but she bit her tongue and decided to wait it out. He was really enjoying this and he wanted her to crack.

This was the part of the job she hated the most. She had her window rolled down. It was a warm morning, the sunlight hit off her cheek and for a brief moment it almost felt like it wasn't Edinburgh. Luckily, they had managed to park in a bay outside the double doors of the mortuary next to a Vauxhall Viva.

The Edinburgh City Mortuary was a modern building, set back from the road, in the Cowgate area of Edinburgh.

Helen looked up at the brown façade. Even with the brass sign next to the door and the metal chimney at the back used to drain the smell, she was doubtful that many in Edinburgh knew what this building was.

'Right then, let's get this over with.' He sighed and climbed out of the car.

Through the double doors, the morgue teemed with life – pathology students, probably. Each one looked relaxed and could have easily been on their way to an art class. In some ways, it was sad how quickly you could become accustomed to death. She remembered her first visit to a mortuary during training and just a few hours later she felt like a veteran. In truth, it was a necessary part of the circle of life. She just hoped one day she wouldn't end up on one of the trolleys.

When they arrived, they brushed past a white-coated pathologist who was having a smoke in the doorway. Craven took in a deep breath of smoke, then popped another mint in his mouth. This time Helen took one as well. The building smelt of clinical bleach and rotting meat. It reminded Helen of a piece of bacon that had been left to fester; a smell she had encountered in her student days and she could almost taste, and it would stick to your hair and clothes. White halls and polished hard lino floors led the way to the postmortem suite: a large room made to feel slightly smaller with the left-hand side taken up by the metal door used to bring up bodies from the cold store underneath.

'Morning, Alex. Let's get this show on the road then.' Craven clapped his hands together as he entered the room. Goosebumps formed on Helen's arms. She rubbed them in the tan leather jacket, a shiver running down her spine.

'Morning officers.' Winston nodded to both of them. He had a scuffed brown apron on with a white shirt underneath. The shirt looked at least a size too small and pulled tightly on his portly frame; patches of sweat pooled underneath his armpits. His pathology assistant was a gangly-looking teenager with tar-coloured, slicked-back hair. He was wearing thick-rimmed NHS glasses which made his eyes look comically large.

'I'm going to be sick of the sight of you at this rate,' Craven said.

'Hopefully this will be the last one this week.' Winston chuckled.

They had the body of the unknown man from the cinema prepared on the metal trolley. He looked almost like a big rubber doll, and, certainly, his swollen, battered face made it look as if he was wearing a mask. His lips reminded Helen of blue pen ink. There was a bulge in his throat, and she could see that Craven had noticed this as well. His clothes had been removed and replaced with a white sheet tucked under his arms. Winston and his assistant moved around the body with expert precision, their tools and scales on the trolley beside them. Their victim's skull was clearly cracked and deep blue bruising lined his wrists and neck.

Helen and Craven stood back. They were required to attend the postmortem for evidence continuity, but neither wanted to see more than was necessary.

Winston made an incision with his scalpel, then slid in his rib shears. It took him a couple of attempts before the crack of his chest bone echoed in the examination room. It was a noise that could curdle Helen's blood. She kept her eyes firmly fixed on the sheet. This had put her off spare ribs for life. 'Well, Jack, you were right about something being in his neck.'

Helen looked up to see Winston removing a plastic bag from the victim's mouth. Craven stepped forward as the pathologist unwrapped it and carefully placed it on the metal tray.

Winston frowned behind his thick-rimmed glasses. The smell was almost unbearable: blood and vomit from the corpse. Helen watched him peel the soggy plastic away, unwrapping a small gold-coloured watch. The hands had stopped on seven twenty-five. Winston's face creased. 'I have never seen anything like this before.' He looked at Helen. 'Any ideas on this one?'

Helen shrugged her shoulders and looked at Craven. 'If the blood painting in the picture house is a picture of a clock face then it could be that time has meaning in the murders.'

'Who would want to ram a watch down somebody's throat?' Craven crunched on another mint as he spoke. Helen grimaced. It sounded as though his teeth would break. 'Well, it's clearly a message.' Craven stepped forward and peered at it. 'I agree with you, now. This was calculated.' He paused. 'The watch looks expensive. We can see if there's been a watch reported stolen recently and speak to the antiques shops.'

Winston rubbed his hands on his apron. 'This young man really suffered, I can tell you that.'

Helen looked down at the corpse.

'Do we have any idea who he is yet?'

Winston read from his clipboard. 'Not yet, but he's in his mid-twenties and had a last meal of what looked like stovies. I would say that was about twenty-four hours ago.' Winston sounded bored. Helen wondered how many of these postmortems he'd done over the years. He tutted. 'From the rate of decomposition I can say he died sometime between eight and midnight the night before he was found.'

Craven nodded. 'Right, so we have a more specific timescale, that's a start at least.'

When they were back in the car. Craven asked her to radio the control room and get Stanley's address. It was in the Portobello area about five miles to the east of Edinburgh. The mid-morning rush of traffic had died down and it would be a twenty-minute drive at most. Something Helen was quite glad of. Her stomach wasn't settled and the smell of the petrol fumes made her slightly nauseous. There was something about a postmortem that seemed to make her hungry.

# Chapter Sixteen

Helen slumped back in her seat and stared out the window. She looked over to the promenade. There was one person out in the sea – crazy. The tide was moving in. A jogger was losing a battle with the wind and staggered along the promenade. They passed both without a word. The area had been known as a holiday destination but that had started to fizzle out when the package holiday became affordable. Not that her family ever really did holidays. Dad was always too busy with work and he didn't like travelling either. It must've been different before her brother died though because mum had a box of holiday snaps. Helen was too young to remember. She wound her window down, letting in the smell of the beach and the salty air. A red sky hung low over the horizon. Cars hurried past.

The ground was still shiny from last night's rain. A fat seagull pecked at a dropped fish supper. Passing the Mr Whippy van, she remembered a time when she pestered her dad for some ice cream on a rare day out. Then he'd given her a lecture on all the chemicals in it. There was an open-air swimming pool but, with the wind of the North Sea, she couldn't imagine the appeal. Perhaps if Sean Connery were still a lifeguard there she would be more tempted to try it. Panic rose in her at the thought of getting into water. She forced the thought from her mind.

They pulled into Portobello High Street then took another right turn.

'It's that one.' Craven pointed to a stone cottage with a red-painted front. The garden was freshly mown, and hanging baskets hung each side of the door. The house showed no outward sign of life. They parked at the bottom of the street. Out of sight. A woman walking a Labrador passed them. She muttered 'Good morning' and smiled. A man was working underneath his car, only his legs visible. His radio was playing some classical-sounding track. They stepped over his feet. Craven lit his cigarette. She followed him into the garden.

'Do you know him personally, Jack?' Helen asked, the windows were closed and the curtains open.

'Not really,' he said, between puffs. 'He was in another division to me. Never had any cause to work with him and I know he spent a lot of time down in the Met with the Flying Squad.'

'It seemed more than that in the cinema.'

'Did it?' Craven flicked the ash onto the path and thumped on the door. It shook but there was no movement inside. He gave it a minute then peered through the letterbox. Without saying a word he headed around the back of the house. Helen followed him. There was a small garden covered with paving stone and a plastic deck chair in the corner. Craven shook on the handle of the kitchen back door. Locked. A tabby watched them suspiciously from the wall. Helen looked up to the second floor. A window was open; it was frosted and had a ledge underneath.

'I could get up there, Jack.'

'Nah.' He stubbed his cigarette out against the door. 'It's a wee bit high, love.'

She tugged on the rusty drain pipe it didn't budge. She took off her duffle coat and handed it to him. 'I can climb up through the window and let you in.'

'What if he is in the hoose but just no' answering the door?'

Helen shook her head. 'We both know he's not inside.'

'You sure you can climb up there?'

'Definitely. I used to do rock climbing. C'mon, I wouldn't suggest it if I didn't think I could do it.'

'Right,' he pointed. 'Just dinnae fall whatever you dae, and if you're not out in five-minutes ah'm coming in after you.'

She laughed. 'Inspector, I didn't know you cared.'

He shrugged and gave her a lift up onto the drain pipe. She wedged her foot in the gap then pulled herself up. The ledge was slippery from the overfull guttering which she hadn't noticed. She got a knee up and slid off like butter but she managed to grab onto the pipe. She tried again to get a foot up and this time put her foot onto the window frame and, bobbing the top of the frame, she managed to get in. Her blouse sleeve caught on the handle, and she swore as she heard it tear.

# Chapter Seventeen

When she opened the door, Craven took a step forward then stopped in his tracks. A wide grin spread across his face. He pointed to her sleeve and laughed. 'I thought you said you could climb?'

'Don't.' She shook her head. 'Don't bother. Just don't.' Helen let out a giggle more from the shock than anything else.

'Didn't think you would've had that in you, love. Nothing a wee bit of lipstick won't solve, eh?'

Helen took her jacket, buttoned it up fully then wiped her hands down her trousers to get rid of the muck. She had grazed her palms on the ledge and they stung.

'Well…' Craven patted her on the back. 'Hopefully, it will all be worth it.' He turned the latch back on the door. 'If Stanley shows up, we'll just say the door was open and we heard a noise inside.' He closed the door then pulled the handle, testing that it wasn't locked. Once satisfied, he headed into the lounge-cum-kitchen.

The faint aroma of Dettol lingered. Plates were stacked beside each other on the drying board. A plastic box full of empty whisky bottles sat in the space intended for a fridge or a washing machine. This kitchen had neither.

Craven looked around the room. 'This is a bit too bloody homely.'

Helen shrugged, 'I don't know.' She picked up an opened bottle of aspirin. Empty. She put it back down. 'It doesn't look all that homely to—'

'I half expected him dossing somewhere,' Craven interrupted her. 'Maybe he has a woman staying over.'

'I thought you didn't know him? But yeah, he does. There's women's laundry hanging up in the bathroom and some toiletries'.

'He's always got a bird on the go.'

'He's led a disciplined life with the police and the army before. Why would you expect him to doss somewhere?'

He waved a hand. 'I know what the army is like, sweetheart. They might tell you things in psychology books, but I know many men couldnae take the discipline. Ending up in doss houses or squatting.'

'What are we looking for exactly?' She followed Craven through to the lounge area; it was compact but still big enough to be comfortable. A television was set on a stand in the corner. The aerial was positioned on the floor and they both looked like they had not been used for a while. A small wireless sat on the coffee table beside a pouch of tobacco. Two empty tins of lager and a Babycham glass were on the floor. Last night's *Evening News*, reporting the picture house murder lay folded on the two-seater sofa. Craven picked it up and skimmed through a few pages.

'Stanley's hiding something.'

'How do you know that?'

Craven shook his head. 'Why do you keep questioning me about Stanley? I'm the one who should be asking you.'

'What are you talking about?' There were a few scuffed paperback books on a table in the hall. Helen flicked through them. You could always learn a lot from the books and music someone listened to.

Craven scoffed then started for the stairs. Helen placed the books back down. Her gaze firmly fixed on him. 'Jack, tell me.'

'Well, your old man must have known him. That's what I mean.'

'You don't know that.'

'I cannae mind—'

She crossed her arms over and let out an exasperated breath. 'Is this why you have a problem with me?'

'No,' Craven shrugged. 'Your Dad was Stanley's Inspector.'

'I thought you didn't know Stanley?' Helen paused in an

attempt to calm herself down. 'My father was a good officer. He wasn't bent.'

'Look, I didnae mean anything by it.' He walked along the hall and pushed open the bedroom door. The bed hadn't been slept in and a pair of silk pyjamas lay draped over the chair. She couldn't tell if he was actually being serious or if that was a dig at her father. The scent of aftershave and smoke hung heavily in the room – almost as if they had just missed him.

After a moment of silence, he spoke. 'Was just rumours.'

Helen clenched her fists; he just couldn't resist having a go. 'You can't help yourself, can you?'

Craven shrugged and changed the subject. 'He keeps this place clean as a whistle, eh?' He rubbed a hand along the bannister and made a show of examining it for dust.

'Jack, my father has nothing to do with me being in the police and I certainly don't police like him either... Wait.'

'What?'

'Look.' Helen had a jewellery box in her hand. She handed it to Craven. It was stuffed full of fivers.

***

'I wish I could ask you about George Stanley.' Helen put her hand on the headstone. He'd been dead nearly seven years now. A heart attack from all the smoking and drinking. He'd only been retired six months when it happened. The stone felt warm from the sun. She brushed away some of the dirt that had collected on top. 'I... I wish I could believe that you can hear me rambling on.' She leant down and took out the dead flowers from the pot. The petals disintegrated in her hand and stunk of rot. Hot tears stung her eyes. 'I'm sorry I've left the grave so long.' She hated visiting the cemetery; it always brought out everything she wanted to keep inside. She took a shaky breath. 'I've got a mix of flowers here.' She placed them on the grass. 'Pansies, daffodils and I don't know what these pink ones are.' Birds sang in the tree behind her. 'Please, Dad. If George Stanley was corrupt, please don't be involved.'

# Chapter Eighteen

'You're going to do what?' Blake rubbed his greasy hands on his overalls.

George Stanley shook his head. 'I don't know, learn a trade, work in an office – just pack all of this rubbish in.' He sighed. 'It's just one thing after another. If ah'm not getting paid, ah'm either getting battered or ma car is being smashed.' Stanley was leaning against the counter. He noticed Blake trying to suppress a smile.

'I'll tell you one thing, though. I'm going to find out who attacked me at that house and I'll bloody kill them. I had mare money and less hassle when I was in the polis. Can you believe that?' Stanley gulped, his mouth felt dry, and he badly needed a drink. If it wasn't so early he would have popped into the pub next door for something strong. The air was thick with the smell of petrol, adding to the nauseous feeling in the pit of his stomach.

'The trouble is you just don't know when to quit.'

'Ach!' Stanley waved a hand dismissively in the air. 'One thing at a time, eh?' He motioned to the vending machine. 'Do you mind if I…?'

'Away and help yourself, you look as though you need it.'

'Cheers.' The glass front of the vending machine was cracked and most of the trays for sweets were empty. He reached in and grabbed a Fry's fruit bar then slumped down on the bench.

Blake returned a few minutes later and handed him a mug of what looked like tea. The side of the cup was marked with his greasy fingerprints. 'Are you sure you shouldn't be going to the hospital or at least go and see a doctor?'

'Nah. I'll live.'

Blake nodded to the vehicle ramp. 'The car's out in the forecourt. I've had a few of the apprentices work on it. You had nae luck with that car o' yours though, pal. You need to think about scrapping it.'

Stanley nodded and took a sip of the tea. The cup felt slippery in his hands. 'Aye, well. What can I say? Last night wasn't really how I wanted to spend the night. ' His head still ached, and he winced as he pushed away a stray strand of hair that had stuck to his cut. 'I thought I was going tae listen to some old wifey going on about how her husband might be cheating on her...' He paused and bit into the chocolate bar. His jaw still ached, so he let it melt in his mouth rather than chew.

Blake pulled out a notepad from the front of his overalls. 'You sure you're no' wanting me to buy it off you?' He scratched his head and then added, 'I'll dae you a pal's rate on it?'

Stanley shook his head and glanced over to the forecourt, where a few sorry-looking cars sat with "for sale" signs slapped on them. The light blue Morris Major boasted having one owner, but he remembered Blake's old granny had it then his dad. It was more of a family heirloom than anything else.

He shook his head when he had finished with the chocolate bar and said, 'If ah'm ever that desperate, I'll let you know.'

'Nae bother but maybe you should start taking the bus.'

Stanley laughed and his jaw ached. 'Well, if people keep wrecking my car, I will be.'

'Are you going to want it on the tick—' He stopped talking as a woman in her thirties with Monroe-styled hair walked up to the counter with a scowl on her thin features. She was wearing a mink fur coat, and clutching a brown leather handbag with both hands.

Stanley was tempted to say. 'You're alright love, I'm not going to steal it.' Instead, he flashed a smile and waved the mug at her.

'Your car's almost ready.' Blake smiled at her. He pointed to the chairs. 'It won't be long, sweetheart.'

She wrinkled her nose then sauntered to an area with plastic tables and chairs.

Stanley slipped her a glance as she passed him. He peeled his shirt from the nape of his neck. He badly wanted a shower.

'Right,' Blake motioned to the end of the counter. When the woman was out of earshot, he spoke, 'for me towing you here and doing this work quickly, it'll cost forty quid.'

'Forty quid?' He let out an exasperated breath. 'That includes our little discount?'

'Oh aye.' He nodded rubbing a hand through his salt and pepper beard 'There's more though.'

'Aye, is it going to be what I think it is?'

A twitch of a smile stretched his dry, cracked lips, showing two missing front teeth. 'I'll see you down the pub tonight. You've no got yourself into trouble again, have you?

'Naw this is no' related to that, pal. I promise ye'.'

The car stank of oil. Stanley leaned back into the driver's chair and fiddled with the radio. The news was on and the reporter was talking about the murder in the picture house. There weren't any new leads and he didn't think they would find any either. Inspector Craven was asking anyone who was in the area at the time to come forward. No chance, he thought, and retuned to a station playing The Who. Lighting a cigarette, he rolled the window down and nodded his thanks to Blake. On his way, he made a quick detour home for a clean shirt.

# Chapter Nineteen

It took all of a minute for Helen to decide he was hiding something, and when George Stanley looked up from the whisky he was nursing and smiled at her. She was certain of it. The yellow shirt he was wearing was skin-tight and it was half-buttoned up and messily tucked into his trousers, like he'd got dressed in a rush. His brown layered hair looked damp and left wet patches on the shoulders of his shirt. A purple bruise was visible under his chest hair. He had a matching black eye and angry-looking cut along his brow. He reminded her of someone but she couldn't place who.

'Jack, it's *really* nice to see you again.' Stanley held up his glass and drained it. 'This day just keeps on getting better and better. Cheers.' He put the empty glass down on the desk.

Craven made a show of looking around the office. 'This is no' a social call. Drinking at this time of the day, eh? That was always your trouble, wasn't it?' The men exchanged a look that told Helen they had history.

'No, I didn't think it was.' Stanley raised an eyebrow. 'It's just a wee dram. What do you want?'

'Where were you on Thursday night between eight and midnight?'

Stanley looked down to the ground. 'Emm, I was working, down at Diamond's.'

'Diamond's?' Helen asked.

'It's a dance hall down in Leith. Ah'm surprised you've no' been, darling.'

'Doing what?'

'Doors, security – the usual…'

Helen thought she could hear the hint of a Glaswegian

accent.

'Perfect timing as usual. The kettle's nearly boiled.'

Craven shook his head.

'Suit yourself, Sergeant Craven. Look, let's cut the shit though. What exactly do you want?'

When Stanley tilted his head to the side, she knew exactly who he reminded her of – Frankie Miller, her favourite singer.

'No, you cannae and it's Inspector Craven,' Craven snapped.

Stanley looked at Helen. 'He's such a charmer, isn't he? Inspector Craven. Promotion at last, eh? Last I had heard they were going to give you the boot—'

'Pack it in, Stanley.' Craven stepped forward.

'Who's this wee lassie then?' Stanley asked, dropping some instant coffee into a mug and stirring it with a sugar-coated spoon. 'You work through them all, don't you?'

'I'm DS Carter.'

'Carter?'

She looked at Craven. His hand was trembling.

'How did you get those injuries?'

'I'm clumsy, pet. You wouldnae believe it but I fell doon the stairs.'

'No, I dinnae believe it,' Craven answered, exasperated.

'Well, then you won't mind if I…' He fished in his pocket for his cigarettes then waved the packet at them. 'Ah'm gasping. Are you still on the rollups or can I tempt you with one?' He lit his cigarette. 'How's the wife, by the way?'

'Just look at this photo.' Craven handed Stanley a black and white photograph of the victim in the mortuary. It had been crumpled and the edges dog-eared from being kept in his notebook.

Stanley did not bother to look at the picture. Instead, he put a cigarette to his lips. 'Do you seriously,' – he pointed the cigarette at Craven – 'and I mean seriously, reckon that I would have anything to do with that picture house murder?'

'Just look at the photo, please.' Helen moved around the

desk.

He laughed, shook his head. 'What the hell is this? Amateur hour?' Stanley took the picture from the table and held it up to the light for slightly longer than was necessary. 'Right, I have looked at the photo. Never seen the guy before in my life. Sorry, I can't help you.' He scratched his nose and slid the photo back towards them. 'I've had enough of this anyway. You'd both better leave.'

'That's not very polite,' Craven tutted.

'How do you know we are talking about the cinema?'

'Look, sweetheart, I wasn't born yesterday. I read the papers. I listen to the radio, same as the next person, and mind I used to work for you lot.'

'Are you sure you don't recognise him, Mr Stanley?' Helen stared at him. If he had spent just a second less on the picture she might have felt that she was wrong.

'I have never seen that man in my life.'

'Bollocks.' Craven shook his head. 'Do you want me to drag you to the station?'

Stanley laughed. 'Craven, you would need to arrest me for that, you and I both know that. C'mon, I'm not someone that you can just bully down to the station. You have no evidence that I was at the picture house or that I ken your victim. Me and you, Craven, will no' see eye to eye, but surely even you can see that.' He took a drag on his cigarette. 'Believe me or not, that's completely your choice, Inspector. I don't know what else I can help you with. You know, Craven, I'd love to help you do *your job,* if I could.'

'Did you drive home after your shift?' Helen interjected.

Stanley flashed Helen a smile. 'Eh...' He scratched his head narrowly missing the gash on it. 'I walked home.'

'Why?'

'I had a few jars during ma shift and I like the walk home. Helps me clear my head.'

'Don't suppose you have any witnesses to that?' Craven chimed in.

'I walked home alone, but plenty would have seen me in the club.' Stanley motioned to the door. 'Now if you don't mind, I've enjoyed this wee visit but I've work to dae myself.' Stanley stood from the desk and motioned towards the door. 'Listen, go down to the dance hall if you don't believe me, they'll tell you the same.'

Helen crossed around to the desk next to the door. Business cards were stacked in a plastic tub in front of the typewriter. The same style as the one they had found in the picture house.

A leather appointments book was open on today's date. She flicked a few pages back. 'What was rubbed out?

'Sorry, sweetheart?'

'There was an entry under Thursday and it's been rubbed out.' She handed him the book pointing out the marks.

'It'll be Maud. Our secretary. I don't deal with the appointments. I don't know what would have been in there. Like I said, I was working. '

'One last thing to ask you then we'll leave you to your thriving business here. We found this card.' Helen slipped the evidence bag containing the business card from her pocket.

'Eh, I've got a stack of them.' Stanley turned the evidence bag over in his hand and had a look on his face as though he was just going through the motions. 'I can confirm it's one of my cards.' Boredom crept into his voice. 'You know it's one of my cards and it doesnae mean anything. I give them out like sweeties.'

'That card was found on our victim.'

'Aye, ah thought as much. Like I said, he could've got that card anywhere. Maybe he was going to give me a call? I wouldnae know, would I?'

'There's a time and date on the back of it. Helen narrowed her eyes. 'So, that's not your writing on the back of the card?'

'No, I had no appointment to see anyone then. I have never seen that man before. And no, that's not my writing. If I could help you, darling, I would.'

'Right, well you know where to contact me, Stanley. I'll see you again soon.' Craven turned to the door quickly.

Helen followed.

She stopped in the doorway and turned to Stanley. 'Give us a call if anything springs to mind.'

Craven had already disappeared down the corridor.

'She doesn't know, does she?' Stanley called out behind them.

***

As soon as they were outside Helen stopped and faced Craven, arms crossed. 'What don't I know? What was going on up there?'

Craven brushed past her and unlocked the driver's door. 'I don't know what he was talking about. He's lying anyway, he knows our victim.'

'So were you.'

'What?' Craven shot her a glance, his face darkening. 'You better watch what you're saying.'

'You told me you didn't know him.'

'Are you getting back in the car or what?'

She stood her ground. 'Why have you been lying to me?'

'I don't need to explain myself to you.'

'Did you work with him?'

'I'm not doing this. Get in the car or go back to the station yersell. You're just a WPC with an attitude and I don't need to tell you anything.'

'What don't I know, Jack?'

'Ach.' He waved a hand dismissively. 'You're just a stupid wee lassie who's getting too big for her boots. I could have you out of this department like this.' He clicked his fingers.

'You don't need to take your anger out on me, Inspector.' Helen's heart raced. She had been warned of his temper. There were stories of him punching the constables when he didn't get his way. She hadn't believed it until now.

She shook her head and got in the car. They drove the rest of the way in silence.

# Chapter Twenty

By 4pm, the swollen evening sun had settled low in the red sky. The station was only a short drive from the Diamond's Dance Hall, and with Craven's driving it was taking even less time. The streets showed little signs of life. Helen rolled down the window a crack. A group of lads congregated outside a pub, drinking cans of lager. Laughter erupted into the car and faded just as fast, as the people became a faint blur.

The sharp air cooled her face. Her temples throbbed and a headache swirled behind her eyes. When was the last time she had eaten? She couldn't remember. The car jolted when Craven slipped the car into third gear, pulling her from her thoughts.

They'd borrowed one of the pool cars – a low-key Ford Granada. Helen had offered to drive Craven in the Mini but he had refused. He had his right hand on the steering wheel, dog-end dangling from this bottom lip, eyes firmly fixed on the road ahead. She leaned back in the passenger's seat and stared out of the window.

They were now driving along Leith Walk, a wide street lined with shops and tenement blocks, not far from the docks. The shops were shut but a few cars were still parked in front of them.

'It's no' far now,' Craven said as they turned past a statue of Queen Victoria. 'Have you been to this place before?'

'Never heard of it.' She looked over to the abandoned Leith station building. Peeling paintwork and smashed windows. The buildings now were only used by drug addicts and alcoholics as a way to get their fix and keep out of the rain. She wondered how long the space would be left to lie.

A neon sign for a chippie was coming up on the left.

'Jack, pull up over here.' She unclipped her seatbelt as he pulled in behind a double-decker bus. The smell of fish and chips wafted into the car and her stomach grumbled. A poster in the window with a cartoon fish advertised the "balanced meal". A middle-aged man was sitting by the window eating chips.

Dinner was on Helen tonight. Two fish suppers which they ate in the car. Helen stabbed her wooden fork into the fish.

'Well, it's safe to say Stanley's hiding something,' Craven said, in between mouthfuls of chips.

'Yes, but what?' Helen took a gulp of her drink and rubbed her greasy hands on the newspaper. The chips were too white and soggy for her tastes but she was too hungry to throw them away.

'I don't know yet but he's involved somehow,' Craven said, tearing a bit of fish with his hands.

'Have you ever worked with Stanley?' Helen asked.

Craven shook his head. 'I know who he is but that's it.' He stuffed a couple of chips in his mouth then spoke. 'Loads of coppers left the polis at that time.' Craven scrunched the paper that had contained his meal into a ball and got out of the car. Dinner break was over.

\*\*\*

Diamond's Dance Hall was a red brick flat-roofed building that looked tiny from the front. Posters of the acts doing gigs there in the following weeks adorned the walls. Next week: the Frankie Miller band. The gig looked good. The scuffed double doors to the front were locked. The dance hall didn't open for another two hours. 'Do you think anyone will be in?'

Craven nodded and fished in his pockets for his packet of cigarettes. 'I've been here before. There's a back door we can try around here.' They followed a path round to the back alley. Craven kicked a crushed lager can into a bush.

'See.' He pointed to the back door which was wedged open by a bag of rubbish.

'What the hell do you want now?' A man in his late sixties looked up from the bar he was wiping.

'That's not very polite.' Craven chided him.

He let out a sigh. 'Inspector Craven, I dinnae want any bother.'

'Well, if you're helpful…'

'I run this business legal since I got out.'

'I want to talk to you aboot George Stanley. Do you know him?' Craven replied.

'Stanley works as an occasional doorman.' The man rubbed his eye with a shaky hand.

'When was Mr Stanley last here?' Helen asked. She took over the questioning.

'Thursday night.'

'When?'

'Till the place closed.'

'What time was that?'

'Around three, I think'

'Did he speak to anyone?' Craven walked over to the bar.

'Right,' the man held up his hands in mock surrender. 'He spent the beginning of his shift talking to some young lad.'

'Just talking?'

'Aye, it looked important, like. I had to tell him a few times to get back on the doors.'

Helen took out a picture of the victim. 'Was this who he was talking to?'

The man took the picture and slipped his glasses on. He squinted as he looked at it, taking his time to respond. 'I think so.' He flicked the photograph onto the bar.

'You think so?' Helen took the photograph back.

'It's really hard to tell. It looks like him. It's dark in here.' He took a deep breath. You know what, I actually think it is. Go an' let me see that picture again. Aye, it really looks like the laddie.'

'When was the last time you saw them talking?' Helen

questioned.

'It was about nine or ten. I didnae see the boy after that.'

Craven took a whisky bottle from the counter. 'What were they talking about?' He held it up to the light. 'This bottle looks a bit watered down, you know.'

The old man pursed his lips. 'Is it fuck!' He looked at Helen, his face reddened. 'I run this place legal. You don't need to thump me about like you did last time or threaten my licence. I'm telling you everything I know.'

Craven nodded but didn't say anything. He walked behind the counter and took a glass from underneath the bar.

Helen shot Craven a glance. 'Do you know what they were talking about?' She stepped forward trying to ease the tension by putting a barrier between the two men. 'Anything that you can think of that might help us? No matter how small.'

'No,' He looked at the both of them. 'It's loud when the music's on, it's dark, and I've honestly told you everything, I know.' He looked at Craven. 'Take a drink on the house, Inspector, if you want.' The man sneered. 'If I think of anything else, I know where to find you.'

\*\*\*

When they were outside, Helen stabbed a finger into Craven's chest. 'That man in there is in his sixties and you slapped him about?'

'It wisnae like that. I just gave him a wee tap. He wisnae giving me the information I needed.' Helen felt his hot whisky-breath on her cheek. He leaned in closer. 'I'm not like that.'

Helen batted his hand. 'I'm driving.' She started to walk towards the car.

When Craven got back in the car he put a call out to get George Stanley picked up. 'Doesn't look like Stanley's our murderer but he knew our victim,' he explained over the radio.

# Chapter Twenty-One

Wendell Clint looked up just as Stanley landed a punch to his stomach. He yelped and crumpled as all the breath escaped his body. Stanley pulled him back up.

'Don't, please,' he stammered. 'Don't hurt me.' He held out his hands. 'Take anything you want, please.'

'I didnae want to do this.' Stanley grabbed Clint by his shirt and dragged him round into the close. 'But no, you had to be awkward, didn't ye?'

He had waited until it was dark and Clint was alone. Stanley slammed him into the wall and two rats scattered with a squeal. 'You could have just paid me but no.' Another body blow. 'You think I would have just left this?' He slapped Clint on the face.

'No. No, I just didn't think—'

'No, you didnae think.' He slapped Clint again. The sound echoed in the empty alley. *Never leave any visible marks on the face.* 'I could've accepted a loss of money but having someone following me? Now, that's a different story.' He shook Clint. 'Why mess with me?'

'What... I don't... understand.' Clint furrowed his brow. 'I haven't done anything like that.' He blinked hard. Tears welled in his eyes. 'I'll give you the money, please!' His face twisted in pain. 'You've broken my ribs.' He winced.

'Not yet, I've no.' Stanley stabbed a finger and twisted it into his side. 'But I will.'

'I... I've had nobody follow you. I've just not got the money to pay you.'

The words hung in the air. Stanley could see he was telling the truth.

Clint reached into his pocket and pulled out his wallet. 'Just take everything in this.'

'Fifty quid?' Stanley snatched the leather wallet and fished through it. A credit card and a few dry cleaning slips and a couple of five pound notes. Stanley pulled them out and dropped the card and slips into the puddle at his feet.

'It's all I have. The shop's making no money and my wife emptied all my accounts when she left.'

Stanley slipped the notes into his pocket. 'If you even think about going to the police, I'll come back here, finish the job.' He stabbed a finger into Clint's chest.

'I won't, I won't, I promise.'

Stanley hadn't enjoyed that as much as he'd hoped.

# Chapter Twenty-Two

He'd been round all the jewellers and pawn shops in the area, this pub was now his last option. Stanley shoved his way through the group of regulars who blocked his path to the bar. They were debating football – apparently Hibs were going to win this season. They didn't notice him, or if they did they didn't bother to look in his direction. The leader of the group was waving his arms in explanation, spilling his own pint down his purple crushed velvet shirt.

Two younger-looking lads in decorators' overalls squinted through the smoky haze; one of them threw a dart at the board. The shrill crack of a breaking glass followed by a roar of drunken laughter erupted behind him, dying into the sea of noise.

The smell of sweat and days-old alcohol stung him. Beside him, slumped at a bar stool, sat a drunken lump of a man, a cigarette dangling from the creased corner of his grey lips. His yellowed eyes met Stanley's before they sank back to his pint.

Stanley made eye contact with Blake who was sitting at a table in the corner. He held up three fingers, Stanley nodded and ordered the drinks.

'Cheers, pal,' Blake said, taking his drink from the tray. 'This is Slippy Jimmy by the way.' He gestured to the skinny man next to him who was slurping down the last of his cider.

Slippy Jimmy looked up and smiled through his missing teeth and slid the glass across the scuffed mahogany-coloured table. 'You'll need to fill that up, son, and then we'll talk.'

Stanley put the bitter in front of him. 'No, you can drink this and talk.'

Jimmy shrugged and took the glass. Stanley sat down opposite him and took a foamy sip.

'I cannae tell you much, like. I wis just saying that to Blake before you arrived.' Jimmy took a gulp of bitter, and wiped his mouth with the back of his hand. A gummy smile spread across his face. 'That's gid that, ah wis dry as a bone. You got any fags oan ye? Ah'm bloody gasping.'

Stanley snorted and slipped his packet of Lambert & Butler across the table.

'Ta.' Jimmy snatched them off the table and slipped them into this pocket.

Jimmy had got the nickname Slippy Jimmy from having his crooked fingers on most of the stolen goods in Edinburgh. He used to be a notorious burglar and safe-breaker in the Fifties, but after spending time in jail he got married, had a few kids and settled down as a rag and bone man. Yet he still seemed to know about every dodgy deal that went on.

'I've mentioned to Jimmy about how you got attacked in that house. He was telling me he might know something about that necklace you found,' Blake added.

'Really?' Stanley raised an eyebrow. He was probably just talking his way to a free drink.

'Aye,' Jimmy was nodding. 'A wee gold necklace wi' two love hearts oan it?' The old man ripped up a beer mat and used a corner edge to dig dirt from under his nails.

'That's right.' Stanley took the necklace from his pocket and put it on the table. The gold chain had knotted. He rolled it in his thumb to untangle it. 'You've seen it before?'

Jimmy cocked his head to the side. 'Aye, that looks like wan o' them. There was a young lad in here aboot a week ago and he wis trying to flog some jewellery.'

'What young lad?'

Jimmy paused to drain his glass then burped. 'Gonnae get me another wan, son? Ah'm thirsty.'

Stanley sighed and rose to his feet with the two glasses 'This is your last one. You'd better tell me something useful.'

Jimmy shrugged his shoulders and took the fags from his pocket.

The barmaid looked up as he approached. 'Same again?' She tucked a strand of her blonde hair behind her ear.

'Aye.' His stomach rumbled. 'Have you got any crisps?'

'I might have some.' She rustled in a box under the bar. 'You're in luck. That's the last packet.' She put them on the bar.

'Thanks.' Stanley took the last coins from his pocket and slid them across the counter. The barmaid nodded and eyed him suspiciously. 'You're not a regular in here, are you?' she said, pouring the pints. 'I'm Gina, by the way.'

'No, I'm not a regular.' Stanley looked up from the sticky counter and put his cigarette to his lips.

'Thought not, although I just started here a few weeks ago.' She smiled at him. There was something funny about how she looked and it took him a few seconds to work out what it was. Her blue eyeshadow had a much thicker coat on one eye lid than the other. She turned her head to the side and he could see a smudge of it on the corner of her temple like she had been rubbing her eye. 'I'm finishing at ten this evening.'

'Aye, that's good.'

The barmaid leaned over the bar and motioned towards Jimmy. Her white blouse slipped down her shoulder exposing a pink bra strap. 'I'd watch him if I were you. He's right dodgy. Always trying to sell stolen gear, I wouldn't buy anything off him.' She smiled again, her freckly cheeks dimpling. She looked Scandinavian, he thought and she reminded him of an old girlfriend.

'Aye? I'll keep that in mind, love.' He lit the cigarette and took a deep drag, blowing the smoke towards the ceiling. Stanley looked over to Jimmy, who was laughing with Blake about something. If it wasn't for Blake he would have just knocked Jimmy about a bit and got what he wanted and not need to spend any money. He took a gulp of bitter and headed back over to the table.

Blake was staring at him as he approached.

Jimmy squinted and held the necklace up to his eye. 'Ach, I'm no' sure now.' He screwed up his face and threw the necklace on the table. 'I'll take it oaf y're hands though.'

'No you'll not, and give me my fags back.'

Jimmy snatched the necklace from the table. 'Right, it's got hallmarks on it. It wis assayed in Ireland.' Jimmy paused and cleared his throat. 'And it's pure gold, gid quality.'

'Is that it?' He grabbed Jimmy by his scruffy collar.

'Mon, pal, calm doon.'

Stanley released the collar. His hand felt greasy so he rubbed it on his trousers.

'Hinking aboot it, this might be wan fae the house burglary, like. Actually, am sure this was wan o' the bits he tried to flog.' He turned the gold chain over in his hands. 'Aye, it's nice. Do ye' want to keep it?'

Stanley narrowed his eyes. 'When was this?'

'Tuesday or Wednesday night, mebbe. He was hanging aboot in a few o' the pubs trying tae sell stuff oan the cheap.' Jimmy weighed the necklace up in his hands. 'This is a nice solid wee piece, though, quality. I could get a gid price for this, you know.'

'Have you seen him before?'

'Nah.' Jimmy shook his head. 'Ah stayed well away fae him. That bloody Inspector Craven would hae me back inside.'

'Is that so.' Stanley sneered. 'Craven's not who you should be worried about. Now, would you recognise the man again?'

'Am no' sure, really. He wis a young lad with a smart suit. Ah've no' seen him aroond here before. I think he might've been a weegie, if that helps ye. He had a nice watch on but he wisnae interested in flogging that. Oh, and he had red hair.' Slippy Jimmy looked pleased with himself for remembering that last part.

Stanley took the necklace back. 'Right, thanks.'

'I'll keep an eye oot for him and let me ken if you want

rid of that necklace,' Jimmy said before he left.

Blake went up to the bar and returned with two glasses of whisky. He sat down and shook his head. 'I saw Denise down Safeway yesterday. When were you going to tell me she left you?'

Stanley downed his whisky to give him some time to answer. 'You know what she's like. She'll come around.'

Blake made a face and puffed out his cheeks. 'Not from the way she's talking. She's cancelled everything for the wedding, did you ken that?'

That hit Stanley like a punch to the stomach. She'd left him countless times and always came back a week or so later to try again and give him one last chance. The room spun around him. Denise always came back.

'Cake, dress—'

Stanley didn't let Blake finish. 'No, I didnae know that.'

'I don't know what else to say. Every time it seems like you're going to get your life sorted, you bugger it up.'

'It's no' like that.'

'She's a fucking grafter. How long's she been in that damn baker shop? Two years? The lassie's saved up mare than you've drunk and gambled away. I'm saying this to you as a pal.'

'Aye, I know that.' He leaned back in the seat. 'It's no' as bad as she's making out. Ah've had a few money problems but am sorting it out.'

'Sorting it out?'

'Aye, I wis owed money. I was going to use it to get her an engagement ring and make it proper. I've been putting away money fur the wedding.'

'Aye.' Blake took a sip of his whisky and sneered. 'Tell me you've no' been going out with that wee lassie you've hired?'

'Of course no'. What's Denise been saying?'

'Well, you cannae blame her for thinking like that, can you?' Blake pointed a finger at him. 'And it wouldnae be the first time either.'

'No.' Stanley nodded. He couldn't blame her for that, at

all.

'Why don't ye just forget about whoever attacked you and just give Denise that necklace?'

# Chapter Twenty-Three

'Finally!' Craven said, to whoever he was speaking to on the telephone. He said something else but Helen couldn't hear what. The radio was blasting out some nondescript disco tune. Randall briefly looked up from his typewriter.

Helen thought about turning the radio off but knew Craven would have a fit if she did. McKinley followed her over to her desk, and dropped the case files onto it with a thump nearly knocking her cup over.

'Sorry about that,' McKinley mumbled. He rubbed his hands together to get rid of the dust then brushed the marks off his shirt and trousers. A bead of sweat trickled down his temple.

Helen flicked a glance over towards Craven's desk.

'Who do you think he's on the phone to?' McKinley asked.

Helen shrugged. Craven was now busily writing something down on a piece of paper, the phone receiver balanced between his head and shoulder.

'Not sure… probably the forensics.' She slumped down at her desk. 'I'll start going through—'

Craven burst through into the main office interrupting her. 'We now have the identity of our picture house victim. His name's Derek Leckie. We've got a match on the fingerprints.' He went over to the board and scribbled Derek Leckie on it. 'He was arrested in Glasgow five years ago for stealing out of a department store. I have an address for him as well in the Gorbals.' Craven smirked and looked at Helen. 'You're with me on this one, sweetheart.'

Her dad had worked the Gorbals in his early days. She had to promise him she wasn't going to be on those streets – even though there were other areas just as bad. Very different to the big 19ᵗʰ century villa in Thorntonhall, she grew up in. The slums that were currently being ripped down in the Gorbals were infamous. The name synonymous with razor blade gangs, gangsters, drug problems and loan sharks. It wasn't a place where a police presence was often welcome.

'Any idea what he was doing through in Edinburgh then?' Randall spoke with a thick Aberdeen accent. He flicked through to an empty page of his notebook. 'It makes some sense now that no one aroond the area of the picture hoose recognised him then.'

# Chapter Twenty-Four

It had taken them the best part of an hour to drive to the Gorbals from the station. She wasn't surprised to find a lot of the tenements had been demolished since her last visit but enough of the old still remained. The pubs and undertakers would be the last standing and still doing a roaring trade. It would take a lot more than modern tower blocks to lose the desperation that dripped from the crumbling tenements and the people who lived there.

She rolled her window up as they passed the Palace Theatre. The building next to it had been gutted by a fire and was now propped up by scaffolding. At the junction, a bunch of wilted daisies had been tied around a rusty lamppost. She wondered who they were for.

'Slums must go, eh?' Craven said.

'It's just past here.' Helen pointed to a street on the left.

They took the turning into the street lined with semi-derelict tenements and crumbling shop fronts. Four young girls were playing with a broken pram and some sticks outside the stairwell. They parked behind the only other vehicle on the street – a solitary car propped up on bricks. A demolition gang's ball and chain loomed over the block. The high-rise flats behind the street looked like they could block out any chance of morning sun. Sadly, she didn't think those modern blocks would solve anyone's problems.

Helen sighed. A man who looked to be in his late sixties was leaning out of a window smoking a fag. He eyed them both suspiciously as they headed into the stairwell. A baby was crying in one of the flats. There was no lighting in the stair and all Helen could smell was damp and piss. They kicked up bits of rubbish as they walked. There were scurrying sounds around them but she couldn't tell where they were coming from.

Helen shivered, 'I really hate doing this.'

Craven paused before answering. 'I thought it's what we had women like you for. You should have had plenty of practice for this.'

'You're unbelievable.'

'Let's just get this over quick and get back to some real work.' He took the stairs two at a time.

Helen stood to the side of Craven. He knocked on the front door; it was badly scuffed and dented and looked as though it had been kicked in before. Someone had done a poor job of repairing it by covering it with a badly-nailed plywood panel.

After getting no answer, he rattled on the glass panel. The light in the hall went on. She could hear a bolt being unfastened and then the mortice lock.

The door opened a crack and the old man from the window peered behind a rusty security chain. His leathery face hardened instantly. Craven fished out his warrant card and held it up to his face.

'I am DI Craven and this is DS Carter. We need to have a chat with you. It'll be best to do this inside.'

Helen watched the colour drain from the old man's waxy face. He flicked looks between the pair of them. 'Fuck, I knew you were the polis when I saw you come in the stairs. He's no here and I dinnae ken where the fuck he is so ye can both just clear off.' He tried to push the door shut but Craven stuck his boot in the gap.

'So are we going to do it here or inside away from prying eyes?'

'I cannae help you with anything, just leave me alane will you!'

Helen stepped forward. 'Mr Leckie, this really won't take long and it's about your son. It's really important that we speak with you.'

'Making my life a misery. Bloody round here all the time...' Before he could finish the door of the flat opposite opened.

An emaciated-looking woman with straw-like blonde hair that was stuck down to the sides of her spotty cheeks gawped at them. She opened her mouth like she was going to say something, showing a row of broken brown teeth. A little girl of about four or five was holding onto one of her drainpipe-like bare legs.

Leckie sighed. 'Right, let me close the door and I'll take off the chain and let ye in.'

Craven took his boot from the door.

He opened the door for them and hushed them inside. 'Make this quick. Am just no' wanting that nosey wee bitch hearing my business.'

Helen nodded. 'I understand, Mr Leckie, this won't take very long. Is there somewhere we could sit down and talk?' She could hear the television on in one of the rooms, an Open University programme.

'Mon then, ye can come into the living room.'

Helen stepped into the hallway followed by Craven, who was putting his warrant card back in his pocket. The smell hit her straight away: the cat litter tray. Her stomach turned – it looked like it had not been cleaned in weeks. She made a conscious effort to only breathe through her mouth.

Craven closed the door behind them and stumbled over a cat that had run through his legs.

'Need the cats fur the rats.' The old man manoeuvred past a broken bookshelf and stacks of old newspapers. He turned to face Helen before going in the living room. 'He's not been back in days. Y're wasting your bloody time.'

'Please take a seat and we can talk. Is it just you and your son who live here?'

'Aye.'

She ushered him onto the sofa. The bedroom doors were open and broken furniture had been crammed into what seemed like every spare inch of space.

The old man nodded nervously rubbing his tobacco-stained fingers together. He smelt of alcohol and stale smoke. The wool jumper he was wearing was ripped at the sleeves and stained with paint. He rubbed the side of his cheek and Helen could see faint bruising.

'Who did that to you?'

The old man shrugged. There was no obvious place for them to sit. Clothes were stacked in piles on the sofa; the brown armchair in the corner was covered in white fur. Helen moved the pile of clothes onto the coffee table and helped the old man to sit down. Craven sat in the armchair which instantly sunk under his weight.

'Look, what's it y're after him fur anyway? I dinnae ken nothing and he disnae like me talking to the polis.'

'I'm very sorry to tell you this, Mr Leckie. Yesterday morning we found the body of a young man which we think may be your son.'

Tears began to well in the old man's yellowing eyes. 'What do you...? No, y're talking rubbish.' He started to pull at the thread on his jumper. 'It cannae be. I dinnae believe ye!'

'We also found this wallet that we believe to be your son's. It was found nearby. Helen took the wallet out of her handbag. She folded back the plastic evidence bag it was in so he could see it more clearly.

'Naw,' he looked at her blinking back tears. 'It's no' him. He doesnae have a car.' He looked everywhere but at the wallet in her hand.

'We've also had a match on your son's fingerprints.'

'No, It cannae be he's...' He put his head in his hands. 'You're wrong, you have to be wrong.' He reached out and snatched it from her. His son's name was on the evidence bag, with "deceased" written next to it in brackets. He traced the word "deceased" with his fingers.

Craven leaned forward in his chair. 'Right, when was the last time that you saw your son?'

He looked up, his lip quivering.

Craven lowered his voice. 'Yesterday? A week ago?'

He looked bewildered by the question then answered. 'Eh, about two nights ago, he was...' He looked back down to the wallet and traced his son's name with his finger. He rubbed over the word "deceased" as if he was trying to get rid of it.

'He's a good laddie just had a bit of bad luck, that's all.'

'A good laddie doesn't have an arrest record in the double—'

Helen cut Craven off before he could finish and shot him a look. 'Is it normal that you wouldn't see him for a few days?'

'Sometimes.' He wiped the tears away on the sleeve of his jumper.

Craven sighed and took out a photograph of the driving licence and address book. He waved them at Leckie. 'Recognise these, do you? These were retrieved in a bin close to where we found your son.'

The old man took them from him reluctantly. He opened his mouth as if to say something then stopped and just nodded his head. He rubbed more tears away with the back of his hands.

'They're ma son's but he might have just dropped them there, that doesnae mean that it's him. How did it happen?' He looked at Helen. 'What happened tae him, hen? Wis it some kind of accident?'

'No, we are treating the case as suspicious—'

'Any ideas of who would want to hurt him?' Craven took out his notebook. 'Just the first ten or so names will do for now.'

Leckie bunched his fists. Helen put her hand on his to stop him getting up. She glared at Craven. 'The circumstances of his death are still to be investigated, Mr Leckie. Was your son due to meet with anyone? Did he tell you where he was going?'

'My son wouldnae tell me where he was going. He would just usually go oot for a few days come back when he fancied. I thought he had a bird he was seeing but am no sure. You know what a young laddie can be like.'

'Did he have any problems with anyone? Is there anyone that might have wanted to hurt him?'

Leckie looked back down to the wallet. 'You shouldnae have his name on this it might not be him. It cannae be him.

As usual, you have got it all wrong.'

Helen pressed on. 'Anyone who might be trouble for your son?'

'Nobody, nobody would want to hurt him. He's a lovely laddie. He's not had bother with anyone.'

Craven looked at his watch.

Leckie started to shake. 'It wis probably a robbery.'

'That's a possible line of enquiry. We are doing everything that we can to find out what happened to him. Where's your kitchen? I'll go get you a cup of tea.' The man pointed towards the door.

He reached for her arm and tugged at the sleeve of her blouse. 'Can I see him? I want to see ma son.'

'Yes, we will need to bring you down for formal identification.' She paused before continuing. 'Do you have any recent photographs of your son that we could see?'

'Is this some kind of joke? If you ken it's ma son why do you want a photie?'

'Mr Leckie. I'm afraid we are more or less certain that this man is your son, I'm very sorry for your loss.'

Helen swatted a fly away as she walked into the kitchen. Some chipped mugs lay out on the drying board along with plates and empty tins of beans and spaghetti hoops. She rummaged through the empty cupboards and managed to find a dented tin with tea in it. There was no milk or fridge. She looked around the kitchen two mugs, plates and bowls. She shook her head and poured the tea.

The man looked up as she handed him the cup but didn't say anything. He had the wallet on his knee. 'Is it okay if we have a look at your son's bedroom and see if there is anything that will help with our enquiries?'

Craven got up from the chair. 'Is that his room through there?'

'Aye.' He took a sip of his tea. 'You'll no' find anything though. He's a bit of a lad but a good boy really.' His hands were shaking violently and some tea spilled onto his lap but Leckie didn't notice. 'He's no' like I wis.'

Helen took the mug from him and placed it on the table

before sitting down beside him. 'Is there anyone I could call to come and stay with you? Or anywhere we could take you to stay for a few days?'

'No.' He twisted the wedding band on his finger and caught Helen looking at it. 'My wife died five years ago. Cancer.' He held his hand up and let out a laugh. 'This is all I have now. What am I going to do?' He broke into a hacking cough.

Helen handed him his crumpled handkerchief from the table. He coughed into it, peppering it with blood. Leckie looked down at it.

'Ave no' got long either.' He said, rubbing the blood from his chin.

'I'm very sorry, Mr Leckie.'

Derek's bedroom was just big enough for the single bed and writing desk in the corner of the room. Dusty paperbacks were stacked neatly on the desk along with a couple of notebooks. A board on the other side of the room had some photographs tacked up on it. A picture of one of the kittens curled up on the bed. It looked like the same bobbled red blankets peppered with cat hair were still on the bed. Helen approached the desk and opened a leather photo album. The pages had yellowed and curled at the edges. Pictures of Derek as a baby, chubby with a toothless grin. Cute. Reg Leckie, with a thick head of black hair and muscle on his frame. In most of his pictures, his arm was draped around a waif-like woman with long blonde hair, both smiling broadly.

'She was beautiful, wasn't she?'

Helen turned to see Leckie behind her. 'Yes.' She flicked the pages over finding two newspaper clippings taped to the page.

**Edinburgh Evening News.**
*17ᵗʰ November 1957*
*Jewellers Robbery. Man shot and killed. Second man arrested. Last month four men attempted to rob Clifton's Jewellers. One of the men, Harold Walter, fired a shotgun*

*at police, and fatally injured security guard Robert Andrews, who died later in hospital. Walter was apprehended at the scene. This morning Police arrested a second man, who was subsequently named as Reg Leckie. Police are appealing for witnesses to come forward.*

### *Obituary*
*Robert H. Andrews.*
*Suddenly at Edinburgh Royal Infirmary,*
*on 15ᵗʰ November, aged 30.*
*Loving husband of Sylvia.*
*Sorely missed*
*Family flowers only, please.*

'You don't mind if we take this photo?' Craven held up a recent photo of Derek Leckie.

'Aye,' the old man said without looking at Craven. He pointed to the album Helen was flicking through. 'I keep them to remember all the things I've done wrong in my life and so that Derek wouldnae make the same mistakes I did. He kens everything I went tae prison for and he's trying to make a good life for himself.' He let out a cry and broke down. Leckie's emaciated body leaned into Helen, heaving as he sobbed. 'How can ma son be deid?'

'Were going to do our best to get these answers for you.' Helen replied. 'We found your son in Edinburgh. Do you know what he was doing there?'

'He had a job as a handyman and it gave him lodgings but I cannae remember where.'

'Was it a hotel or a school maybe?'

'I dinnae ken. I'm sorry.'

When they both got back in the car, Helen wound her window down. She shook her head. A hard knot formed in her stomach. 'That old man will not survive without his son. Whoever murdered Derek Leckie may as well have killed him too.' Her shoulder felt damp and she blotted it with a tissue. She thought back to the two cups in the kitchen and the photos of a smiling Reg Leckie with this wife and son.

Two little boys ran past the car with a rusty wheelbarrow. The smaller one with scraped knees gave her a wave and smile.

She waved back.

Craven lit a cigarette and exhaled the smoke slowly before speaking. 'He's no saint and his son wasn't either.'

'Saint or not. No-one deserves to die like that.'

He slipped the car into first and pulled out into the road. 'Back to some real police work, eh? Bet you're glad that you didnae go on your holiday after all?'

'Why do you have to be like that?'

'Like what?'

'So horrible.'

'Ach, that old man up there has hurt loads of people in his time.'

# Chapter Twenty-Five

There was a time when Helen used to roll her eyes when she heard the remarks again and again, but now she didn't even bother. '*You're too pretty to be a copper*' or '*You can stick your handcuffs on me, sweetheart.*' Those were the favourites. It might have been funny once, if only they all didn't say the same thing and every one of them thinking they were being clever and witty. Helen looked at him as she walked past. She didn't mean to do so but his strong Glaswegian accent cut through the noise of the several other football hooligans and drunkards who were being propped up by the arresting officers, typical for the weekend.

One man was skeletal, in his fifties, prematurely aged by booze and fags. He raised his eyebrows at her and offered a gummy smile. His slicked-back silver matted hair, bloodshot eyes and whisky nose made it clear he would spend a drunken night in one of the cells. A constable had a pincer-like grip on his arm and swung him over around to the other side of the desk without any effort. As much as he tried to resist, the man was whipped off his feet with ease, his face contorted in pain.

She headed through the building and jogged quickly up the stairs into CID. DC McMaster hurried past with files bundled under each arm and two tins of tape in his hands. He kept his head down, she moved aside to let him past. Friday nights and the weekends were always fun at the station, and tomorrow the station would smell of sweat, sick and cigarette smoke diluted with cleaning fluid. Then it would be cleaned, ready to start all over again the next night.

Helen sat down at her desk thinking about George Stanley. It was something that had never appealed to her, being a private investigator or agent as she had heard them being called. Most of the private investigators she knew were the old types who couldn't give up the job when they retired, and that she could understand.

She flicked through Stanley's service record and it read like her own dream. He had joined the police straight out of national service aged twenty. A few years in uniform and then moved into Serious Crimes in the Met and worked his way up to Detective Inspector aged just twenty-nine and finished off his career in Glasgow. His career couldn't have worked out any better than if she had written it herself and she couldn't help but feel envious.

She flicked over the next page to find Stanley had abruptly left the police in June, 1971. 'Why?' she mumbled and closed the folder.

'Why, what?' Randall look up from the pile of papers on his desk with a friendly smile. His circular glasses had slipped down the bridge of his nose. Helen looked at him; this was the first time he had spoken to her directly and no doubt only because his buddies had finished shift. Ever since she'd arrived he had made it difficult by ignoring her, making sly comments, withholding information and "forgetting" to tell her things. Lots of new officers had arrived when the serious crimes squad was created, yet he acted like her being there was a personal insult to him. But when his pals weren't around he became one of the nicest men around. *Arsehole.*

Helen shook her head. 'It's nothing.' She resisted the urge to look round and make sure it was her he was actually talking too.

A couple of other officers were sharing a desk at the top of the room. It looked as though they were going through fingerprints.

Randall leaned forward, looking keen for her to explain what she was looking at. No doubt he would have a look through her desk when she was away. She had caught him in the act before.

Helen slipped Stanley's case file back in the desk drawer;

that way it would be easy to find later and hence less chance of Craven moving it or taking the credit for her work.

Randall took off his glasses to clean them. 'It looks like you've been busy there, pet. How many of the statements have you gone through?'

*What's it got to do with you?* 'I've just finished going through the missing persons register.' Helen looked back down at her work. She had to get back to sorting those witness statements for the DCI for his briefing in the morning. She massaged her temples, easing the throbbing that had slowly built up behind her blurry eyes. She had suspected for some time now that she needed reading glasses but she hadn't actually got round to visiting the optician.

A telephone rang and they exchanged glances. It was Craven's. They both thought about answering but Helen decided to wait until it made the rounds and reached her phone.

Randall looked back down to the papers on his desk. Helen had her hand braced on the telephone, picking it up on the first ring when it hit her.

'Sergeant Carter.'

'Finally got through to one of you,' the staff Sergeant growled down the phone. 'I've got someone down at the front desk asking to see you, well, demanding to see you.'

'What, to see me?' Randall looked at her and put his pen down. Helen swivelled slightly in her seat and lowered her voice. 'Do you know who it is? I'm not expecting—'

'Your fiancé, or so he says, anyway. He sound familiar?'

Helen looked up at the ceiling tiles. She could feel Randall's stare. 'Tell him I'll be right down.'

'Is everything alright, Helen? Got a wee visitor?'

'Never better.' She scooped up her jacket and headed for the door. 'I'll see you tomorrow.'

'Have a good night, Helen.'

That sent a shiver down her spine.

\*\*\*

117

Ted looked up and smiled as Helen walked through the double doors. He was sitting on a Formica chair under a poster that said 'Thieves beware.' He put the plastic cup on the floor as she approached, and got up from his seat. He looked tired, and for the first time, she noticed how deep the creases were around his eyes.

'I didn't expect you here.'

'I know love. Sorry…'

'I didn't mean it like that.' She looked down to the holdall that was sitting on the other chair. 'I'm sorry; I couldn't come down to your mum's for the weekend but I've had a nightmare of a day.'

He kissed her on the cheek. 'You could look at least a little pleased to see me.'

'I'm just in the middle of a case. I've got a pounding headache and I expected you…' She paused and looked at the clock on the wall. 'Yes, I expected you to be at your mum's party.' She relaxed and let herself smile. 'Of course, I'm pleased to see you. We've all been working double shifts. I don't know whether I'm coming or going.'

'Good.' He smiled. 'I'm sorry I snapped on the phone, I know it's not your fault that your work is so demanding.'

'I just can't take time off, but I'm glad you're here…' She motioned towards his bag. 'I appreciate the gesture, though. I really do.'

'I went to your flat but there was no answer. I thought that it was better to come here than waiting for you to come home at God knows what hour.' He looked down to her jacket. 'Please, please say you're finished for the evening at least, right?'

'Has something happened, Ted? You don't seem…'

'That coffee is awful by the way, but I needed something to keep me awake.' He reached down to the foam cup and took another swig, grimacing.

'You must really be desperate to drink that rubbish,' Helen said, slipping on her jacket.

'I just needed to see you.' He moved the cup and some of his coffee splashed onto his hand. 'Dammit.' He rubbed it on his trouser leg and placed the cup on the chair.

'Have you had your hair cut?'

'Yesterday.' He put a hand in front of his mouth to stifle a yawn. His brown hair had been styled in a side pattern; a few strands had strayed onto his forehead. He made no mention of the change in her own hair style, a few weeks back.

'I've really missed you. I don't want to argue. I know this job adds a lot of pressure and I only want what's best for you. For us. I don't want us to be apart for so long ever again.' Ted leaned in to kiss her mouth.

Helen turned her cheek to him. 'I can't talk about this here.' She could see the desk Sergeant glaring at them from his pile of papers. Ted hugged her tight; his six-foot frame dwarfed her. She took his hand and led him out of the station.

They stopped talking as they headed over to her car. She watched him puff rapidly on his cigarette. The frosty air felt like a stab to the chest and made plumes of smoke out of their breath.

Ted was ten years older than her, but the new rockabilly spectacles he had started to wear since his last optician's appointment made him appear even older. He was wearing the lilac shirt Helen had bought him with a floral cravat which was partially tucked into his shirt. Her mother always liked to say he had classic good looks, even comparing him to Dick York from TV. Maybe in certain lights he *did* look a bit like him.

Home was the top floor flat of a tenement block in Newington. The area was most popular with students who went to the technical college. There was a whole range of boutique shops that she would at some point visit, when she could get a day away from work. So far she had only been to Diane's café on the corner and the chip shop. Both had always been more than adequate for her needs, considering the amount of time she had spent there. They did not speak until she was locking the door.

'This is…'

'You can say it.'

'I was going to say it's nice. Well, once it's done up it could be nice. Anyway, this is only temporary.'

'Is it?'

Ted followed her through to the kitchen then dumped his bag onto the table, right on top of her notes. He took out a cigarette, putting it to his mouth. Helen looked in the cupboards for an ashtray, eventually settling for an old chipped tea plate.

She watched him look around the kitchen, taking in every detail. She motioned to the peeling floral wallpaper above the cooker. 'I'll get around to sorting out the décor at some point.'

'You'll need some new tiles too.'

'Are you going to put up the tiles?' Helen rummaged through the cupboards. 'Well, I have a tin of pie and some Smash. Sound okay?

'Is that all you've got?'

She waved the packet of Smash at him. 'This is quite nice, honestly.'

'I'm into Italian at the moment. Have you got a Yellow Pages? I'll see if one's open.'

'For mash, get Smash.' She rummaged further behind some tins and managed to find some rice pudding and a tin of peaches for afters. She set them down on the worktop. 'You'll enjoy this, honestly! Or I've got a couple of Vesta meal things…'

'Those tins are fine then. Anyway, I've got a bottle of red in my bag.'

'I thought you were going to cut back on the drinking after last time.'

'I am. It's only the one bottle, to share.'

Ted had gone through to the living room and she heard music coming from the radio, something classical. She couldn't help but smile at the thought of someone else in the flat other than her. Helen picked his woollen overcoat from the chair, still damp from the evening's rain. As she hung it up on the corner of the kitchen door something hard in the lining thumped against her thigh. Reaching into the pocket, she found a ring box. Her heart raced. She resisted the urge to open it. It felt heavy in her hand.

'Is everything alright, darling?' Ted's head was peering around the kitchen door, a glass of wine in his hand. His brow furrowed. 'You should have just left my jacket where it was—'

'It was damp. It won't dry folded on the chair.' She slipped the box back in the pocket, feeling like a child caught with her hand in the biscuit tin.

# Chapter Twenty-Six

Helen rubbed the sleep from her eyes. The smell of burnt toast wafted into the bedroom. She groaned but could not force her drained body to move. It was still dark and not even the hint of morning leaked through the gap in the curtain. Helen shivered and pulled the duvet over her head; she would only wake when there was actual daylight.

The sound of clattering pans and cupboard doors opening and thumping shut pounded through her head. She strained to see the clock. Seven-thirty. Not that bad, she supposed, considering this was her first full night's sleep in as long as she could remember. Damn, it must be at least two weeks. She closed her eyes again. Another crash, this time followed by a muffled shout, then the dreaded rattling of the water pipes.

'Bloody hell, Ted,' she called out getting up, but the thumping continued. The lino felt icy against her feet. She grabbed her dressing gown from the hook, tying it tightly. The kitchen door was closed but she could still hear him crashing about inside. He was like that – always up impossibly early, always had to be busy doing something.

The living room door was wide open along with a window, the netting billowing against the wall in the wind. She rubbed her arms, went through and pulled it shut. Nearly tripping over some half-empty tins of lager and last night's plates on the floor as she did so. One tin had drained its contents onto the carpet. She made a big step over it, and then went through to the bathroom, grabbing a hand towel to mop up the spillage. The telly was on, and some kids programme flickered on the screen. She took the damp towel through to the bathroom and dropped it into the sink.

Against her better judgement, she glanced at her puffy,

tired face in the mirror. A shower would help, she thought, and turned the nozzle, holding her hand under the spray of water until it started to warm. She stepped in closing her eyes as the warm water washed the night away.

As soon as she went back through to the living room, the phone started to ring. The noise in the kitchen stopped abruptly. A second later she had the receiver in her hand and before she could say even her name, Ted emerged from the kitchen, carrying a mug. He took a sip and eyed her carefully.

'Woke you up from your beauty sleep, have I?'

Helen waved a hand at Ted and pressed the receiver to her ear. 'Morning, Jack. No, I've been up a while.' She could see Ted shaking his head from the corner of her eye.

'You better skip the face powder this morning, sweetheart. I'm going to need you down here. We've been called to another one.' It sounded as though he'd had a hard night.

'What! Another one?'

'Male found dead this morning.'

'How?'

'Gunshot wound. He hasn't been dead long. I can get a car to pick you up if needed.'

'No,' she shook her head, 'I've got the Mini.'

Helen massaged her temples, avoiding Ted's stare.

'Give me thirty minutes and I'll be there.' From the corner of her eye, Helen could make out Ted shaking his head again. She put the receiver down and shook hers too.

'Listen, I have to do my job and this is all part of it.'

He waved a hand at the phone. 'Yes, but I just didn't expect....'

'Didn't expect what?' She started to mop the up the mess on the carpet. 'You just heard my phone call, didn't you? It's not like I'm volunteering to go in or anything.'

'I thought we could at least go out for breakfast. I had a whole day planned...'

'I don't have a choice. It's my job.'

'Don't you even want us to work?'

'That's really not fair!' She sighed. 'I'm just trying to do my job the best I can. I explained to you last night that we were in the middle of a big case.'

'For goodness' sake, Helen. All the more reason to leave that job! I have more than enough income, you don't need to resort to this.' He took a sip of his coffee. 'Especially if you expect me to be here when you get back.'

'*I am the spirit of dark and lonely water,*' sounded out from the television, as the camera panned in on the black and white grim reaper. Goosebumps prickled her skin and her throat tightened. The narrator's deep voice echoing in her ears. She ran over and shakily pulled the plug on the TV.

'I was watching that.' Ted pointed at the screen, his brow furrowed in annoyance.

'It reminds me of what happened to my brother.' She looked at the blank screen. 'I can't watch it.'

'I'm sorry. I forgot.' Ted held out his hand. Helen shook her head, grabbing her bag. She headed for the door.

'Fantastic,' she mumbled to herself. 'Fan-bloody-tastic.' Last night's weather had covered the Mini's windscreen in a thick coating of frost. Helen rubbed her freezing hands and stomped on the spot. She had forgotten her gloves up in the flat and her damp hair still stuck to her face.

After scraping away the frost, Helen tugged the driver's side door open. Thankfully the engine purred into life with one click. As the winter months had progressed, she found the car sometimes needed a little persuading to start. After she was more settled, she would get a more up-to-date vehicle, but for now it had to do.

Mini in gear, she manoeuvred through the morning traffic, through Fountain Park and the smell of the Fountain Brewery then onwards down onto Princes Street. By the time she passed the Princes Street Gardens and The Scot's Monument, the frost had been replaced with rain and the sky was now the same colour as the imposing rock of the Edinburgh Castle.

Helen leant forward, straining to see through the rain that began to lash against the windscreen. Her eyes felt hot and stung as she rubbed them with a heel of the hand. She stopped near the Edinburgh Waverley train station, slowing for two buses that pulled out in front. Undeterred by the rain, people poured in and out of the shops that lined one side of the street. She sighed, shakily trying to push the thought of what happened to her brother from her mind. He'd be nearly thirty-five now. Still, life is for the living, as her dad used to say. She looked up at the Castle which also served as barracks for the army. She didn't have the time to admire it today though, as she slipped the car into second.

Ten minutes later she pulled up into Mayfield Place with tenements flanking both sides of the street. The only cars parked were police vehicles.

# Chapter Twenty-Seven

'What's his name?' Helen approached the dead, fat man, who was slumped over in his leather armchair in the back room of the sweet shop.

'Arnold Richard Heath, he's the owner,' the uniformed officer said, following her.

'Was the owner,' she corrected him. 'Age?'

'Fifty-six.'

The room was not much bigger than a cleaning cupboard. Pathologist Alex Winston was mumbling to himself as he rummaged through his briefcase. He didn't look up as she entered. The door frame had grooves for hinges but no door attached. Heath's chin rested on his chest, eyes closed. He could almost pass for sleeping had it not been for the crimson stain. The blood had seeped from his stomach and collected in a pool on the floor and over his slippers. Helen looked at the angle of the chair. It was positioned so that he could sit in the back and still have full view of the shop. The pungent aroma of shit, vomit and stomach bile hit her suddenly. It was like that rotting cat she had discovered under her shed in the back garden a few years ago. She dry-retched a few times and covered her mouth.

Craven chuckled as he walked up behind her and patted her on the back; she leant onto the door frame for support.

'C'mon, hen. You'll need to be a bit harder than this to last in CID. Bloody women, eh? This is what we get when nepotism exists in the force. If you're going to be sick, go outside. I'm no' wanting you ruining my crime scene and I could do wi' a cup of tea anyway.'

Helen batted him away. 'I'm fine, thanks. Go get your own tea.'

She glared at him and took a few short breaths through

126

her mouth to steady herself, her face scarlet and sweaty. *Fuck off!* She wanted to shout. *Nobody has done me any favours.*

She leaned down so that she was level with Heath's forearms. His nails were filed short and clean. His hands were free of any defensive wounds. Three stab marks were visible under his rolled up shirt sleeves. The wounds were distinctively star-shaped rather than like a blade.

She felt Alex's eyes on her and he pre-empted her question.

'It looks like he was stabbed with a screwdriver in the arms before being shot in the stomach.' He shook his head. 'What a way to go, eh?'

'Our victim yesterday was stabbed with a screwdriver as well.' Helen swallowed and looked at Craven.

'It's too similar to ignore.' Craven stood in the doorway rustling a bag of Treets; he popped a handful into his mouth and stood waiting for the crime scene officer to take the last of his photos at the back of the shop.

The victim's final meal sat on the table beside him. A half-eaten spam sandwich and a nearly full mug of milky tea. An Agatha Christie paperback looked as if it had been knocked off the table.

'He's been dead a couple of hours at most. The killer would most likely have been known to him, or they might have looked like they were nothing to worry about,' Craven stated. 'It doesnae look like he tried to get out the chair.'

She pressed the back of her hand against the smooth surface of the mug. Stone cold.

'Rigor has started to set in… I would say he's been dead for aboot two to possibly six hours. Not very long at all,' Winston chimed in.

'Ugh.' Craven looked down to his boot and picked off three feathers that had stuck to the sole.

Helen looked down at her shoes. Feathers were stuck to hers as well. She scraped her shoes on the ground to get them off. Feathers lay scattered the floor. A cushion lay at Heath's feet and Helen could see a circular hole with singed edges.

Winston looked at the cushion then at Helen. His round cheeks were red and sweat glistened on his forehead. The cheery demeanour of yesterday was long dead and it was understandable why. This could easily be one of the busiest weeks he'd had and he too would have been dragged out of bed far too early in the morning.

Winston looked her up and down then closed his bag. 'What the hell happened to you? Rough night, eh?'

Helen rubbed a hand through her damp hair in a vain attempt to stop it sticking to the back of her blouse. 'Has anything been taken from the shop?' she asked Craven.

'Nah.' Craven reached over the counter and opened another bag of Treets.

Helen felt her blood rise. She gave him a hard stare, not that it would do any good.

Craven took time to chew a sweet before speaking again. 'Disnae seem to be anything missing in the shop. Till's full and booze and fags are still behind the counter.'

'That's apart from the stock that's disappearing into your mouth.'

Craven shrugged. 'I've been around the back of the building. There's no sign of forced entry, no disturbance and no one has seen or heard anything either. Uniform are out combing the bins and side alleys in case the killer dumped the murder weapon. '

'I don't think they'll find anything.' Helen glanced at the door; most of the glass was covered in sale stickers and special offers. This was probably a good thing and stopped passers-by and reporters getting a good look in. She could just about make out the shapes of the two constables blocking the scene and talking to potential witnesses.

'Have you got the list of employees?' She manoeuvred past the magazine rack. Her gaze fell upon the bridal magazines on the bottom shelf.

'McKinley is getting a list together now. You're probably going to have to come with me later,' Craven added.

'I'm finished here.' Alex stood up then slipped his

glasses off, rubbing the sides of his nose where they had pinched and left red indentations.

A constable was dusting for prints near the door and counter but Helen would be surprised if they managed to get anything useful from them. Lots of people would touch them on a day-to-day basis.

Helen nodded. 'You said he was found by the cleaning lady? Does she clean every day?'

'She comes round once a week and she does his flat upstairs as well.'

Craven slipped another chocolate in his mouth and crumpled the empty packet into his trouser pocket.

'You still shouldn't be eating the stock, sir. '

'Calm doon, hen. He's no' going to miss it, is he? I was on shift all night. And I've no had ma breakfast yet.'

Winston let out a sigh. 'I'll see you both later on. I've got to get to court.'

Helen moved out of the room so that Winston could get out. His stomach nearly knocked over the cup of tea as he struggled past.

'A few more things before you go,' Helen said. 'Do you have any idea what kind of gun?'

'I would say a handgun.'

'And did he die in the chair?'

'He's been struck at downwards angles. See this?' He pointed to Heath's belt, where the skin had turned a purplish blue. 'After death, the heart stops pumping blood around the body and collects around any bit of the corpse that has pressure. So, yes, he has been sat here, long story short. Right, I'll see you down the mortuary for the postmortem. Hopefully, it will be a few days at least before our paths cross again.'

Helen picked up the black and white photograph of Arnold Heath, his wife and smiling child, a seaside shot then another on a white beach; France or Spain maybe. She turned the frame over in her hands. It was by no means a recent shot judging from the bloated cadaver that was slumped in a chair. The muscular man in his forties in the photograph had since lost all his hair and gained at least five stone.

'Where are the wife and child, then?'

Craven shrugged. 'The photo looks auld; that wee lassie might be in her twenties and as for the wife…'

'He's been on a lot of holidays. That must have been expensive.'

Craven took one of the photos from her hand. 'He does look familiar but I don't recognise the name, Heath.'

She motioned to the ceiling. 'I'll take a look at the flat upstairs.' Craven nodded. 'It's through there.' He pointed to a door behind the till and followed her up the stairs.

A winding set of creaky stairs led to a studio flat. The door was locked but Helen located the key on a hook on the staircase. She moved through a narrow hallway and into the bedsit. Rain battered the attic skylight and the floorboards groaned under their weight.

Helen looked around the room. A faint smell of polish still lingered sweetly. Framed photographs of his family adorned the walls, pictures of his daughter at all stages of life covered the cracked plasterwork. A television set with TV guide magazines underneath sat in front of the window. A little stained glass lamp still illuminated the room. A bookshelf in the corner was crammed with art journals and yellowing travel books and paperback novels, mostly crime ones. There were more family photographs on the top shelf. Smiling faces on holiday and passing milestones.

The living room-cum-kitchen area was pristine. The sofa bed was made and orange cushions had been placed at each end of it. Dishes set out to dry on the drying rack and an orange spotty tea cloth hung over the oven handle. Helen felt them – the cloth was damp to the touch but the dishes were bone dry.

The bleach smell got stronger as she moved towards the fridge. A speckle of red caught her eye on the faded cream lino floor. It looked dry. 'Jack, we might have some blood here. Get forensics up to the kitchen area.'

She heard him shouting to someone in the corridor.

'Forensics are on their way up. This is not bad, is it?' She turned to see Craven looming in the doorway. She walked over to the bin and lifted the lid, empty apart from a carton of eggs and the previous day's *Evening News*.

Helen looked at the block of knives. One was missing from its slot. She slid open the cutlery drawer to find a serrated bread knife placed on top of the butter knives, its plastic handle still damp.

'Sir, I think we should have a look at this. She waved Craven across and he looked over her shoulder. 'What do you think?'

'Possible, it looks out of place. We'll get it dusted for dabs.'

He shouted through to the hall. 'Alan, got some knives I want dusting when you're done with the door.' He turned to Helen. 'We will probably get nothing from it anyway. It looks like it has been thoroughly wiped clean.'

She nodded. 'I don't get why it wouldn't have been put back in the knife block through. Someone cleaned it up but at the same time made it stand out.' It was probably the knife he used to make his sandwich, she thought.

'They might have been in a rush to get cleaned up because they know the old bag from next door comes through to clean.'

She walked through to the bathroom. Just big enough for a bath, a small hand basin and toilet. It boasted a modern avocado suite, with pink towels folded neatly on the handrail and another at the corner of the bath. There was a laundry basket but that was empty. Helen examined the sink, and the towels felt dry. The sink looked clean and the taps freshly polished.

'It's all clear through here, Jack.'

'Well, it's no' all clear through here, sweetheart.'

Craven was leaning over the sofa. He had picked up a book on Aztec culture. 'Guess what he is using as a bookmark?' He flicked the card with his finger. It was George Stanley's business card, dog-eared in the middle of the book. A smile spread across Craven's face. 'I bloody knew he'd pop up again.'

Helen shrugged. 'That could just be coincidence, Jack. It doesn't mean that Stanley had anything to do with—'

'Well, I want him picked up *now* and waiting in the station for me in an interview room when I get back.'

'As you wish.' Helen replied.

Craven put the book back down on the side table. Helen headed towards the hallway.

'Bloody Hell! What have we got here then?'

'What?' Helen turned back to see Craven looking up the fireplace.

He pulled a little torch from his pocket and pointed it towards the chimney.

'What is it?' Helen asked again.

'There's a shotgun suspended up there with rope.'

'A shotgun?'

'I didn't think I stuttered…'

Helen bit her lip. She came back into the room and peered up the flue beside Craven. The brick fireplace was wide and the shotgun had been hung just a few inches up from the opening. It swayed back and forth. There were some charred remnants of paper at their feet.

Craven stood up, knocking a duck ornament off the mantelpiece with his shoulder. 'He must've been worried for his own safety then? Or hiding it for someone, maybe?' He brushed some coal dust from his hands.

Before Helen could say anything, McKinley popped his head around the alcove. 'Helen, the DCI needs a word with you outside.' She exchanged a confused look with Craven.

'Do you know why?'

'Yeah, he wants you to have a word with the wee old woman who found Heath. She's very emotional.'

# Chapter Twenty-Eight

Beryl Butler, the shop's cleaning lady, shook her head. She smoothed out her pinny with a shaky hand and scraped off some muck with her nail. Her silvery hair was in rollers and half-covered with a floral scarf. She picked at the threads on the apron as she spoke. 'I cannae believe, I just cannae believe…' All the colour had drained from her tear-stained cheeks.

She looked up at Helen with bloodshot eyes. 'Who would go and do that to a poor old man? Edinburgh's always such a safe place. You dinnae get this kind of thing.'

*Oh, you do*, Helen had wanted to say.

She continued. 'I just wouldnae expect…. Oh hen, he's such a lovely man.'

'Beryl. You don't mind if I call you by your first name do you?'

'Aye.' Beryl muttered. 'Who would have wanted to dae this?'

'We are doing everything that we can to find that out.' Helen sat down beside her on the sofa. The woman lived next door to the shop. Helen still wasn't convinced that she shouldn't have been sent to the hospital for shock but the DCI had managed to get her to calm down enough for Helen to speak to her.

'I would make a few meals for him and clean, to help him out. This is so horrible, I cannae believe… He's been murdered.'

Beryl shook her head as Helen handed her a cup of tea. 'Okay Beryl, Can you help me with some questions?'

'I'll try.'

'When was the last time you saw Arnold?'

'Yesterday morning when I went through for some

bread.'

'How did he look when you saw him?'

'He wis fine, everything wis normal.' She took a polka dot handkerchief from her pocket. 'I got to the shop, the door was ajar and all the lights were off.'

'Okay, and normally the door would have been locked?'

'Aye.' Beryl nodded and fished in her pocket, pulling out two brass keys on a ring. 'I let myself in with these.' She separated them and handed them to Helen. 'This is the back door one, and this is the front door.'

'Do you know anyone else that might have a key to the shop?'

Beryl shook her head. 'No, I think it's just me that has the spare. The shop normally doesn't open until eight, sometimes a little afterwards depending on how Arnold is feeling that day. Sometimes he likes a lie-in.'

'And what time did you get to the shop this morning?'

'Just after seven.'

'Did you see anything out of the ordinary? Did you hear a disturbance?'

Beryl took a deep breath and looked up to the ceiling. 'No, it was all quiet. I heard nothing at all. I went into the shop, shouted for him, and then I went through to his little back room and found him like that. For a wee second, I thought he was sleeping. I walked up to him and…'

'I understand that this is really difficult for you but can you think of anyone that might have a reason for doing this?'

'Does anyone hiv' a reason tae commit murder, officer? Ah bloody doated on him. You'll no find anyone that could say a bad word against him, that's for sure.'

'Does he have any family?'

'Yes, he was married but his wife died a few years back and his daughter works as a secretary in London.' She gasped and covered her mouth. 'His poor wee daughter! That wee lassie has gone through enough already.'

'Gone through enough?'

'Aye wi' her mum and that. It's a bloody sin.'

'I will speak to her, Beryl. But can you think… is there… was there anything out of the ordinary in the past few days or last night?'

Beryl looked away to the carpet and took a few seconds to think before she looked back at Helen. 'No, not really.'

'Not really? It doesn't matter how small you think it is. Anything little bit of information might be what we are looking for.'

She nodded. 'I am not sure if it's any use but there was a van parked outside last night – aye, I thought it might have been deliveries, last night parked on the pavement. It was there late last night and gone when I went through to clean for him this morning. But it's probably nothing.'

'Do you know what kind of van it was?'

Beryl grabbed onto Helen's arm. 'I don't really know anything about vans or cars. I can't tell you what kind it is, except it was dark blue, maybe black. And it quite looked old.'

'That's okay Beryl – what made you think that it looked old?'

'Well…' She rubbed her chin before responding. 'It's one of the old style vans and it wis rusted at one side. I noticed it when I walked past.'

'Was there any writing on the van, a company name?'

'I don't know… I don't think so, I wasnae really paying that much attention.'

'Did you happen to see the driver?'

'No, I didnae see anyone inside it at all and the lights were off in the shop.'

'And you're sure you haven't seen the van around before?'

'It's probably nothing but it's all I can think of. I've called ma son, he is going to pick me up soon.' She looked at the clock on her mantelpiece. 'He'll be here any minute.'

\*\*\*

Outside, Helen rubbed her boot on the wet grass. It had been recently cut; she took a deep breath, inhaling the smell. She closed her eyes. The wind added a chill to the air and the rain that had whipped violently before had eased to a gentle drizzle. The smell of shit from the shop still stung her nostrils and she could see Arnold Heath and his injuries every time she closed her eyes.

Helen started for the phone box on the corner. Ted might still be in the flat. A hand tapped her on the shoulder. She batted it away and whipped around to see Craven. He pulled away with an expression on his face like she'd gone mad.

'You gave me a fright.'

'I know women are over-emotional but bloody hell, Carter.'

'Sorry.' Helen shook her head. 'I was just in a world of my own. Two murders in two days, what are the chances, eh?'

'Aye.' Craven looked up to the sky. 'This is a first for me too. Did you get anything useful from that old cleaner?'

'Not a lot. She might have seen a van parked outside the shop. She's in shock though; she should be going to the hospital, not have me interviewing her.'

'A van?' He flicked the butt end of his cigarette into a puddle and watched it fizzle out. 'There was a van parked outside the picture house.'

'If this is the same murderer, he's evolving. This is much less frenzied and it's more organised.'

'What are the chances that both victims would have a business card for George Stanley and not be related? Even though they were both killed with different weapons, both had marks on them from a screwdriver. It's too much of a coincidence for me.'

'They're going to kill again. It's only a matter of time.'

'I've had a couple of officers tailing George Stanley since the picture house. He wasn't anywhere near the shop at the time of the murder. He's a bastard, but no' a murderer, anyway.'

His lip twitched and he looked away. She wanted to ask

about Stanley. He wasn't giving her the whole picture but she decided to leave it for the time being.

'Anyway,' Craven shrugged. 'We've done a thorough door-to-door but it's just the same situation as yesterday, no one has seen anything or heard anything useful.' He scoffed. 'No one can understand what happened and he's such a quiet old man who everyone loved.' He shook his head and took a cigarette out from his pocket.

'Why am I not surprised?'

'Check at the station for any witness statements that mentioned any hint of a van.' Craven cupped his hands around the cigarette and lit it.

The wind blew the smoke into her face. The sweet smell burned her nostrils. She breathed it in deep.

'And another thing, go and check for known criminals with vans.'

She could see a few police officers talking to people on the streets. They had just cordoned off half the street to stop people walking past.

Craven looked as if he were about to say something else but stopped as Keaton approached.

\*\*\*

The CID room stank of damp clothing and rain. Helen draped her jacket over the radiator to dry it off. The sash window behind Craven's desk was open. Rainwater had collected on the windowsill. She shut it and went back to her desk. Helen picked up the phone and had started to dial Ted's number when McKinley crashed into the room with folders in each hand. She put the phone down.

'Thank goodness. I've been going through all this myself.'

'Terry, has anyone you've spoken to mentioned anything about seeing a van at the cinema or the sweet shop?'

McKinley rubbed his head and walked over to his desk. 'Eh, I can't remember off the top of ma head but I'll check.' His face looked flushed, his blond hair, which was normally up in a quiff, lay flat against his face, and his shirt was damp with sweat.

'Are you feeling alright?' Helen asked.

He nodded, cupping his hand over the telephone receiver, and began to dial a number. 'Yes, I'm just rushed off my feet this morning with the DI. He has us both doing the dog's work as usual. Is everything alright with you? You're looking a bit—'

'I've had a hell of a morning, Terry. Just don't go there.' Helen slumped down in her seat with her first coffee of the day in her hand. She tried to pat down her hair after catching sight of her reflection on the photograph of herself and Ted on her desk. The photo had been taken at her sister's wedding; that was a good day. Ted had even talked about getting engaged, but that was before everything changed. She looked away from the photograph. She had run out the house this morning minus her makeup and her hair felt damp and frizzy from the rain. She raked in her handbag for her hairbrush and cosmetic bag. Damn, they must be at home.

Instinctively, she looked down at the telephone receiver, her heart pounding faster at the thought of calling Ted. She dialled the number but hung up the phone before it rang. Taking a sip of coffee to calm her nerves, she tried to push away the thought of him packing his stuff and the flat being empty tonight when she got back. She couldn't deal with a day of work if she knew he was doing that. Picking up the photograph, she rammed it into her top drawer. Out of sight, out of mind.

Helen forced herself to go through the files from the collator's office and was now thumbing through information about all the vans in the area and vans owned by known criminals. She couldn't find any that matched the description given by the cleaner. When Helen had transferred to Edinburgh. She'd gone through most of these files to get a feel for the area.

She leaned back in her chair; in all probability, the van meant nothing. Afterwards, she would need to go through the shop's accounts and see who made the deliveries, on the off-chance it was their van.

McKinley was sitting opposite her going through the list of employees who had worked in the cinema before it had closed down. He had the telephone receiver balanced on his shoulder, using his hands to scribble things and find the right pieces of paper. A lot of the records had been destroyed in the fire and McKinley was having trouble finding out information from the former manager. He looked up and flashed Helen a smile, before pretending to bang his head on the desk.

'Right,' he said to Helen as he hung up the phone. 'A woman saw a van outside the picture house at around ten that night, and it was gone by the time she got up in the morning.' He turned the page over. 'A dark blue van, possibly a Leyland.'

Sally strolled in with an envelope in her perfectly manicured hands. Helen watched McKinley straighten in his seat as soon as he noticed her. Sally flicked her hair as she walked past his desk. She put the envelope on Craven's desk and pursed her lips, avoiding eye contact with either of them before marching back out.

Helen arched an eyebrow. 'You're in the doghouse?' she whispered when Sally was safely out of earshot.

McKinley hunched his shoulders. 'Story of my life.'

'Right, we'll make this quick. Carter, get the kettle on,' DCI Whyte barked as he stomped into the CID room followed closely by an irritated looking Craven. 'I want everyone through in my office for a briefing. *Now*.'

Before Helen could reply, Whyte marched out of the office and down the corridor.

Helen avoided eye contact with Craven and stuck the kettle on to boil, spooning instant coffee into stained mugs. The briefing had already begun when Helen entered with the tray of coffees in front of her. Craven had his arms crossed and was leaning against the wall.

'Okay, before the press publish the names we need to make sure the family is informed.' Whyte was sitting at his desk, hands clasped. His golf clubs were stacked in the corner and an oil painting of Edinburgh Castle was hanging on the wall behind him. His receding grey hair had been freshly cut and he was wearing a crisp white shirt.

He continued. 'I've spoken to the press this morning to appeal for any information that may help us.'

Helen squeezed past Randall and a nervous McKinley who was chewing on a fingernail. She put the tray down on the mahogany desk then thumped one of the chipped mugs in front of Craven. He snatched it and his hand lingered against hers.

'Get Carter to speak with Arnold Heath's daughter.' Whyte took his mug. 'Woman's touch and all that.'

'Aye,' Craven took a sip then crinkled his nose. 'Bloody Hell, Carter go easy on the instant will you, this tastes like tar.'

'Sorry, Sir. Perhaps you should make it next time if that's not to your taste.'

Detective Constable Randall spoke next. 'We've found a diamond head screwdriver thrown near a bin bag in the back garden of a nearby house. The wee lassie that lives there has no' seen it before. It's been examined for prints and Alex said that it looks like the right size and fit for the stab marks on Arnold Heath's arm.'

DCI Whyte looked down to his notebook. 'I'm still waiting on forensic reports. They've been rushed through so hopefully we'll have them by tomorrow at the latest.'

'Right, that's everything. Inspector Craven, I want a private word with you.'

# Chapter Twenty-Nine

Helen found an address for Sylvia Heath in Shepherds Bush, London. While she was on her last telephone call she scribbled the symbol found in the picture house. She traced over it with her pencil. After making the call, she was going to try and find out what that symbol meant. Others on the team had been trying without any luck.

She also managed to call in a favour from a WPC she had met on training and now worked in the Metropolitan Police. She would speak to Arnold Heath's daughter, Sylvia, in person. After the news was broken to her, Helen would try and call and see if there was anything that she could add to the investigation. She snatched up the receiver as soon as it rang.

'Hello, Sergeant Carter.'

'Hiya, Helen, it's Kelly. Just to let you know I have spoken to Sylvia Heath.'

'Thanks, I really appreciate it.'

'That's alright. She didn't take it well.'

'Did she say anything useful?'

'Not really, she's in shock.' Kelly paused. 'She phones her dad every Sunday and last time they spoke he was in good spirits. He was looking forward to retiring and moving down to London to be with her and her kids. She told me he was well-loved and ran that shop for over thirty years, and he's never mentioned being in trouble with anyone.'

'Thanks, Kelly. I hope you're doing well.'

'Getting there. Tired as usual. You take care now.'

She hung up the phone and it instantly rang again.

'Hello, Helen. It's Alex here.'

'Hi, Alex.' Helen took a sip of her coffee. 'What can I do for you?'

'It's more what I can do for you.'

'Okay, you've got me interested.'

'Remember the tramp from the park? It looks like he died of a heart attack.'

'That's not—'

'You've not let me finish, my dear.' Winston cleared his throat. 'He was branded.'

'Branded?' Helen sat up in her seat. McKinley looked up from his desk, his brow knitted together. She beckoned him over. 'What do you mean, branded?' McKinley perched on the end of her desk.

'He has the circular mark that we found in the picture house branded onto his stomach. It looked like it happened just before he died. And do you want to know the most important part of the puzzle?'

Helen sighed. 'Of course.'

'This is your first victim.'

'I don't understand.'

'This man died *before* the one in the picture house.'

Craven approached her desk just as she hung up the phone. 'Let's go and see this Parson again. '

'Ok, but there's something else you need to know first.'

# Chapter Thirty

'This looks good, doesn't it?' Craven said, holding up the menu. 'I quite fancy the summer pudding.'

'We're not here for the food.'

Helen and Craven took a seat at a table for four by the bay window. *Discreet*. She sat down and brushed crumbs off the plastic tablecloth. After reading through the rest of the menu, Craven ordered fruit scones and a pot of tea. A few minutes later, the waitress returned with a stained tin teapot and four small scones on a tray. Helen turned over the cup and poured herself some tea. She took a sip. *Overbrewed*. Craven was busy spreading butter over a scone. Helen spread hers thinly with raspberry conserve and took a bite just as Parson appeared, his eyes darting around the room. He was still wearing his food-stained apron and rubbing flour from his hands.

'You're looking a bit pale, Mr Parson,' Craven said. Another couple, in their forties, sat at a table near the door in the middle of a heated discussion. Helen couldn't make out the words but the man had reached out for the woman's hand and she pulled away.

'I can't help you, Inspector,' Parson said, as he looked over to the couple.

'That's okay, we can wait for your wife.' Craven took a bite of scone and chewed slowly.

Parson sat down opposite Helen. She fished in her pocket and placed a picture of Derek Leckie on the table. 'Do you recognise this man?'

Parson picked up the picture and stared at it a few seconds then turned it over and placed it back on the table. 'Yes, he worked here.' Parson started to rub his arm. 'I can't talk long. I need to get back to the kitchen.'

'Worked here?' Helen asked.

'Well, he's dead isn't he?'

'You almost look relieved,' Helen said, looking down to her notebook.

'No, I... I'm shocked. I don't know what to say.'

'You don't look that shocked,' she replied.

Parson looked away and mopped his forehead with a napkin.

'Right,' Craven cleared his throat. 'Derek Leckie stole your car and now he's dead?'

'Well...' Parson rubbed his arm vigorously leaving a red friction burn.

'Any idea why he would steal your car?'

He shook his head.

'Will your wife know?' Craven made a move to stand up.

'Wait, please.' Parson looked towards the door then leaned forward. 'Right, I'd let him borrow it from time to time. He didn't steal it.' Tears welled in his eyes. 'I had no choice... I had no choice.'

'Why did you tell us he did?'

'I didn't want my wife to know.' He sighed. 'He caught me with another woman and said he would tell my wife if I didn't help him out.'

Helen shook her head. 'And how exactly did you help him out?'

'I gave him money as well.'

'How much?'

'Am no' sure. Last time it wis, forty quid.'

Craven straightened up in his seat. 'Maybe he threatened you a bit too much and you wanted rid?'

'No, I didnae. I wouldnae!' He stared at them both, wide-eyed with an open mouth.

'Okay,' Helen said. 'When did the blackmail start?'

'Last month. Oh, God!' Parson rubbed his head again, and sneaked another glance towards the door. 'I gave him money from time to time just to keep him quiet and I would let him borrow the car. That's it! Now, I know what you're thinking but I didnae hurt him.' He shook his head. 'I didnae hurt him.'

Helen slipped the picture back in her pocket. 'Why were you going to report the car as stolen?'

He exhaled a shaky sigh.

'This is a murder investigation, Mr Parson.'

'I knew he had previous convictions and if he was caught with a stolen car...'

Craven wiped his hands on a napkin. 'So Derek Leckie being dead is like you winning the lottery.'

'I didnae do anything to hurt him. I just knew that if he was charged wi' stealing my car I'd be rid of him, and I know my wife wouldnae believe a word that he said. I didnae lay one hand on him.' He motioned to them. 'You lot would have arrested him and that would have been the end of it.'

Helen shook her head. 'Is there anyone around here who would want to hurt him?'

Parson scratched his bald head. 'No.' He swallowed. 'Everyone seemed to like him. All the lassies fancied him.' A sneer twitched his lip. 'Ma wife said he could charm the birds out the trees.'

It took all of Helen's willpower not to reply with, *Well, they're no' going to fancy you are they?* 'When was the last time you saw him?'

'Two days ago. He said he was going to take the car when he finished his shift... I think he was going to see some girl. I gave him the keys and that was it.' He reached out for Helen's hand. 'Please, dinnae tell my wife. It's our anniversary next week.'

Helen moved her hand away. 'You should have thought of that before, Mr Parson.'

Parson looked up at her with watery eyes. *Pathetic little man.* She threw a napkin in his direction. 'Dry your eyes, that won't work with us.'

# Chapter Thirty-One

It was a rancid chip-fat smelling shit-hole, but from this seat, Stanley was able to watch the police. The old woman behind the counter had noticed the police presence across the road as well. 'Terrible business that, son, eh? Terrible business.' She had muttered when she poured his coffee.

'Aye,' he replied, as she limped back over to the counter. Stanley took a long drag on his cigarette. He listened to the cars slosh past outside. A few people had passed in the sleet but apart from that, the streets of Edinburgh were deserted. He grimaced, putting the mug back on the table. The coffee was like piss. The cup still had a greasy feel and a smudge of lipstick from the last person to have drunk from it. The woman watched him from the counter.

'Do you know anything aboot that sweet shop?'

The old woman shrugged her shoulders. 'I just keep myself to myself, son. Want a bacon roll with that coffee?'

He slid the coffee cup away. 'Nah, you're alright.' Stanley brushed fag ash from the check-patterned cloth as he waited. He looked up as the door opened. A man in a wet mac entered. He waved to Stanley.

'You took your time.'

'Sorry.' Mike Savoy closed his umbrella, a spray of water hitting Stanley in the face. 'I got completely soaked out there.' He pulled out a plastic chair and sat down. 'You've seen better days.' Savoy motioned to his own face. 'What happened to your...?' Savoy's hair had clumped together like rat tails. He separated the strands with his fingers.

Stanley sighed. 'Some fucker jumped me.' He looked over to the old woman who was staring at them both. He lowered his voice. 'I dinnae want to talk about it. Now, what's this information that you said you had for me?'

'I can't tell you a lot, it's Craven's case.'

The old woman eyed the both of them. Savoy leaned in and whispered. 'You were right, the dead man in the sweet shop is Arnold Heath.'

'I knew that. I was expecting this.'

The old woman asked from the counter, 'Do you want a wee cup of tea, son? Or a roll?'

Savoy looked at Stanley's greasy cup then shook his head.

'Aye, he'll take a cup, darling,' Stanley said lifting his up.

The old woman muttered something under her breath.

When she was out of earshot Savoy continued. 'He was shot while he sat in a chair in the back of his shop. I couldn't get more information. Craven doesnae take backhanders.' Savoy shrugged. 'He'll not talk to me since I published details about a case he told me to keep quiet about.'

Stanley clasped his hands together and raised an eyebrow. Mike Savoy had always been pretty thick. 'Did you manage to find out anything about the house?'

'Is that where…?' He motioned to his own face again.

'Aye, and stop doing that.' Stanley slapped Savoy's hand down.

The old woman put a mug down in front of Savoy.

'It's owned by the council. I couldnae get the name of the last tenant. It's been empty for years.'

'Is that it?'

'Aye, well there are a lot of houses lying empty like that.'

'Any more information about the picture house murder?'

Savoy sucked air through his teeth. 'Some young laddie was tortured to death. I've been asking locals nearby. Apparently, there was a van parked outside the building that evening, an old-looking blue one.'

'What kind of van?' Stanley clenched his fists as he thought back to the van that followed him.

'A dark blue one, maybe a Leyland or a Morris.' Savoy stood up and slid his cup away. 'You know, both of these murders might no' be related.'

There was an off-licence two doors down. After dithering at the doorstep Stanley bought the cheapest half-bottle of whisky they had. He took a shaky sip while standing in the doorway. It burned his throat. 'Ahh.' He took another sip. The shakes had started to ease. He took another then another as rainwater soaked through his shirt.

He got back into the Vauxhall and slipped the bottle into the cubby. He rubbed his mouth with his shirt sleeve then pulled out into traffic. The roads were quiet but he got stuck behind a red light just before Princes Street. He could get another sip in before they changed. He leaned over to grab the bottle when an authoritative rattle on the glass startled him. 'Aww, fuck.' He rolled the window down. 'What can I do for you, officer?'

'George Stanley?' the PC enquired as he pulled open the driver's side door. He had an expectant grin on his face, almost like he had waited for Stanley to have a quick swig before stopping him.

'Yes.'

'Turn your engine off, please.'

'What's this about?'

'Turn your engine off.' The officer sniffed. 'You like your whisky, eh?' He looked down to the whisky bottle that had fallen onto the passenger's side chair.

'I've no' been drinking it though.'

'Aye, right and I'm Doris Day. Now, I'm going to need a breath specimen.'

# Chapter Thirty-Two

'You're a naughty boy,' Craven said sitting down in front of Stanley. 'You worked in the police when drink-drive limit was introduced, right?'

'I wasn't over the limit.' This was a first for George Stanley, to be sitting on the opposite side of the interview table. He looked up to the polystyrene ceiling tiles. Still, he would grin and bear it, then get himself out of here. 'I had a little sip.'

They both looked to the door when Helen came into the room. She sat down next to Craven. The room was barely big enough for the scratched plastic table and four chairs. Each scratch on the table told a story. The stuffy air was thick with the smell of days-old sweat, and smoke.

Stanley cleared his throat. 'I wasn't over the limit. I've not been charged with anything. I could just get up and walk out the door.'

'That would be a waste of time, Mr Stanley, especially since you have come all this way to assist in our enquiries,' Helen said as she flicked through her notebook.

'Oh, is that what we're calling it nowadays?'

Helen carried on. 'We've been down to Diamond's Dance Hall.'

'Aye, I thought you would.' Stanley clasped his hands and slipped them under the table.

'Your manager gave you an alibi for our victim's time of death.'

'Aye.'

'However,' she slid a picture across the table, 'I want to know what you were talking to this man about earlier that evening. You might have been the last person to see him alive.'

Stanley creased his brow and stared at the picture. 'I can't remember.' He sighed.

'Why aren't you helping us? This man was murdered.'

'Listen, darling, he might have been asking about what band was playing. It's busy in the Diamond.' He put his hand to his lip then winced.

'I hope you went to a doctor about your face. Looks sore,' Craven said.

'It's nice to see you're so concerned about my health, Craven.' Stanley slipped a cigarette out of his packet of Marlboro. He lit the cigarette and blew the smoke out slowly through his nostrils. 'Such a nice man. So caring, eh?' he said to Helen.

'Perhaps these will jog your memory.' Helen slipped two photographs out from the folder – black and white Polaroids, one of the victim in situ. The other a close-up of the victim's face and neck on the trolley. The photographs held a certain kind of horror that only the camera could capture after death. The face white as snow, the matted hair slicked-back, it looked almost like tar rather than hair. The hollow eyes grey and lifeless, like that of a porcelain doll.

'You've already shown me this photo.' Stanley held both photographs up to the light and surveyed them both.

\*\*\*

In the silence, Helen could hear the sound of Stanley's breathing, rapid and shallow. 'I dinnae ken him.'

'Try again. You were talking to him in the Diamond.'

'Oh, aye…Well, it's really dark in the Diamond,' Stanley finally said. 'I didn't recognise him at first but I did speak with him. He said he was worried about someone following him. Someone wanted to hurt him. He wanted me to look into it and offer protection. I fobbed him off. Gave him my card. Told him to call me.'

'Why not help him?' Helen asked.

'Am only interesting in making easy money. He couldn't really tell me why he thought someone was going to hurt him and wasn't clear how someone was following him. I just thought he was pished.' He shrugged. 'Didn't occur to me that he was the one murdered in the pictures.'

'Rubbish,' Craven added.

'It's the truth. When he left the club, I never saw him again after that.' Stanley stood up and slipped on his jacket. 'You're barking up the wrong tree here.'

'Stanley, don't go far. We're going to be speaking to you again soon.' Craven shook his head and stood up.

# Chapter Thirty-Three

Helen stretched out her shoulder blades until it gave a satisfying crunch. The muscles between her shoulder blades were tight and aching. No doubt from slouching in that uncomfortable chair with the broken back in the office. She looked up at the flat; the lights were out. She didn't really expect it to be different but she had hoped. Slinging her handbag over her left shoulder, she turned to the doorway and caught the twitch of her downstairs neighbour's net curtains.

It was old Mrs Hatchet, a nosey old cow who seemed to see and hear everything. In Helen's experience every tenement block seemed to have one. A prying neighbour seemed to come with every flat she had rented; an obligatory nuisance. Helen locked the door to the Mini and headed towards the stairwell – the door had been propped open with a half-brick. She kicked it aside and shut the door, scrunching her nose at the chemical smell of bleach that hung in the air.

Old Mrs Hatchet's door opened a crack before Helen had a chance to walk past. 'Here, hen.' The old woman waved. She was wearing a scarf over her head and her rollers stuck out underneath it.

Helen was half-tempted to pretend she never heard the old woman, to just carry on up to the flat, but instead, she stopped, one hand braced on the bannister, and let out a deep breath.

The old woman stepped out into the alcove. 'Hen.' She hissed just a little louder and waved Helen over. The old woman had a moth-eaten cardigan wrapped tightly around her bony frame. She held out a shaky liver-spotted hand. 'I hope you dinnae mind... I just...' The old woman cut off, a look of concern washing over her face.

'I saw that fella o' yours leave your house and I thought I heard raised voices coming from your flat this morning.'

'I'm fine, Mrs Hatchet.' Helen rubbed her eye. 'Look, I'm really tired. I just want to get up to my flat and get to bed. I'm really sorry about any noise and I can tell you it won't happen again.'

Mrs Hatchet looked up the stairs. Her leathery brow creased. 'It's alright, hen. I was up anyway. I'm always up early in the mornings.'

Helen followed her gaze but couldn't see anything. She forced a smile. 'Now, if that's all you wanted to speak to me about. I really need to just get up to my flat.'

The woman stepped out further and grabbed Helen's arm. 'It's no' that ah'm wanting to talk to you about. There was a strange man up there.' She pointed up to the stairs and whispered in Helen's ear, 'I didnae know what to do.'

Helen smiled again then patted her on the hand. 'I know there was, you just said you saw him leave this morning.' Helen wiggled her arm free and started for the stairs but before she could the old woman stopped her again.

'No, I came out to say there was a man hanging around up there.' She lowered her voice and looked up the stairs. 'Am no' talking about the one you brought home the night before.'

'What?' Helen turned to face her. 'When was this?' She leaned back against the wall to try and see up the stairs. 'Are you sure?' The lights were flickering but she couldn't see or hear anyone up there.

'Aye, there was just something no' right about him.' The old woman shuddered and wrapped her orange cardigan tighter around herself. 'I was going to phone the polis but am no' wanting involvement with any of that lot.'

'I can't see anyone. When did you see the man?'

'About an hour ago when I was washing the stairs.'

'Did you see him leave?'

Mrs Hatchet shook her head. 'There *wis* someone there, am telling you.'

'Could it have been one of the neighbours?'

'No, I've no' seen this man before.' She grabbed Helen's arm again.

'Did you see him leave?' Helen repeated.

Helen felt the hairs on the back of her neck stand on edge. She put a finger to her mouth to silence the old woman. She peeled her arm away, and tiptoed up two stairs just far enough to see all the way but not enough to be noticed. There was no one on the landing. Her front door looked untouched and so did her neighbour's.

'There's no one up here,' she called down to Mrs Hatchet. 'Are you sure it wasn't someone visiting? Or a workman or something?'

'I was out here mopping the landing and he wis just staring at me, smoking a fag.' She pointed. 'Just standing on the top stair there by the window. I jumped right out my skin, hen. He just didnae stop staring at me. His face was blank, he looked like a right nutcase. I nearly had a heart attack, swear to God. I just ran inside ma hoose and I've been waiting for someone to get back.'

'Okay.' Helen nodded and motioned to the old woman's flat. 'Just you go back inside.'

'I just thought I would say, like. I have been bloody terrified, ken, wi' what you hear in the papers.'

Helen forced a smile. 'Seriously, there's no need for that, just go back inside your flat. I'll take a look but I can't see anyone up there.' She went back down the steps and led the old woman back to her door. The old woman did not look convinced. Helen tapped her on the hand. 'I mean it. Just go back in your flat and I'll call the police if it's anyone to worry about, but I'm sure it's nothing. Go and get yourself a cup of tea.'

Helen had been here six months and still not met all her neighbours. The old woman was nosey but people came in and out of the buildings so quickly, she probably hadn't seen everyone that lived here either. The technical college was around the corner and the flats were popular with young students. If there was someone up there now there would be nowhere else to go. She made a quick job of the stairs, not really sure whether to believe the old woman or not. For all she knew it was just Ted leaving but stopping to have a quick cigarette in the landing before he decided to leave her.

Her neighbour's door was shut and their hall light was out. There was no smell of smoke either but a couple of cigarette ends had been dropped under the window. They hadn't been there this morning. She nudged them with her shoe.

A crash from behind. She dropped her keys onto the concrete. She screamed and jumped around the see her neighbour's plant pot lying on its side, and a small black and white cat moving the soil with its paw. It looked at her with almost the same shocked expression.

'Bloody cat.' Almost as if understanding her, it gave her a triumphant look and trotted past. Her heart pounded and adrenaline coursed through her body. She picked up her keys and got into her flat as quickly as possible.

'Ted?' She flicked on the light and then locked the door and placed her keys in the empty fruit bowl. 'Ted?' Helen slipped off her shoes and headed into the kitchen. She touched the kettle – stone cold. A ghostly smell of aftershave still lingered. There were a few side plates stacked on the drying rack and a half-empty bottle of red sat beside the sink. Helen picked up the bottle. She didn't recognise the brand or remember them opening it. Although wine was one of those drinks she could take or leave happily enough.

She poured the remnants into a glass and swallowed back a couple of paracetamol. Her box of Milk Tray was open on the counter. She ate one of the truffles.

The kitchen window faced out onto the shared back garden. Washing fluttered on the lines. She thought she could see the shape of someone from the corner of her eyes but when she looked again she couldn't see anyone. She rubbed her raw eyes. 'Don't be stupid, Helen,' she murmured then headed back through to the lounge, picking up what was left of her glass of wine. It was too quiet, so she put on the wireless as background noise, and curled up on her three-seater sofa. She had a pile of books on the unit to read and her records. A country radio show, *Hits of the 1960s,* played on the radio. *'Now it's time for Johnny Cash at San Quentin,'* the presenter announced. She wasn't going to argue.

Helen slumped back onto the sofa. The telephone was beside her; she picked it up and dialled Ted's number. There was no answer. She shut her eyes – praying the music would keep away the thoughts. She listened to the rumble of traffic outside. Helen took a gulp of wine to calm her nerves. Her heartbeat thumped in her ears and the room swirled around her. The glass fell from her hand, the red wine dissipating in the carpet in a blood-like stain. Tears burned her eyes. The walls closed in on her.

A clicking sound pulled her back into the present. It took her a few seconds to work out what it was. It was still dark outside and static purred on the turntable. She heard the front door close softly. The floorboards creaked. She looked around the room for something she could use as a weapon, grabbing her empty glass. The living room door opened, just as she scrambled up to her feet. Ted appeared in front of her with a gaping jaw and raised eyebrows.

'What's the matter?'

'You scared me!'

He looked at the stain on the carpet. 'I'm sorry. I didn't mean to.' He took the glass from her hand and placed it on the mantelpiece.

'I fell asleep. I thought you had gone home.'

'I came back, love.' He pulled her in and hugged her tight. She could smell beer and cigarette smoke on his breath.

'Where have you been?' She pulled away.

'I just went for a walk. I'm absolutely shattered, let's go to bed.'

Her heart sank. He always seemed to escape to the pub after an argument – and he started them all too frequently.

'I'll need to go home tomorrow night, though.' He kissed her forehead. 'I've got lots of things to get sorted. I'll get a cloth for the carpet. '

***

The next morning, Helen pulled into the car park and looked up at the dull façade of the police HQ. It had just gone past six. It was still dark, and there were only a handful of cars in the car park. She had left Ted still sleeping in the flat.

If she was lucky the canteen would be opening about now, so she would get a coffee and pull open everything there was on Arnold Heath. Wrenching up the handbrake, her mind raced. She thought back to old Mrs Hatchet and the supposed man in the stairwell. The old lady was probably being paranoid but it made her feel uneasy all the same.

She was tempted to tell Craven about it, but he wouldn't be interested. She couldn't really remember the last time they had a pleasant conversation, or he had taken an interest in her personal life without being insulting. Grabbing her handbag off the passenger's chair, she shook the thought from her mind and headed into the station.

A couple of the officers on the morning shift were already in the CID room by the time she arrived. The smell of greasy bacon rolls and a wave of warm air hit her. Nausea sat in the pit of her stomach. Randall picked a bit of bacon fat from his teeth with a nail then made a chewing noise. She looked away, feeling the bile rise in her throat.

With her canteen coffee in hand, she looked up at the board. "Catch him" was scribbled on the board underneath pictures of the crime scene and the photograph they were given of Derek Leckie, Arnold Heath and more recently, the old man in the park.

Before she could even sit down at her desk, Craven appeared from his office.

'Right.' He rubbed his eyes which looked sunken and

157

bloodshot. 'I have some of Arnold Heath's autopsy results back. His stomach was full which puts the estimate of the time of death between four and eight in the morning which is what we expected anyway.'

Helen took a sip of coffee. Craven and Randall had attended that autopsy. Luckily for her.

'He opened the shop at seven.' Helen added. 'So that narrows it down a bit.'

Craven looked up from his notebook. 'We also have a witness who says that a Leyland Sherpa van was parked outside the picture house. Have you found a van that fits the description?'

'No, I—'

'Bloody useless.' Randall's eyes were like slits and a sneer curled his top lip. He directed his next question at Craven. 'Will I double check them?'

Helen took a step towards Randall and gave him a hard stare. 'I've looked through all known criminals with vans like I've been asked but there isn't one that fits the description. I'm still looking though. I'm also looking for any females who have been arrested recently.'

'The priority is finding the van,' Craven stated.

'I understand that,' Helen replied. 'I've been working with the theory that Derek Leckie most probably arrived at the picture house in the Ford. One of the seats was pushed forward, suggesting a female or someone short was potentially the driver.'

'I don't know about a female.' Craven bit his lip and looked as though he was thinking. 'There was too much violence,' he eventually replied.

'Maybe if it was a woman, she lured him into the cinema and whoever was in the van turned up to carry out the murder?' She put her coffee down on the desk. 'Going in there with a woman wouldn't be threatening, would it?'

'I've been out with some right scary birds in my time,' Randall chimed in.

Helen ignored his attempt at humour. 'If he had felt in any danger, he wouldn't have gone into the picture house, surely?'

'Maybe not.' Craven shook his head. 'His father had said he thought he had a girlfriend. He's never met her and didn't have a name.'

'The other thing. We've had the blood results from markings on the picture house wall. It's the same blood-type O, the same as Derek Leckie,' Craven added. 'So it's likely that it's his.'

'Constable Bell has gone to the art galleries to see if anyone knows what the symbol means.'

\*\*\*

Helen had escaped to the collator's office: a dusty room lined with metal shelves, each one rammed with manila folders. There was a Formica table and two chairs at the bottom of the aisle. McKinley was sat there, hunched over some folders.

She had her second coffee in hand, going through the picture books, mugshots of convicted criminals and, so far, it had been a waste of time. She flicked to the last page and sighed.

'No luck?' McKinley said, peering over her shoulder.

'No. What about you? It's bloody freezing in here.' Goose pimples peppered her arms.

'Bingo.' McKinley tapped the page. 'I've found the Clifton's jewellers robbery, 1957.'

'Shit.' Helen snatched a photograph from the folder. Her heart pounding, she stared at the face. He had hair on the top of his head and a full set of crooked front teeth, but it was definitely him. He smiled at the camera with a big grin, and one eyebrow higher than the other. 'This is our first victim.' She waved the paper at McKinley. 'Our first victim is Harold Walter. This is the old man that was found in the park, two days ago.'

A look of confusion swept his face. He flicked through the bundles of statements.

Helen jumped up from her seat and slipped on her leather

jacket.

'I don't understand.'

'Harold Walter was arrested along with our second victim's father, Reg Leckie for robbery in 1957.' She fished through the folder and handed him the statement.

'Ah.' McKinley put his hand over his mouth. He then read. 'Arnold Heath, Harold Walter and Reg Leckie were arrested for robbery, in 1957.'

'I've got Walter's address here.'

***

Helen was expecting Harold Walter's home to be a flea-ridden cesspit, judging from the state of the vagrant-looking old man. Instead, it was sparse but spotless and in very nice area in Bruntsfield in the south side of the city, well out of Helen's price range. She had looked at a flat a few streets away from here but it was more than double the price of hers.

Helen and McKinley stood in the doorway of the ground floor flat in Admiral Terrace. The white front door wasn't locked and opened onto a wide tiled hallway.

'I can smell bleach,' McKinley said. 'I'll go in first.'

'Be my guest.' She stepped back and let him past. 'Arnold Heath's flat smelt the same,' she said, following him through the hallway. White panels adorned the green walls as well as empty shelves. *Strange.* Sunlight filtered in through the big bay window. The massive room, with its green threadbare carpets, looked clean. Helen looked down at the glass coffee table to see a copy of the *Evening News* and a cup of coffee with blobs of mould. A wicker armchair sat in the corner, next to a little oak telephone table, and a wireless set.

McKinley rubbed the back of his neck. 'I'll go have a look in the bedrooms.'

'Okay.'

A black coat was draped over the radiator. Orange and brown floral curtains framed the window. Damp spots peppered the wall next to the window and the plaster smelt wet. That was a problem with a lot of these old buildings.

'Helen.' She could tell from his tone something was wrong. 'I'm in the bathroom.'

Helen ran through to where McKinley was.

McKinley pointed at the symbol on the wall. Painted in red above the bath was the same symbol they had seen in the picture house. It looked flaky and darker in colour. It was interesting how the colour of blood could vary. Sometimes it would look like melted chocolate other times bright red, Helen thought.

# Chapter Thirty-Four

'I'm going into a meeting.' Savoy didn't bother to look up from his typewriter as Stanley closed the door to the journalist's office.

'I want an update on what the polis knows. They've been sniffing around for days.' Stanley went over to the window and parted the blinds. A nondescript car had parked behind his.

Savoy looked up, his eyes narrowing. 'Why are you coming into my office then? I don't want Craven to know I'm supplying you with information.'

'What's Craven's problem wi' you anyway?'

'Ach.' Savoy adjusted his tie. 'I published some details about a case he had asked me to hold off on.'

'Right.' Stanley smirked.

'I had my editor twisting my arms. I had to. Anyway, you didn't come here to talk about Craven.'

'Have they mentioned anything about a necklace?'

'A women's one?'

'Aye.'

'No.' Savoy sat back in his chair and clasped his hands together. 'They are looking for a male and female suspect, though.'

'Anything else?'

'One of the victims was branded.'

'Branded?'

'Aye, with some weird symbol.'

Stanley fished in his jacket pocket for some paper and pulled out the one Savoy had given him before. It had Stanley's blood on the corner of it. He handed it to Savoy.

A look of disgust spread on Savoy's face when he noticed the blood. 'Wi' a symbol like this.' Savoy drew the picture on the back of the paper. 'It was also painted on the wall of the flicks in blood.'

'Do you know what it is?

'Aye.' Stanley snatched the paper. 'I've seen this before.'

# Chapter Thirty-Five

Helen was starting to hate coming home like this, alone. Left with her thoughts; reliving conversations; thinking about the cases. Colleagues treating her like an idiot. Exhaustion made her head spin. How could she have been so stupid in thinking things would be different in CID?

Maybe she hadn't done the right thing in transferring from Glasgow. It made it almost impossible to see friends and family with the long shifts and the attitude towards her was not much better in the Lothians. At least no-one had yet pinched her bum which was a bonus.

She hung her handbag up on the boiler cupboard door, kicking off her shoes against the wall with a clatter. Helen sighed, her heart rate slowing. She'd been hopeful when that bloody Sex Discrimination Act came out. *Arghh.* She stormed through to the kitchen and pulled the loaf from the bread bin and the knife from the drying board. There was some cheese in the fridge and maybe some pickle. The bread was crumbling but she couldn't see any mould on it and she'd only bought it a couple of days ago. Carefully carrying her plate, she headed through to the lounge to enjoy her sandwich.

Sorting this flat out into better order would help, she thought. Paint a watercolour for above the fireplace, perhaps. Her easel was in front of the window, holding a blank piece of card. The view outside the grey tenement was hardly inspiring. The flat faced out onto identical flats and fat grey clouds hung above them, but at least it never seemed to rain as much here as in Glasgow. Mumbling and TV noises from surrounding flats filled the living room.

The phone rang just as she was about to sit down.

After hesitating for a few more rings she decided to pick

it up. 'Hello.'

'Helen, it's me, love.'

'Ted…' Helen slumped down on the sofa. 'How are you? I didn't expect—'

'I know. I'm sorry. Don't bite my head off but I've got a psychology job position that would be fantastic for you.'

There was silence in the line and Helen could almost hear him grimace.

She remembered having to declare her relationship with Ted so that he could be vetted while other male officer's relationships were like a revolving door. It was one of the reasons they were probably still together. She chewed on a nail, thinking about her confrontations with Craven. She didn't want to spend the night alone, stewing. It wasn't going to help. She thought about going to the pictures but she couldn't face that either. She could see her trainers at the front door. Maybe she'd go for a run along the streets; run until she could feel her lungs burn. Anything to not be alone tonight.

Ted pulled her from her thoughts. 'Look, it's a great role. You'd be doubling your pay and still helping people; you'd get more time off and work office hours. It would be perfect for you and for us. I'm not forcing you but I want to talk to you about it, at least.'

'You know what?' she said finally. 'Why don't you take me out for dinner and tell me more about it?'

'Really?' He sounded genuinely surprised. 'Be ready in half an hour. I know just the place. Put something nice on.'

'Ted,' she searched for the right words. 'I've heard rumours about my Dad.'

She could hear his breath on the line. 'I heard he played golf with the MacPherson brothers.' He replied. 'Before they were arrested. A long time ago.'

Helen's heart raced. The MacPhersons were Glasgow's equivalent of the Kray twins in the Fifties. 'Are you sure?'

'Helen if I was you. I wouldn't start digging into this.'

'I need to know, Ted.'

'That's all I know. That would be enough to cause

rumours but it was twenty-odd years ago.'

She was probably being stupid and Ted was right. 'I'll see you shortly, Ted.'

Helen hung up the phone and slumped down on the sofa. Corruption had been rife within the police. She read in the papers last week some officers had been arrested in London during a large-scale police review; that's what probably brought this to her mind. Coppers tended to close ranks though either not wanting to damage the reputation of the police or to protect their colleagues. *This was ridiculous.* She got up and went through to her bedroom. She didn't have long to get ready.

# Chapter Thirty-Six

'Does this mean anything to you?'

George Stanley cast a glance over the space he was in. St. Margaret's Nursing Home: an old converted Edwardian house, surely once a prized residence of some old rich bastard. The place smelt like a hospital and had the same clinical feel. He was standing in front of a sunken-cheeked man who didn't look up. Stanley stared at him.

'The past is really coming back to bite you in the arse, isn't it?'

If he got to this age he would rather be taken out and shot. Stanley glanced around the room. There was a small bay window with yellow curtains that faced out onto the car park. The bedroom had been easy to find and it was barely big enough for the single bed, chest of drawers, chair, and sink in the corner. It was a blank space, no clues to who might live there.

'Right, are you going to start talking?'

Silence. The man was staring into the distance. His mouth set in a macabre expression, revealing a couple of brown teeth that jostled out awkwardly. He sat stiffly, arms hanging down the sides of the chair.

Stanley moved forward and pressed two fingers to the man's throat. No pulse. Ice-cold and as stiff as a board. Sighing, he rolled up the man's sleeve. A tattoo, trying to hide under his arm hair. The one painted on the wall at the picture house.

'Who's murdering all your pals, then?' Stanley leaned down beside the man and felt his pockets. Empty. 'If you don't talk, I cannae help you.'

He crossed over to the drawers and pulled them open.

The top one was full of underwear and socks. He rummaged through them. Nothing. The next drawer – more clothing. Closing them, he looked back at the man.

'What am I going to do about you then, Harry?'

He called for a nurse and a little blonde thing in a cap came to the rescue. She touched Harry's corpse then recoiled like she'd been burnt. 'He's dead,' she gasped then turned to him, hands trembling.

'Aye, he looks like he's been deid a while.'

'I'll need to call the doctor,' she said, shakily.

'You stay here with him, darling. I'll go and phone.'

He jogged down the tiled lobby towards the front desk. There was no one around. He could hear a trolley being pushed but he couldn't tell where it was coming from.

The visitor record book that he'd had to sign was behind the counter. He reached in and grabbed it. Flicking back a few pages to a couple of days ago, he found the last person to visit Harry Jones. 'Arnold Heath!'

'Can I help you?' Authoritative. A matron, maybe and old. He closed the book. A stern-looking woman was leaning over his shoulder, frowning at him.

'Aye, I was looking for the telephone. Harry Jones is dead. A nurse is with him and has asked me to phone the doctor.'

Her eyes narrowed. 'Well, you'll not find the telephone there.'

The matron shook her head as she made her way behind her desk and picked up the telephone. As soon as her back was turned, Stanley headed straight out the door.

When he was safely out in the car park, he punched the concrete wall. 'Fucking hell!' It tore the skin of his knuckles and a single drop of blood trickled down his index finger, he rubbed it on his shirt.

A plane rumbled overhead.

# Chapter Thirty-Seven

They took a taxi to the La Fiesta Café in the Rutland Hotel. As she got out, Helen tugged at the hem of her black dress as it rode up her thigh. The late night fish and chips were taking their toll on her waistline. She'd need to start running again. She was met with the smell of steak as soon as they entered the restaurant. Harp music played gently in the background. It was cosy with crisp white tablecloths, and artsy pictures on the walls. She manoeuvred past an overweight man in his forties who was ripping a steak to pieces with his knife and fork and eagerly talking to the woman opposite him with his mouth full. She looked around the restaurant. It was buzzing with happy couples gazing at each other.

Ted squeezed her arm. 'You look lovely, darling.'

She tensed her shoulders. He was wearing a white linen shirt, brown suit jacket and expensive silk tie. His spectacles slipped down the bridge of his nose as he looked down to guide her to the booth seat.

A waiter eagerly followed them clutching two menus. There were flickering tea lights and fresh flowers in tiny vases.

'I'm surprised you managed to get a table like this,' Helen said, sitting down in the red leather booth.

'I have my means.' His hand around hers felt clammy and sweaty. 'I wanted this to be special.'

Helen could already smell alcohol on his breath. She wriggled her hand free as the waiter slipped the menu in front of her.

Ted sat down opposite her and scratched the shaving nick on his cheek. He muttered something in Italian to the waiter who grinned at the both of them then scurried away.

'I've ordered us a nice bottle of red.' He was looking at the menu intently. 'I fancy a steak. I'm starving.'

'I thought you were going to cut back on the drinking,' Helen said, flicking through the menu.

Ted managed a rueful smile. 'I'm just going to have the one glass, darling.'

Before she could say anything else. The waiter returned with a bottle of wine. He turned over the glasses on the table and poured Ted's. Helen stopped him when it came to her glass.

'I'll just have a glass of water, thanks.'

'We'll have the prawn cocktail and steak Diane,' said Ted.

'Actually,' Helen pointed to a dish on the menu, 'I'll have this instead of a steak.'

'C'mon and have a real drink, darling.' Ted motioned to the empty glass on the table.

'I don't want a real drink. I just want water.'

'I'm really looking forward to this,' Ted replied, rubbing his hands together.

'Telling me about the job, or the food?' Helen closed the menu.

'Both. This is a celebration.'

'I don't know about that. I haven't agreed to anything yet. Let's just talk about it.'

'I know.'

She thought about the engagement ring. A wave of nausea surged over her. She looked around the restaurant. He wouldn't do it tonight, not here.

They didn't have to wait long for the starter when the server returned with two glass bowls of prawns in a pink creamy sauce. She took one forkful which slid straight off and onto her lap.

Ted didn't notice. 'This role I wanted to talk to you about.'

'Aye.' Helen furrowed her brow as she peeled the prawn off her dress and rubbed the stain. 'What is it exactly?'

'A friend of mine has a private practice in London.' He

paused to take a gulp of wine. 'He wants a psychologist and… well, I thought of you.' Ted reached out for her hand. 'This could be a new start for us. You'd have a real opportunity to do everything you want in life.'

'London though?'

'In the centre.' Ted had finished his drink and poured himself another. 'And I've seen a stunning house in Shepherd's Bush that would do us.'

'God, you've got this all planned out, haven't you?' Helen bit her lip looking at his glass.

Ted sighed and lifted the glass to his mouth. 'I want you to be happy. You mean everything to me and we have nothing keeping us here.'

'I have my family.'

'Who you rarely see.'

'We're seeing my mum tomorrow.' Helen sat back in her seat and took a sip of water. The waiter who had shown them to their booth was standing in the corner ready to pounce. She avoided his stare.

Helen's chest tightened; Craven thought she was useless. Nobody wanted her in the department. She would be doing them a favour. She took another sip just as the main course arrived. Craven could click his fingers and send her from the department so why shouldn't she just go?

She felt hot tears welling behind her eyes, she tried to blink them away.

Ted pursed his lips. 'What's the matter?'

'It's nothing. I'm just overwhelmed. I didn't expect this.'

'Okay,' Ted looked off to the side, 'I'm worried about you.'

'It's just been a hard day.' She stuck her fork into the prawns. 'This looks lovely and I'll think about the job.'

Ted shrugged his shoulders.

When the waiter returned to ask how their meal was Ted asked for a glass of their finest single malt. 'I want to celebrate, darling,' he said. 'Just tonight.'

Helen sighed and they carried on with their meal. 'I'm really worried about you. Ever since your dad died your

171

drinking has got out of hand.'

Ted nodded, chewing on a fingernail. 'I know,' he finally agreed. 'I just want to block out the pain.' He looked down at the table.

'Ted...' She didn't know what to say, so reached out for his hand instead.

The mains arrived on big white plates. Ted barely touched his. 'It's lovely, I've just lost my appetite.' He pushed the food around the plate with his fork and poured himself another glass of wine.

Helen's pasta was spicier that she had expected. She took a few mouthfuls but she had lost her appetite as well. She signalled to the waiter for the bill.

Ted leaned forward. 'I'm buying the meal. I want to treat you.' He slurred his words and fumbled in his pocket for his wallet. It fell onto the floor.

Helen picked it up and pulled out twenty pounds' worth of notes from it and placed them on the table. She helped him up to his feet. 'Let's go home.'

Ted stumbled out of the restaurant and into the rain, holding onto Helen's arm for support. Helen leaned away to avoid his hot whisky-breath on her face. The icy air stabbed her in the chest. The torrential rain poured down in a thick sheet, soaking her through to her underwear and her dress stuck to her stomach. 'Ted, let's go back inside and try and get a taxi.'

'We can get a taxi up here. I'm really hot.' He tugged at his shirt.

They walked past a couple who were huddling in a shop doorway.

'Ted, please.' The words escaped her mouth in a smoky plume.

'Let's go and get a drink, sweetheart.'

'No, you've had enough. Let's just go home. I'm freezing.' She could see the pink of his skin under his shirt.

'Go home?' He spluttered. 'Go home... You go home, you're b... fucking boring.'

Helen exhaled shakily. All his weight was on her

172

shoulder and it ached.

'I'm going home then. Ted, you can't go on like this.'

'You do that. I'm going to get myself a drink.' He let go of her arm and staggered across the road. The oncoming car swerved and sounded its horn. Ted waved his hand at the driver.

Helen watched him disappear into the pub. She turned the other way and headed up the road to find a bus home, tears streaming down her cheeks. She rubbed her face with the back of her hand. Her mascara left a black streak on her fingers.

\*\*\*

'Aren't you a sight for sore eyes?'

Helen didn't reply. She could see from the corner of her eye that a yellow car had pulled up beside her. Helen carried on walking and pulled her handbag tight against her chest.

'Should I call you Sergeant? Will that get your attention?'

Helen turned to see George Stanley peering out of his car, his forearm resting on the window. He stared at her with big green eyes. The bruise on his chiselled jaw had faded.

'If this is about the case, call me at the station tomorrow.'

'No, I was just passing and thought…' He brushed a hand through his thick brown hair. A cigarette dangled from his mouth.

'I'm not interested in whatever it was you thought.'

Stanley smiled cheekily. 'I thought I would offer you a lift since I nearly knocked your date over. C'mon.' He motioned to the passenger-side door. 'I'll drop ye' off at your house. You're soaking wet.' He flicked his fag out onto the road and blew a circle of smoke. 'I'm a gentleman. I cannae leave you like this.'

'I'm getting the bus.'

'Ach, I'll give you a lift and you can ask me any question you want?' He winked.

'No.' Helen crossed her arms.

'You'll catch your death. You look like a drowned rat.' His brow sloped downwards. 'You cannae catch a bus like that.'

'Just watch me.' Helen started walking again. Her shoes were wringing wet and made a squishing sound as she walked.

'Your makeup is all down your face,' he called out after her. 'Right, you're not related to Richard Carter, are you? You look similar. He was my Inspector for a while.'

Helen looked over to the pub. Where was Ted when she needed him? One panel of the frosted-glass window was smashed and covered with a wooden board. She wished Ted would come out the door but it remained firmly closed.

'Alright,' she finally said. 'You can drop me off at the station.'

The car stank of stale smoke and there was dirt along the dash. Without a word Stanley slipped the car into first and drove down the street. The radio crackled softly with some rock music but she couldn't hear the song properly. Helen peeled her hair away from her cheeks and found a balled up tissue in her handbag. She rubbed away the streaks of mascara. The hot air from the engine drifted in from the grill; it felt nice on her face and was doing a good job of drying her hair.

'I've no' got anything to do with those murders,' Stanley said, making the turn onto North Bridge, a big road bridge that ran above the railway station. He looked at her expectantly.

'How do you know Jack?' Helen asked, looking out the window. The streets were quiet looking, the wind and ran keeping most people away.

'We worked on a case together,' he replied.

'Is that it?'

'Well,' he shrugged, 'he had an affair with my ex-wife and it cost him his marriage.'

*Hardly surprising.* 'What about my father?'

'He didn't.' He said with a half-smile.

Helen glared at him. 'I'm not in the mood for jokes.'

174

'I can see that. He was my Inspector, a nice man.'

'Is that it?'

'Well, we worked together for a few years. I didn't know him that well.'

Helen thought about asking him about the rumours her dad was bent, but then if he wasn't, she would be broadcasting that she thought he was.

He took a right turn and drove along behind the Meadows and the Royal Infirmary. A long way round but it gave them the chance to talk.

'How many years did you work with my dad?'

'I dinnae ken. Just a couple of years, I think. What's with all the questions?'

She shrugged. 'Did you take backhanders while my dad was your inspector?'

'People always talk, that doesn't mean it's true. But to be honest with you, so many coppers did that because the pay was so bad and lots of men didn't last in the force that long.'

'Is that what happened with you?'

'I left the police because I'd had enough. I've never killed anyone.'

Helen headed into the station. She'd grab a shower and a change of clothes from her locker then see how far they had got with the case. There would be no point in going home now waiting for Ted to stagger in and start a fight.

# Chapter Thirty-Eight

The telephone call hadn't given much away – did he even want to see him? His dad had walked out on them both for his assistant. McKinley tried to think back how many years it had been. Seven or eight, maybe. A pack of students had congregated beside the revolving door, and he threaded his way through them. Self-conscious, he tucked a stray strand of hair behind his ear then slipped his hands in his pockets. The Theology Department was on the first floor, if the garish metal sign was anything to go by. A copper-haired girl sat in a chair by the window. She looked up from the book she was reading with big green eyes. A smile crept to his lips.

He gazed up at the traditional Georgian architecture. It was a stunning building. A gold carpet led him to the office. The brass faceplate proclaiming "Professor McKinley" gleamed at him, as he took a deep breath and knocked on the door.

Those eyes are him alright. Even through the grey beard, it's him. Age had changed him. He'd lost his wiriness too. Bit of a paunch there now and the jowls were filling out too. Time hadn't been kind to him.

'Afternoon, Dad.'

'Terry,' he exclaimed, half getting up and waving to the chair in front of his desk. 'Come in and take a seat. What a surprise.' He arched a bushy eyebrow. 'A surprise indeed.'

'Thanks…'

'I heard you had joined the police.' His dad sat back in his seat.

McKinley nodded. 'You're looking well, Dad.'

'Aye,' he patted his stomach. 'I need to lose some weight though.'

McKinley didn't say anything and sat down, silent, finding his knees higher than his hips on the uncomfortable office chair.

'I haven't seen you or your mother for years, so I'm guessing this is not a social call?'

'No... well.' McKinley shrugged.

'You've got so tall.'

'Aye.' McKinley looked away. 'How is Stella?'

'We're getting divorced... What did you want to speak to me about?'

'Well...' McKinley fumbled in his pockets for his drawing. 'It's about this. This drawing has been left on the wall at the scene of a murder. It was painted in blood.' Giving up on the chair, he stood up and smoothed out the drawing on the desk. 'Do you know what this could mean? I thought you might recognise the symbol.'

'Let me have a look then.' A couple of silvery hairs were visible on the top of his head. He took the picture in his tobacco-stained hand and puffed out his cheeks. 'No, I've never seen this image before.'

'I appreciate you looking anyway.' He swallowed hard. McKinley put it back in his jacket pocket and backed off towards the door.

'Wait, Terry.' Dad bobbed his head towards a filing cabinet that had a few chipped mugs on it. 'Stay and have a cup of tea, please.' He smiled, the corners of his eyes creased. 'I've missed you.'

McKinley pinched his nose and looked away. 'You could have got in contact with me... Anyway, I can't. I've got to get back to work... Some other time though.'

His father nodded and took a breath. 'I suppose if you were taking it as a clock then the hands could be pointing to five and seven, so it could symbolise Psalm 5:7: "Blessed are the merciful, for they shall obtain mercy". Stay for that cup of tea and I'll have another think.'

'Okay...'

His father poured some water from a flask, dropped two tea bags in the cups and put them on the desk.

'How's your mother these days?'
'She's doing better now. How are the girls?'

# Chapter Thirty-Nine

Rain battered the windows. Helen looked around the office; in the pale yellow strip light it looked dank and claustrophobic. The powers above had managed to squeeze ten desks into a room big enough for six at most, not including the bank of telephones and filing cabinets that lined the back wall.

The radio was on quietly in the background playing The Doors' *Break On Through (To the Other Side)*. Helen stood in front of the dog-eared road map of Edinburgh that had been pinned to one of the walls. She had the Yellow Pages in front of her and had marked down the five hardware shops that were within a mile of both crime scenes. If the rope could be matched up then they had a chance of getting a description of the possible murderers. Helen stifled a yawn and stretched her neck.

She closed the Yellow Pages and picked up her coffee mug, taking another gulp of the cold remnants. She had been alone in the CID room for the past half-hour and her eyes felt gummy. She looked out over the distant lights of the city through the window. She was able to see out to Arthur's Seat in daylight, the benefit of being on the third floor. The window was open a crack and she could hear the sound of the occasional car sloshing past; a fire engine wailed somewhere in the distance.

She slipped on her jacket just as Craven emerged from his office.

'Where are you going?'

'I'm going to see if I can find out where the rope that's been used on the bodies was bought.' Helen answered wearily. Helen had pictures of the screwdriver that was recovered on her desk but it looked old; the red handle had faded and the silver discoloured. They wouldn't have much chance of chasing that. There was dried blood on the tip of it but not enough for any blood analysis and it had been wiped clean of any prints.

'I'll get my jacket,' Craven replied.

'Terry's coming with me.'

'No he's not. I am.'

'Fine,' Helen nodded. 'I just need to put these files away first.' She scooped them up from her desk and headed through to one of the empty meeting rooms with a telephone. Helen had asked her old colleague to get her the dates of robberies that her dad had investigated. Her hand shook as she dialled the number and thankfully they picked up on the fourth ring.

Helen twisted the phone cord around her finger as she spoke. 'Hi, it's Helen. Did you get the dates of the robberies I was after yet?'

There was some silence on the line and the phone crackled.

'Aye, I did.'

'Just keep this to yourself, Alice, alright?'

'Of course, have you got a pen there?'

Helen bit down on her lip hard as her colleague listed the dates of the robberies.

# Chapter Forty

At lunchtime the pub was dead, apart from a couple of grey-faced regulars supping pints, entranced in a game of dominoes. The barman was flicking through a copy of the *Evening News*, with his chubby hand resting in a packet of crisps.

'Are you going to tell me what's going on?' Blake strode up to him, pint in hand.

Stanley drained his glass and nodded for him to sit. He stubbed his second cigarette out on the tin ashtray and immediately lit another.

'It's not Denise, is it?' Blake furrowed his brow and sat down opposite Stanley. The top of his pint spilled onto the table as he pushed his chair in. He tutted, and wiped his hands on his trousers.

'Naw, it's no' about Denise,' Stanley sighed.

'Right, start talking then. What couldn't you tell me over the phone?'

Stanley glanced around making sure no one was within earshot. 'About twenty years ago, I helped with a jewellers robbery. I was starting out in the Police.'

Blake nearly choked on his pint breaking into a hacking cough. 'You didnae!' he spluttered and rubbed the lager that had spilled down his velvet shirt.

Stanley could see the disappointment harden Blake's face. He looked away. 'I had tae. I was desperate for the dosh. You ken what it was like in those days, couldnae pay my rent. I was gambling wi' the wrong crowd. Lots of officers were doing it. My Inspector as well. The money was bad in those days.'

There was a long silence and Blake shook his head before speaking. 'I always thought joining the polis wis your dream? Anyway why are you telling me this?'

'Aye, it wis, I just got desperate. I didnae want tae.' He took a deep drag on the cigarette. 'Because everyone that was involved in the robbery is deid, except me.'

Blake gasped. 'I dinnae understand though, why now? This is the stuff in the papers, aye?'

'I dinnae ken. The jewellers robbery went wrong. They got caught. A security guard was shot and died in hospital.' He trailed off.

'I cannae believe this. How could you?'

Stanley shrugged. 'I didn't mean for anyone to get hurt. I only wanted to make some easy money. Now were all being punished.'

'You're being paranoid.'

'No, everyone that took part in the robbery is dead.' Stanley shook his head. 'Arnold Heath's been murdered, and Reg Leckie's son, Derek. Harry Jones too, and I doubt Harold Walter's still alive or if he is, he'll no' be for long.' Stanley rubbed the back of his neck. His muscles had been sore since that attack in the house. 'Harry Jones wasn't even caught during the robbery. Everyone was too scared to name him, and he's dead.' He swallowed hard. 'My DI at the time was a Richard Carter. He would take payments to lose evidence as he did for this robbery. His daughter's a cop now and she's probably in danger too.'

'What are you gonnae dae?'

'I'm gonnae find out who's behind this.'

# Chapter Forty-One

Helen and Craven parked outside Best's Hardware in Davidson Mains. 'I really cannae be bothered with this.' Craven turned off the engine and slumped back in his seat.

*Then why did you insist that it would be a waste of time, in front of everyone? Then come in place of McKinley?* she had wanted to say.

He carried on. 'How many people thought it was a good idea to open a bloody hardware shop?' He shook his head. 'Two hours and what have I got to show for it?' He nodded to the pub across the road. 'I want a quick one in there after this is done.'

'I don't mind carrying on if you want to go back to the station.'

'Naw.' He glanced at the clock. 'I'll go back shortly.'

No doubt dodging DCI Whyte because they were no further forward with the case. She was about to get out when she noticed a doll sticking out of a carrier bag on the back seat. She reached around and picked it up. A Sindy doll, and underneath that a big box of Dolly Mixtures. 'Trying to impress someone are you?' Helen smiled. 'You've made a good choice there.'

'Aye, they're for ma kids. I was meant to go see them on Thursday but ended up having to work late.'

Helen nodded. She was working late, and remembered seeing him leave early that evening.

He looked at her as though he was about to say something.

'Right, shall we get this over with then?' Helen had a sample of the rope in an evidence bag. She got out the car. 'Third time lucky, eh?'

The shop front on the left was filled with paint pots,

stacked up in a pyramid shape. Various paint brushes were hanging off a board behind them. The window on the right displayed numerous tools and a dirty-looking mop and bucket.

Craven was a few steps behind her and was chewing on the last piece of a Marathon bar. 'Hopefully this will be the last one,' he said.

She walked straight to the counter. The store was gloomy. Very little natural daylight leaked through the window display. The smell of mothballs assaulted her nostrils and dust. She looked around – paints, brushes, wood and rolls of wallpaper. No rope. She could only see some parcel string and the same stuff she had used to hang her own washing out in the back green.

A teenage girl sat behind the counter. Chewing on bubble-gum and flicking through an issue of *Jackie*, her feet on the counter. She eyed them both as she turned the page.

Craven held up his warrant card. 'Police.'

She took her feet off the counter. 'I'll go get my Dad.' The girl plodded out of sight. They could hear some muffled voices then a man in his fifties appeared. He rubbed his hands on his brown apron and smiled at the both of them. 'What can I help you with?'

Helen handed him the rope in the evidence bag. 'I've had a quick look in the shop but it doesn't seem like you stock any ropes like this. We're trying to find the shop that might sell this.'

He felt the rope in the bag, then moved to the back of the counter and turned on a lamp. He held it under the light.

'It looks like camping type stuff. We don't have anything like that.' He turned off the lamp and handed it back. 'Sorry, I cannae really help with this but there's a camping store up the road. I would try that in there. They've got all this kind of stuff.'

Craven had already started down the road. Helen had to jog to catch up with him. The shop was big and spread out over two floors.

Helen noticed them straight away. She tapped him on the

arm and pointed towards the various rolls of rope on a stand in the corner. You were able to cut your own lengths. She went over and compared them to the one she had in the packet.

'This looks like the rope, what do you think?' she said pointing to one on the far left.

'Aye,' he nodded. Helen cut a sample, they looked identical. She ran her fingers over it. The fibres felt spiky. It had the same hardness and the same thickness.

'Can I help you?' A boy in a green T-shirt with long greasy hair approached. He had flecks of dandruff on both shoulders.

Craven lifted up the piece of rope. 'Has anyone bought rope of this kind, recently?'

The boy scratched his head releasing more dandruff, 'I don't know.' He took the rope from Craven and weighed it up in his hands.

'How long have you worked here?' Craven asked.

'Just about six months.' The boy looked up at Helen and smiled. 'Actually, I think a woman came in for some rope like this. I think she bought a hammer and some lighter fluid, you know for a stove and maybe a screwdriver.'

'When was this?'

He scratched his head again. 'It must've been last week sometime. Wednesday, I think. It might not have been this rope, though. She seemed in a rush. That's the only person I can remember buying rope. I don't really pay that much attention to be honest.'

'What did the woman look like?'

'Eh.' He bit his lip and looked down to the carpet. 'She had long brown hair, I think. Quite pretty. She was with this really tall guy and I think he was wearing overalls. I didn't really see his face.'

'Would you recognise her again?'

'No.' He shook his head. 'I dinnae think so.'

\*\*\*

When Helen got back to the office, McKinley was through in the collator's office pulling out every piece of information on George Stanley. She would head home when he was back through. She wasn't sure what they were expecting him to find other than what they already knew.

The door thumped open and McKinley bounded in, folders in each hand. 'I'm almost finished.' He rubbed his forehead with his shirt sleeve. He dropped them onto his desk with a thump and a plume of dust exploded into the air.

'Is it?' Helen said, stifling a cough. 'Bloody hell, is that after eight?' She squinted at the clock, and rubbed her blurry eyes. 'What exactly is the Inspector expecting you to find anyway?'

'Aye, it's just gone ten past.' McKinley slumped in his seat and laid his head on the desk. 'I'm absolutely shattered and I don't know. I think he's trying to keep me busy. He wants me to look at every case that might be similar to what we have here, as well as any cases that George Stanley so much as sneezed upon once upon a time.'

'Are there any?'

He shrugged. 'I think he thinks I'm useless, and is just trying to keep me out of the way of all the real work.'

Helen shook her head. 'If he thought that he would have you straight out the department. Anyway I've been in work for over twelve hours now so let's just call this a night. There's nothing else we can do right now, is there?' She stretched her arms above her head. 'We have everything ready for the briefing tomorrow.' She felt her stomach twitch as she said this; she couldn't face going home but she couldn't stay here all night either.

'Fancy a quick one down the pub then, Helen?' McKinley put the last folder on his desk and was in the process of slipping on his jacket.

She paused then closed the Yellow Pages. 'Just at the wee pub on the corner?'

'Great.' He slipped his jacket on. 'I was hoping you would say that. I really need a drink.'

She nodded. 'Sure. Are we waiting on Sally then?'

'No, I think she's finished her shift anyway.' He paused. 'We broke up.'

'I'm sorry, Terry. Maybe you can both sort it out.'

He shook his head and looked down to the ground. 'I just want a quiet night, a quick drink then away off home.' He puffed out his cheeks. 'She might even be in there tonight. Who knows?'

'You never know.'

***

It had stopped raining by the time they had left the station. She crossed her arms to keep some warmth. McKinley took off his Norfolk jacket and tried to slip it over her shoulder.

She smiled and nudged his arm with her elbow. 'The pub's just around the corner. I'll let you keep your jacket.'

His cheeks flushed red and he looked away.

Two men were chatting in the doorway; they didn't move as they brushed past. Once inside, they were greeted with a waft of stale booze and cigarette smoke which stung her eyes. Roars of laughter and applause came from a group in the corner playing darts. The jukebox was playing *Don't Give Up On Us* by David Soul. Helen thought it was that, anyway. She turned towards McKinley. There was a smell of BO coming from the guy in a crushed velvet shirt, who was swaying to the music with an empty pint glass in his hand. McKinley took a packet of Mayfairs from his pocket.

'Didn't know you smoked, Terry.'

'I keep trying to give it up.' He shrugged and put one to his lips. 'I only smoke when I'm out.'

Sally wasn't hard to miss, her cackle pierced through most of the noise. She was perched on a bar stool and wearing a flowing purple dress with an open back. 'So much for just a quiet drink in here, eh?'

McKinley said something but she couldn't hear over the music. He must've been able to tell from the expression on her face because he then leaned in. 'What do you want to drink?'

She looked up at the board then pointed to an empty beer barrel table with two stools, by the window. 'I'll just take a Blue Nun and I'll grab us that table.'

Once they were both seated. Helen raised her drink. 'Here's to a productive day.'

McKinley half-smiled. 'I'm just glad it's over.'

Sally glowered at Helen as she sipped from a wine glass. Judging by the empty glasses around her, it looked like she had been here a good few hours already.

McKinley turned to see what Helen was looking at. 'This is harder than I thought.' Helen noticed his lip quiver; he looked down to his pint and shook his head. 'We probably should have gone somewhere else. It gets a bit old in here after a while.'

'What's happened between you and Sally? She keeps staring at me.'

'I just couldn't deal with the drama anymore. Told her I needed a break from it, she didn't like it.' He lit another cigarette and exhaled the smoke through his nostrils.

Helen doubted this but wasn't going to push it. Sally had turned back around and was leaning on the shoulder of one of the officers.

Helen nodded and took a sip. 'I'm sure it will work out in the end, Terry. Maybe she just needs a break at the moment or something like that?'

'I made a lucky escape. She doesn't care anyway, that's for sure.'

Helen shrugged. 'She looks to me like she's trying to make you jealous.'

McKinley smiled apologetically. 'I'm not very good company at the moment.'

Before Helen could say anything. Sally appeared at the table, smelling like she had bathed in Love's Baby Soft.

'Can we talk?' Sally put a hand over McKinley's and squeezed it.

'I'll go,' Helen said, getting up.

'You do that.' Sally sat down on Helen's chair and slid

the glass of Blue Nun out of Helen's reach.

Helen overheard McKinley as she left.

'I'm not an idiot, Sally. If you want to be with the Inspector, stop playing games with me.'

She smiled to herself.

# Chapter Forty-Two

Stanley wrenched up his handbrake when he reached Arthur's Seat, and rubbed his aching eyes. This morning's newspaper, had featured a story about the death of an old man, and the description sounded exactly like Harold Walter. It had to be him. No one had seen him for days. He reached for the door handle but waited until a couple – holding tight to each other's hand – had walked past, before he climbed out of the car.

He headed up the gravel pathway, towards the area where the old man was found, using the location details that had been given in the newspaper. Under his feet, stony fragments twinkled as he crunched his way up the rise to where he could see remnants of police tape that had been tied to a tree, and now flapped merrily in the wind. He picked up his pace until he reached the area. Unsure of what he would find. A twig snapped behind him. He whipped around and clenched his fists.

Silence.

He fumbled in his pockets for his cigarettes and carried on to where he thought the body might have been found every now and then glancing over his shoulder as he picked his way across the open space. A second piercing snap had to be deliberate. He felt the warmth of someone watching him.

'Fuck this,' he whispered.

Nothing but bare branches swayed in the wind and the sound of traffic in the distance mumbled softly. Doubling back, he aimed for the car.

When he reached the Victor, another car had parked behind it. He wondered if that was who had followed him into the woods.

Footsteps clattered behind him. Hard shoes slapping the concrete.

'H-have you got a light, p-please?'

Stanley could see from the corner of his eye. A man in white overalls was smiling, holding up a cigarette.

'Aye, wait a minute.' The hairs on the back of Stanley's neck bristled. He clenched his fist, but before he could properly turn a punch landed squarely on his jaw. Stanley fell backwards onto his car bonnet with a thump. The sound of a knife flicked open and the blade plunged into his thigh.

# Chapter Forty-Three

Helen couldn't think of any other way. She rammed her handbag under the driver's seat. Her radio weighed her down enough. The wind whipped the car door, slamming it shut. The noise echoed in the desolate street. She had parked behind two other cars. It wasn't one of the best areas of Edinburgh but the rent would be cheap.

She looked up and could see light spilling out of Stanley's office. She followed the winding staircase to the varnished frosted-glass panel door. It was ajar. Beethoven played softly.

'Hello, Mr Stanley?' She pushed the door. The hinges squeaked as it moved. Someone walked past the second internal glass door. She froze, listening for voices, placing an unsteady hand on the handle.

A brown-haired woman, mid-twenties, sat at a desk reading papers in a folder.

'Hello?' Helen approached.

The woman looked up and swiftly rose to her feet. She pursed her lips, an expression of confusion spread on her face. 'Can I help you, Miss?'

Helen nodded and pulled her warrant card from her duffle coat. 'I'm Detective Sergeant Carter. Is George Stanley around?'

'No, it's just me here. I'm Mr Stanley's secretary, Maud Bevis. '

'Really?' Helen looked around but couldn't see anyone. 'I thought I heard voices.' Helen backed off and looked into the small alcove kitchen. The door was wedged open. Part of a cluttered worktop and a small sink were visible.

'Mr Stanley's not here but you can wait.' She looked over at the clock. 'I'm sure he'll be back soon.'

'I'll wait then.' Helen slipped her warrant card back into her wallet.

'Is this about a case he's working on?' She waved a hand. 'I know everything that goes on in here.' Maud's blue eyes were framed by a thick coat of eyeliner and her eyelashes were caked in mascara, some of it had pulled under her eyes, leaving a dark shadow. 'There's not much that gets past me,' Maud added.

Helen nodded. The room smelt faintly of menthol smoke and lavender perfume.

A few folders had been piled on Stanley's desk since her last visit. Helen skimmed through them: a case about a cheating spouse, another about a missing painting.

'Are you sure I can't help? I bet you're really busy and I don't want to waste your time.' She took a step towards Helen. 'Also, those cases are confidential.'

Helen put them back down on the desk. 'I don't think Mr Stanley will mind me having a look at what he is working on at the moment.'

Maud motioned to one of the empty chairs. 'Take a seat, if you are going to stay.'

Helen didn't budge.

'Tea?' Maud moved round her desk.

'Yes, thanks.'

Maud picked up two mugs and headed through to the kitchen area.

Helen rummaged through the folders again and found a folded-up piece of paper with an address near Cousland on it and the symbol from the picture house drawn in pencil on the other side. The paper was dog-eared and had blood on the corner.

She grabbed it and shoved it into her pocket. Just as Maud emerged with the tea.

'Tell Mr Stanley that I will catch him another time,' Helen said as she left the office.

***

Ted was waiting by her car after her shift clutching a big bunch of mixed roses wrapped with a pink ribbon. He reached out to her as she approached. 'I'm so sorry for leaving. I shouldn't have left you like that.' He tried to hand her the flowers.

'No, you shouldn't have.' She batted them away.

The glow from the lamppost emphasised his sunken eyes, and his normally clean-shaven chin had a day's growth of stubble on it. From the stiff way he stepped forward, he looked like he might have been standing there for a while and he was wearing a thick looking tweed jacket.

'I'm so sorry.' He offered an apologetic smile.

She brushed past him, unlocked the driver's side door and slung her handbag inside.

Ted sighed and puffed out his cheeks, 'I know they don't mean anything but—'

'No they don't. You think you can just throw money at any problem and it'll be okay but it won't.'

'I'll get help with my drinking. Whatever it takes. Please.'

'Ted.' She shook her head. 'You've been saying that for ages. You always seem to find an excuse to have a drink.'

'Don't leave me, Helen. Please. Let me change.' His voice broke. 'Please.'

A young-looking constable walked past them. He gave them both a sideways glance, a smirk twisting his mouth.

Helen's cheeks burned and she whispered: 'I don't want to talk about this here.' She shook her head and got into the car.

'Helen, please.' He held onto the driver's door and lowered his voice. 'I know I've got a problem. I've poured all the drink in the house down the sink this morning.'

He leaned in closer. She smelt for alcohol on his breath but only got the faint odour of yesterday's Musk. That was a first for a long time.

He stared hard at her and put his hand to his mouth before speaking again. 'When I lost my Dad, things got out of hand. You know how close we were.'

Helen looked away and brushed some dust off the dash. It was a shock for everyone when his dad died. He was doing some DIY and fell from a ladder. It wasn't even a bad fall but he'd had a drinking problem. She shuddered as she remembered arriving at the hospital with Ted to be told that his dad died a few minutes before they'd arrived.

'I can't...' She tugged the door from his grasp.

'Please, I'm sorry. I've treated you like rubbish. I know that. Let me make it up to you.' She could hear the desperation creep into his voice. He stared at her. 'I've been on a self-destruction path but you know what I'm going through. You've been through it.'

*Still going through it.* 'Just stop. I can't deal with this.' She swallowed hard. 'I'm going to Mum's house for tea.' She popped open the passenger's side door. 'You can come. She'll be expecting you there anyway but we'll need to sit down and have a good talk. If you have another drink though, that's it.'

'Thanks, Helen. I'm so sorry.'

She let out an exasperated breath. 'I've already had enough people around me struggle with drink. I thought that was behind me.'

'It will be behind us both. Last night was the wake-up call I needed.'

Helen reversed the car out of the bay and wished that she could believe him. The drive to her mum's house near Livingston would give them plenty of time to talk.

# Chapter Forty-Four

Ted was in the front room with her mum sharing a joke. Helen smiled when she heard them laughing. Mum hadn't laughed in a long time. Long-forgotten memories flooded back of her dad working at his desk, reading his magazines and drinking coffee. She closed the door softly. Dad's office had been preserved exactly as he had left it. She kept expecting him to walk in after her then moan about her messing up his office or not letting him work in peace.

Helen ran a finger over the scratches left in the bureau by his silver letter-opener. A pile of *Economist* magazines from three years ago had been stacked neatly next to the typewriter, gathering dust that she brushed away. A black and white photo of her dad in his uniform sat on the window ledge. Her eyes stung. She sunk into the leather chair behind the desk. The last time she had seen him was at this desk, just before she started in the police. She could almost smell his aftershave.

She took a deep breath to steady herself.

'Helen, the dinner's ready.' Ted popped his head around the door. A look of concern washed over his face. 'Are you okay?' The smell of the lasagne drifted in with him.

Helen nodded. 'I'm trying to see if I can find anything about a case I'm working on.' She bit on her fingernail. 'I'm just not sure where to start.'

Ted came into the room. 'Why, do you think your dad's got anything to do with this case?'

'There's been two murders where the business card for an ex-cop has been left for us. My Dad was this officer's Inspector for a while.'

'I don't think you'll find anything, Helen.'

'I'll be out shortly. I just need a minute.'

Ted nodded. 'I'll wait in the lounge but don't be long. Your mum's worried about you.'

When he left, Helen turned her attention back to the desk. The top drawer was stuck. She wiggled it back and forth until it gave and spilled its contents out onto the floor, then rummaged through the papers. Most of them were bills, along with a couple of betting slips and a stack of business cards wrapped in an elastic band. She flicked through them. There it was: a business card for George Stanley. Helen's stomach lurched. Her mind raced. It was the same style as the ones found at the crime scene. She dropped the other cards. Her father might've picked up the card at some point. *It didn't have to mean anything.*

Helen turned to the metal filing cabinet behind her. She pulled out her notebook from her pocket and flicked to the page with the robbery dates on it. She sifted through the bank account statements in the bottom drawers. Dad would never get rid of anything. The first robbery was July 22$^{nd}$, 1952. She traced a finger along the yellowing paper. On July 24$^{th}$, £500 had been deposited into the account. Her heart sank. She flicked through more pages. December 1$^{st}$, 1955 – a robbery; again two days later another deposit of £500. She looked on but 1957 was missing. She shoved them back into the folder. The month after that robbery the money was there and the month before. Nausea settled in the pit of her stomach. The rain clattered off the window drowning out the sob that left her body. *No, you have to keep it together,* Helen told herself. She slipped the business card into her pocket and headed for her car. Ted shouted as the front door slammed behind her. She heard it open again and his footsteps clattering behind her.

# Chapter Forty-Five

McKinley's hands shook as he pushed open the door to Craven's office. He didn't mean to but he must've shoved it hard because it slammed against the wall.

Craven looked up from the telephone, narrowing his eyes. His face darkened and he put the phone down and made a move to stand. 'What the fuck are you playing at? You've never heard of knocking, no?'

'I'm sorry, sir.' McKinley stepped fully into Craven's office clutching the folder to his chest. 'I'm... I'm sorry, sir,' McKinley stammered. 'But I've made a breakthrough. I've found a connection—'

'This better be good, son.' Craven interrupted and gave him a hard stare.

'It is.' McKinley's heart hammered.

'Right, c'mon, tell me then.' He slapped his hand on the desk and sat back down in his chair.

McKinley cleared his throat. 'Helen has identified the deceased vagrant male found on Arthur's Seat as Harold Walter. I've also found a connection between a worker in the picture house, and George Stanley.'

'Aye.' Craven waved his hand in a motion to talk faster.

'Stanley's secretary, Maud Bevis.'

'What about her?'

'Well, she used to work in the picture house before the fire.'

'Is that it?'

'No,' McKinley replied, 'Maud Bevis's father was a security guard at the jewellery shop that was robbed in 1957. Robert Andrews.' He stepped forward. 'Arnold Heath, Reg Leckie and Harold Walter were involved in the robbery. Stanley was in charge of the initial case. Maud has a twin brother called Larry and his description fits the one given in the camping shop. Bevis is Maud's married name. Her husband died two years ago during a tour of Northern Ireland.'

Craven nodded but said nothing.

McKinley rubbed his clammy palms on his trousers. 'Robert Andrew's time of death was recorded at 7.25 pm.'

Craven frowned and lent forward.

'Maud's mother committed suicide not long after the robbery and the children were taken into a children's home.'

Standing up and moving round his desk, Craven peered into the main office. 'Where's Helen?' He rubbed his stubble and looked at the clock.

'I haven't heard from her. Last time I spoke to her she was going to talk to Stanley in the morning. I think she's out for a meal with her mum tonight.'

Craven put out his hand. 'Give me them.' He leafed through the papers. 'Is she due in shortly?'

McKinley shook his head and took a step backwards. 'She's on the morning shift.'

Craven looked up at the clock. 'Get uniform to pick up Maud Bevis.'

# Chapter Forty-Six

Helen fished in her handbag for her car keys at the side of the road. *Where the hell are they?* Tissues, wrappers, lipstick, purse. *Oh, God!* She trembled; the business card for George Stanley could've been a coincidence but she didn't believe in coincidences. Those bank payments... *Dad must've been bent.* Her mouth felt dry. *Get a grip.* He had lots of business cards, Stanley probably just gave him that one. A car sloshed past dredging up a puddle that sprayed her tights in water and mud. 'Thanks a bloody bunch,' she shouted after it. A hand grabbed her arm from behind and whipped her around.

'What's happened, Helen?' Ted squeezed her arm tight. 'Why did you run out like that? Where are you going?' He looked out of breath and his white shirt was starting to soak through.

She pulled her arm free. 'I have to go to work. There's been an emergency.'

'And you weren't going to tell me? I thought we were going to talk.'

'I'm sorry. I'll explain when I get back...' She found her keys eventually in the side compartment of the handbag.

'I'll come with you. Let me go back inside and get my jacket.'

'No, I'll be back shortly. Go back in and have your dinner.'

'Okay.' Ted sounded exasperated. 'I don't want to do anything to upset you. Phone me when you're finished.' He kissed her on the cheek and headed back inside.

Helen had scribbled the address from the paper that she found in Stanley's office into her notebook. She pulled it out from her duffle coat pocket. The day's sleet made way for the first dusting of wet snow that squelched under her boots. Fox tracks dotted the pavement and fog hung heavy like smoke.

She climbed into the car and turned the engine over, reaching for the street map. A quick scan of it told her it was remote, most likely a farmhouse. It was in Cousland, a small village in Midlothian.

Adjusting the mirror, she looked at the red blotches that had formed on her cheeks. The winter air caused havoc with her skin. She pulled her jumper sleeves over her hands and reversed the car out of the narrow space, its headlights illuminating the falling snowflakes. Condensation crept up the windscreen. She wiped it away with a sponge then shoved a Frankie Miller cassette in the radio from a pile in the dash cubby.

There weren't many other cars on the road, so despite the weather the drive past quickly.

The windscreen wipers squeaked as they scraped away the flakes that fell on the glass. She turned up the radio to drown it out. The car rattled along the winding tree-lined roads that seemed to go on forever, and a lot of them needed resurfacing. She didn't notice the giant pot hole in the road until it was too late.

It happened so fast. The car skidded, so she turned into it. It skidded again. She tried to straighten the steering. She pressed on the brake. The back wheels went. No time to brace. The car mounted the pavement and slammed into the wall. The seatbelt had no give and whipped her hard back into her seat. The steering wheel spun, rapping her fingers and her head thumped the headrest.

Dazed. Helen scrambled out of the car, catching her breath. *Fuck.* The passenger-side wheel pointed out at an abnormal angle and the front bumper was dented from the impact. Her knuckles throbbed and started to swell. The address was just at the top of the street. Candlelight flickered from a room on the first floor. When she looked up at the window again, the light was gone. She pulled her hood up and headed for the phone box that she had driven

201

past up the road. Heavy footsteps crunched in the snow behind her.

She whipped round and could just make out the shape of someone holding up a gas lamp. Shielding her eyes, she strained to see who it was. Male, at least six-foot. Steel toe cap boots. She blinked away spots.

'I've had a bit of an accident.' Helen took a step back. 'Can you help me?'

The man stepped forward.

'Hello?' Helen instinctively took a step back. She swallowed hard, her mouth felt dry. An owl hooted and suddenly she became aware of the roar of blood in her ears.

'Lower that lamp, please. I can't see you.'

'Your car's r-ruined.' He took another step towards her. 'S-skid did you? The roads are s-slippery.' He took another step towards her.

'Yes, I did.' Helen shielded her eyes again and stumbled back a couple of steps. Fishing in her pocket for her keys, she slipped them between her fingers. 'I've told you. I can't see you; lower your lamp, now!'

This time he did so, then looked at the car, and back at her. The man shook his head. 'Th-that looks nasty. I h-have a van just up the road.' He was wearing a white boiler suit and a faded leather jacket. His fair hair clung to his face.

'Are you a mechanic?'

The man raised his chin. 'N-no, I just k-ken aboot cars.' He added. 'Your s-suspension is knackered. W-what are you doin' r-round here, anyway?'

Helen rubbed her swollen knuckles. 'I was just on my way to visit a friend. Which house is yours?'

He peered into the car, rubbing his side and wincing as he did so. 'All by yourself, are you? At this time of night.'

'No.' Helen looked up and down the street. Deserted. 'I have a friend expecting me.'

'Come wi' me,' he replied.

She looked back up at the building but it was in darkness. There was no sound of traffic, while tracks in the thin dusting of snow only indicated the man and foxes.

He started up the road towards the house. 'C'mon, I have a ph-phone you could use. Just a girl all by herself. Now, that's n-no' very s-sensible at this t-time of night.'

She followed a few steps behind him. He put more weight on his left leg as he walked.

'I didn't think anyone lived here.'

'Ah'm doin' the h-hoose up, it used to be ma family h-haim. It's been empty a long t-time.' The rust-speckled entrance gates were lying on the verge and almost covered by the grass that grew up around them. A blue Leyland van was parked in front of the farm house, dented at the front and with half the licence plate missing.

Mud squelched underneath her boots as she walked. She guessed from the deep tracks that the van had been up and down the path a few times recently.

'Thanks for your help, but I'm going to try the phone box down the road.' Helen's heart-rate quickened. She rubbed her clammy hands on her jacket.

'The phone b-box is no' working. Ma phone's just in the kitchen. You're welcome to use it.'

She followed him round the side. Leaves bobbed on the murky pond. Helen shuddered and kept as far away from it as possible as she headed towards the open kitchen door. Plastic sheeting had been laid across the floor tiles, peppered with what looked like blood. Helen backed away.

'I'm going back to my car.'

The man laughed and shook his head. 'Detective S-sergeant Carter, ah'm no' l-letting you go anywhere.'

He turned to face her, a grin spread across his face. As he reached out to grab her, she turned to run, tripping over a brick. She landed with a crack and felt him drag her up and into the house. She tried to kick and punch out but they just bounced off him.

'You took your time. Get her car moved.' It was a female voice. Helen could only see her back.

'Will I k-kill…?' The man looked down at her as he spoke. Helen tried to stand but was unable to move.

'This is your mess and you'll need to clean it up. I want

the pig dead,' the female voice commanded.
   He levelled a boot to her head. Darkness.

# Chapter Forty-Seven

'What about it?' Craven stubbed out his roll-up and flicked the dog-end into the wastepaper basket. He had his feet up on the desk and was going through the Green Shield Stamp catalogue. Helen's house a couple of times and in all probability she would be in shortly but he kept finding himself glancing over at her desk. It was too early to go to her house and her shift wasn't meant to start for another half an hour.

'What aboot what?' McKinley asked.

'This telly.'

'Looks like it would cost a bomb. I can't afford it on my salary.'

'Aye,' Craven said stifling a yawn. He had been up the best part of last night and had nothing to show for it, except for being on his third cup of coffee and second Marathon bar. He stretched the side of his neck until it gave a satisfying click.

'You all right?' Randall had his hand over the mouthpiece of his telephone. Before Craven could answer, Randall was back speaking on the telephone again.

'Who is he on the phone to?'

'He's going through interviews. Are you still saving the Green Shields for that telly? I can ask my mum if she has any going spare.' McKinley stood up straight and rocked back and forth on his heels, hands in pockets. 'I would go for that washing machine though. You wouldnae need to bother going to the launderette.'

'Just get married and get the wife to do it. That's what they're there for.'

'Is that why my mum sends me down to the launderette, then?'

Craven laughed. 'The colour telly's what I want.' His phone rang. He took his feet off the desk, knocking the picture of the twins onto the floor. 'DI Craven.'

'Hiya, Jack. It's Bobby here. There's a wee lad down here and I think he will worth you having a chat with. He says he thinks he's seen the van you're looking for. He seems serious. Normally, I wouldnae bother you and just take his statement myself, but I know you lot can do with all the help you can get now.'

He looked up at the clock then back to the mountain of papers that he was going to have to go through today. 'I'll be right down then. What's his name?' Craven could hear him rustling through paper.

'Aye, got it here. The wee lad's name's Roddy Smith. He's sixteen and works in a petrol station in Leith. I got one of the WPCs to give him a cup of tea and he's waiting for you in interview room three.'

'Right, have you had him go through the picture books?'

'Aye, he doesn't recognise anyone.'

'I'll be down in a minute.'

# Chapter Forty-Eight

Helen awoke with a start. She pulled against the ropes that tied her to the chair. Thick bristly stuff, the same as the one in the camp shop. *Keep calm. Keep calm.* Tears rolled down her cheeks. A wave of claustrophobia began to rise in her; it wanted to engulf her but she pushed it back. She tried to move her legs but they were tied to the chair. She let out a cry and pushed all her weight against the chair, again and again and again. It was too heavy for her to move. Her head pounded and felt sticky.

A sigh from across the room, followed by a sharp intake of breath. She paused. 'Hello? Is someone there? Help me, please!' The breathing was soft and regular.

She struggled to see in the darkness. Her nostrils stung from the smell of damp and mould. Water dripped in the corner of the room. She could just make out a fireplace and a serving hatch on the other wall. A small amount of light spilled in from the boarded up window but just enough to cast shadows. Her head pounded. She tried to move her hands. They throbbed, she wriggled her fingers in desperation but the rope didn't budge. A sob welled deep in her chest. She closed her eyes and pictured Derek Leckie's mangled body; then Craven and the rest of them finding her the same way. *He was tied to a chair as they murdered him. Tortured him, and it wasn't quick either but what could they want from her?*

Her eyes adjusted to what little illumination there was, and she could see a big toolbox in the corner of the room with some tools laid out in front of it: a claw hammer and a couple of screwdrivers on the same kind of sheeting that covered the kitchen floor. No doubt to help contain the blood and make a quick tidy-up.

'Let me go.' She kicked out, screaming and thrashing against her chair until her throat burned. 'Let me go!' Her cries broke into a cough and her skull felt as though it was going to crack.

A floorboard creaked somewhere in the room.

Someone was in there in the room with her. Watching her. A sharp click of a lock filled the silence.

'Please let me go.'

She felt something hard – the tip of a screwdriver maybe – press into her shoulder. Not deep enough to cut the skin but hard enough to sting. The raspy breaths of the person behind her bristled the hairs on her neck.

# Chapter Forty-Nine

Craven opened the door and a nervous-looking teen looked up from the mug he was nursing. He couldn't see why Bobby had called him the "wee lad". He was nearly six-foot and about two stone overweight. His face looked blotchy and red. The blonde WPC stood up as he closed the door. He nodded to her and she offered a condescending sneer in return. *I'll not bother asking you out for a drink later.*

The room itself was only big enough for a single scratched Formica table and four chairs. Tatty posters telling you to "watch your bags" or "clunk click every trip" had been tacked onto the walls.

'There's no need to look so bloody scared, son. I'm Detective Inspector Craven and I don't bite. Do I, WPC Maloney?' The young policewoman rolled her eyes and he carried on. 'Now, you have some information that I'm gonnae want to hear?' He sat down in front of the boy. 'Sweetheart, away and fetch us a couple of chocolate bars from the canteen.'

'Certainly, sir. *Anything* else, sir? She dragged the word sir out into almost a hiss.

'Not at the moment.' He winked at Roddy who smiled.

The door slammed shut behind him and once they were alone, Craven focussed his attention solely on the youth. 'Now, what have you got to tell me?' He pulled out his notebook from his jacket pocket.

Roddy looked back down at his cup. Craven took out his packet of cigarettes, offering him one but the boy shook his head, so he left them on the table. Roddy looked uncomfortable as he traced some of the scratch marks on the table with his fingers. Eventually, he mumbled, 'Well, it's about that pictures murder and the sweetie shop murder.'

'Right, I gathered that, son. What about them?'

'The newspaper said you were looking for a dark blue Leyland van. I saw one in the garage and I put petrol in it. Last night.'

'You do know that there are a lot of Leylands going about, right?'

The boy nodded but said nothing. He looked up as the door opened and the WPC chucked two Marathon bars unceremoniously onto the table. Craven took one and he slid another to his young witness.

'What makes you think I would be interested in a Leyland van that was being filled with petrol? That's pretty normal.'

'Well, last Wednesday I'm sure I saw the man that was killed in the picture house and he was in the Leyland van with a woman.' He stumbled over the words.

'What woman with what man in the picture house?'

'The man that was found in the picture house, the one whose picture was in the *Evening News*. I'm sure it was them.' He took the Marathon bar, shakily tearing the corner, but didn't bite into it. 'I've seen him a few times before. He normally drives an Escort, a yellow one.'

Craven straightened in his seat. 'How can you be sure that it was them?' The air in the interview room was warm and stuffy. He resisted the urge to open the top of his shirt.

'Well... I was very sure, when they stopped in for petrol. It was the way they looked.'

'The way they looked?'

'Aye, and there was something about the girl. She just wouldn't look at me at all. Then she gave me a fiver for the petrol and told me to keep the change. She's local as well. I'm sure I've seen her around quite a few times. Maybe she goes to Napier College or works nearby. She is very pretty, that's why I remembered....' His cheeks flushed red and he brushed the hair self-consciously from in front of his eyes.

Craven smiled and raised a hand. 'Alright, did you catch the number plate?'

The boy bit his lip and shook his head. 'No, I didnae

really think at the time…'

Craven flipped open his notebook 'Ford Escort you said, right?

'Yes.' Roddy scratched his acne-scarred cheek. 'Yes, it was definitely an Escort.'

'Are you sure now, son?'

Roddy nodded, pausing to think. 'I don't know if this helps but it was dented on the back bumper, like it had backed into a bollard or something.'

'It all helps.' Craven nodded as he scribbled notes but made no comment, he then looked up suddenly. 'What about a description of the van?'

'It was just plain and dark blue. It was old as well.'

Craven leaned back in his chair. 'Now, was there anything special about this old blue van?'

'Not really.' He fished in the pocket of his jeans. 'Here's the licence plate though. I had read in the *Evening News* that morning you were looking for a van, so I took a note of it just in case, like. '

Craven took it from him. 'Right then, what did the woman look like?'

The boy listed every aspect of her description out on each finger. 'Okay, she was a brunette with long hair past her shoulders; she looked really young, early twenties, brown eyes and she was wearing a green dress. She had big earrings in.' He motioned to his own ears. 'The man with her in the van was tall, really muscly, over six-foot, and he was wearing decorator's overalls, and he had brown hair tied in a ponytail.' Roddy shuddered at the recollection. 'He really gave me the creeps, like. He just stared at me.'

# Chapter Fifty

Someone ripped the sack from her head. A bright white light flashed in her face, blinding her. Helen blinked against it, spots peppering her vision. Heavy hands on her shoulders pushed her backwards. The chair landed on its back winding her, crushing her arms behind her back. Hands tore her mouth open, forcing pills down her throat, 'No… please.' She bit hard down onto the hand. Tearing flesh, tasting blood. A shout. Something solid cracked her skull.

'She fucking bit me!'

Helen tried to speak but only a hoarse squeal escaped her. The tablets slipped down her throat.

'There.' He slapped her on the face. 'Y-you'll be better behaved.'

*Helen was swimming in the sea. The tide was against her; the waves splashed off her face. Salty water filled her nostrils and mouth. She struggled to keep her head above water. Tried to swim, gasping for air. Thrashing and kicking. The water filled her lungs as she sank further. 'Help me. Help me. Please.' She tried to scream… but nothing.*

*A burst of energy. She thrashed again. Fighting with every muscle in her body. She started to move. Lights rippled in the water above. She surfaced, panting. A hand grabbed her head and pushed her back down.*

# Chapter Fifty-One

Craven opened the drawers in Helen's desk pedestal, not sure what he was hoping to find. Tea bags. He made a face and threw them onto the desk. Pens, pencils, notebook – nothing in it. Scrap paper. Black and white photos. One in her WPC uniform, long hair pinned up. *Nice.* Another with some lanky looking man with a daft haircut. He held the photo up. 'Who's that?'

McKinley shrugged his shoulders. 'Never seen him before.'

Craven looked at the photo again. He had a familiar look about him. He had seen him somewhere before but couldn't place where. He flicked it to the back. A tattered old book on police surveillance. He leafed through it. Some of the pages were dog-eared. The chapters on cars had slips of handwritten notes shoved between the pages. Craven then flicked through the remainder of the papers on her desk.

# Chapter Fifty-Two

'Let me go. It's not too late,' Helen pleaded. 'I can help you, I can open any investigation.'

'I wish I could, but you had to stick your nose where it didn't belong, didn't you? I investigated the case. I've punished those involved.'

'You can choose to stop this before it gets worse.'

'I can't, Sergeant Carter, I'm sorry.' They had put some kind of sackcloth over her wet head. The cloth and her hair stuck to her face and the fibres were in her mouth. It tasted of mould.

'Why are you doing this? My Inspector will know I'm missing. I should've been on shift hours ago. They'll be looking for me.' Her voice came out muffled. She could hear her heart racing in her chest. A noise came from behind her. Metal on metal. Someone was rummaging through tools in the tool box. Arnold Heath's bloated body flashed in front of her eyes. She clamped her eyelids tightly shut but couldn't blot out the memory of Derek Leckie's smashed skull.

'It will be painless for you. You don't deserve to be punished.' The softer tone of a female voice cut into her thoughts.

Helen recognised the voice, 'Maud?'

Silence.

'Maud, please, this revenge or whatever you're trying to do. It doesn't achieve anything.' Helen could see the stab marks that ran up and down Heath's arms. She closed her eyes and tried to blink them away, a hot tear ran down her cheek and her pulse boomed in her ears. *The puddle. The blood.* 'Please, no.' Helen pleaded. She rocked back and forth in the chair. Somebody clicked shut the toolbox.

'Don't worry, this will all be over soon. I really am sorry. I didn't want to do this.'

Something smacked Helen hard on the back of the head. She floated in and out of consciousness.

'We could let her go.' A male voice. Helen hadn't heard anyone else come into the room.

'No, she'll—'

'We could dump her somewhere.'

'No…'

# Chapter Fifty-Three

Craven stopped the car outside Helen's flat. He looked down to his radio; if she had made it into work, he would have had a call through by now.

'What have you got yourself into, you silly cow?' Craven punched the dashboard before getting out of the car. The curtains of her top floor flat were drawn. Only one flat on the middle floor had lights on. Taking a final drag on his cigarette, he rang the buzzer. No answer, the stair door was locked but it moved on the latch. He shouldered the door and it gave way without a fight.

The smell of piss followed him up the stairs to Helen's faded red door. It still had the name of its last inhabitant on the rusted metal name plate: "Harper". He knocked on the frosted-glass panel. The door showed no sign of damage. The mortice and Yale locks hadn't been tampered with. He peered through the letterbox and saw an empty hallway with all the adjacent doors shut. He could hear the telephone ringing inside.

Craven paused, then looked under the welcome mat in case she had left a spare key, but he didn't really think she would be that stupid.

A pile of cigarette ends near a plant pot at the other side of the landing caught his attention. He walked over to the pile and kicked it with his boot, then looked back towards Helen's door. Someone could have been standing here, watching her. Waiting for her to come home. Most likely one of the neighbours just likes to have a fag on the landing. He knocked on the neighbour's door but there was no answer.

A dark-haired man carrying a Tesco carrier bag was coming up the stairs. Craven recognised him from the photograph in Helen's desk drawer. That daft haircut was a dead giveaway.

'Ted?'

The man looked up. He knitted his eyebrows. 'Who wants to know?' He spoke with a Welsh accent.

Craven recognised him from somewhere other than the picture. '*I want to know.*' Craven pulled out his warrant card.

'Ah, I remember you, you're Inspector Craven, right?' Ted brushed past him. 'What do you want? She's not here.'

Craven recognised him finally from his accent; he was a defence solicitor and he wasn't a very good one.

'When did you last see her?' Craven asked.

'Last night before she went on shift.' Ted put the shopping bag down on the ground. An orange fell from the bag. 'Why are you asking me this; has something happened?'

Craven noticed a nice bottle of red wine and box of Milk Tray in the bag.

Ted gave a close-lipped smile. 'I don't think you've come here to look through my shopping.'

'No,' Craven sighed. 'She hasn't turned up at the office this morning.'

'What do you mean? Where is she then?' Ted rubbed a hand through his floppy hair.

'Did she mention going anywhere else first?'

'Let me think...' Ted slipped the key in the lock. 'We can talk in here.'

Craven followed Ted through to the kitchen. A bunch of pink roses sat in a vase on the windowsill, a box of unopened tiles sat on the counter.

'Well...' Ted dropped the carrier bag on the circular table, on top of a pile of holiday brochures. 'She was a bit distracted yesterday. We went to her mother's house for a dinner party. She spent most of the time in her father's study looking for something. She didn't say what.' Ted leaned against the worktop. 'I think she mentioned going to talk to someone, a private investigator, maybe.' He took a deep and shaky breath. 'I knew something like this was going to happen. That job's so dangerous.'

Craven didn't argue. 'You don't seem that worried though? If someone had told me my bird was missing…'

Ted raised a bushy eyebrow. 'What am I meant to do? I've told her until I'm blue in the face that something like this would happen. I mean you can take a horse to water but you can't make it drink. I've begged her time and time again.'

Craven clenched his fist and took a step forward. 'You're full of shit.'

Ted broke eye contact with him. 'I think you should just leave.'

'Aye, I will. Let's hope I manage to find your girlfriend, eh?' Craven looked him up and down and sneered 'You're not worth my time.' Craven stormed out of the flat, the door banging shut behind him. He heard the key turn as Ted locked it from the other side.

# Chapter Fifty-Four

Helen could hear footsteps in the corridor. The door crashed open and smacked against the wall. The sack ripped from her head, taking some of her hair on its way. Spots peppered her vision as her eyes adjusted to the bright light. She blinked hard. A shape moved in front of her. The harsh light made the scene appear like a photographic negative. The muscly man in the boiler suit threw an unconscious George Stanley onto the floor and the chair shook. Helen tried to squeeze her hand out of the rope, burning and twisting. She gritted her teeth and felt her skin tear.

The man flipped Stanley over and bound his arms and legs. He had the swollen V-shaped figure of a body builder and at almost seven-foot, his frame towered over Stanley. He stared downwards, analysing his prisoner like an insect he was about to pull the legs off.

Then his attention turned to Helen; he smiled, looking into her eyes, a friendly smile. He had a scar from his lip to just beneath his nose and his oil-slicked hair had been tied loosely into a ponytail. Wisps of hair hung at the sides of his face. 'I'm s-sorry, if I s-scared… you before.' He said, as he lumbered up. 'I've t-taken the s-sack off for you.'

Helen struggled to crane her neck to look at him but she forced herself to do so.

'You need to let me go… Let me go, now! My Inspector knows where I am.' Her throat tightened and she swallowed hard. 'You…you'll get into so much trouble for this. But if you untie me now things will be better for you.'

The man's smile changed to a scowl. 'I don't w-want to hurt you. I just don't have a choice. You w-were going to ruin everything. W-why did you have to come here?'

'You do have a choice. Please…' she pleaded. 'It's not

too late to let us go. Just untie me.' She tried to shift forward in the seat. 'All you need to do is untie me. I won't ruin anything. I won't tell anyone, please.'

The man took a few steps towards her. In this light, she could see he was only in his early twenties, at most. He had the same shaped face and small hazel eyes as Maud, but his skin was tanned. No doubt, to make his muscles look more defined. His thick-set jaw had a few wispy hairs sprouting from it and was pitted with old acne scars.

'If w-we let you go, w-we'll get caught. I can't. I just can't r-risk it,' he muttered to himself. 'Y-you brought it on yourself.'

'Please, come back, please! Don't leave me like this.' A key turned in the lock. Footsteps thudded above them, causing a shower of plaster dust to drift down from the ceiling. She didn't try to speak to Stanley until she was sure they were alone and wouldn't be heard.

'Stanley, wake up.' She pulled against the ropes. 'Get the fuck up,' she hissed.

His chest heaved shakily, but he didn't respond. She closed her eyes and sobbed. For what felt like an eternity. 'Just do what you're going to do then! Just do it!' she screamed into the darkness. 'Don't keep us like this.'

Helen had her eyes closed. Stanley's breathing steadied and he mumbled something, as a mouse or a rat scurried behind her chair and squealed. She bit down on her lip hard and shivered.

It felt like hours later when the door finally opened again. Daylight leaked through a gap in the curtains and cast shadows on the floorboards. Maud walked into the room. She had her hair pulled back into a tight bun and wore black trousers and heavy jumper. All of her makeup had been washed off and her forehead looked shiny with sweat. In her left hand, she held a screwdriver. Helen could see the whites of her knuckles.

Helen looked away from her, trying not to think about the damage she could do with it. She gulped. Her heart raced but Helen knew what she had to do now.

'Maud, I can get you the help that you need.' Helen stared hard at Maud. 'I can help you.'

'It's too late for all that,' Maud replied, licking her cracked lips.

Stanley's eyelids fluttered and he slowly regained consciousness. He looked round the room with half-opened eyes, groaning, and spat blood onto the floor. 'You worked with me for months. You're sick in the head. What did you think was going to happen?'

'No, I'm not.' She ran over to Stanley and stabbed him viciously in the forearm with the screwdriver. 'Why would you say that to me?'

Stanley whimpered and tried to kick out. His face contorted in pain.

Helen gagged and looked away. Heath had at least ten of those marks up his arm before they had eventually killed him. 'You're not sick in the head.' She tried to speak as slowly and calmly as possible. Stanley was only going to make this worse.

Maud leaned over Stanley. 'You just made me do that. I didn't want to do it.' She made another stabbing motion towards Stanley. 'Why did you make me do that?'

'Maud, I know why you felt you needed to… to do that and it's okay,' Helen replied.

'It's too late now.' Maud shook her head.

Stanley made eye contact with Helen.

Helen took a deep breath. 'No. No, it's not too late for anything. Maud, I promise. I know why you killed those other men. You thought that it would help, didn't you? That it would take away your pain. But it hasn't. Killing us won't take away your pain. It won't achieve anything. You're a good person. You don't want to do this.'

Maud sighed and shook her head. 'You don't understand.'

'Explain it to me. Help me understand,' Helen replied.

Maud lowered the screwdriver. 'Stanley just got on with his life, while ours ended that day.'

'What happened, Maud?'

She spoke directly to Helen. Her voice was softer now. 'Our dad was murdered in a robbery which he orchestrated with his gambling pals.' She gulped. 'My dad was a good man. We had a happy life.' She paused, her eyes welling with tears. 'Then he went to work one day but never came home. We waited and waited for him... Until the police came.' Maud snorted at Stanley. 'Bet you never thought you'd die like this, did you? You're going to die exactly the same way he did.'

'Maud, keep talking to me,' Helen pleaded.

'My mum was the one who told us he was dead. We didn't believe her.' Tears streamed down Maud's cheeks. 'She killed herself the day after the funeral. We were left with nothing, put into a children's home and forgotten about. The murderers went unpunished. Spending the money they stole. My Dad's murder was forgotten. We were the forgotten,' she spat. 'They got a few years in jail, then out for good behaviour and that was it, all done and dusted.'

'No.' Stanley shook his head. 'I had nothing to do with it. What evidence have you got that I've done anything?'

'Arnold Heath told me and I've worked with you, followed you.' She spat, looking him up and down. 'You'll never tell the truth, will you? I want to hear it from you.'

'I've done nothing,' he replied. 'What about her? She's done nothing.'

Guilt wormed its way into Helen's stomach as the thought of her dad's bank statements filled her mind. They nice house she grew up in. The private schooling... Was she just as guilty?

Helen shook the thoughts from her mind. 'Your parents wouldn't want you to do this. I can help you get justice.'

Maud jabbed the screwdriver in Stanley's direction. 'You haven't seen Denise in a while.'

Helen heard Stanley gulp and his breath quicken.

'You've not? Please... no!'

Helen twisted her arm behind her back. Her shoulder felt like it was going to pop from her socket.

'If you've hurt Denise!' Stanley shouted. 'I'll fucking—'

'What?' Maud laughed. 'Denise has got exactly what she deserved.'

Helen had to do something to change the subject. Calm Maud down. 'I'm so sorry, Maud. That must have been so hard for you,' Helen said.

Maud rubbed the tears away with the sleeve of her jumper. 'Things had got better; I thought I had my life together. I met someone nice at a disco. He took me to the pictures... to parties. Then I learned his last name was Leckie. Like some cruel joke. I asked him if his dad was called Reg. Derek had this expensive watch. It was expensive. He told me it was a family heirloom and it was from that robbery. He was boasting about it like it was something to be proud about.'

'That must've been terrible, Maud.'

She ran forward and slapped Helen hard across the head. 'Will you just stop with the counselling rubbish, Sergeant Carter; I've heard it all before. It doesn't help. I've been through it a thousand times.' She then pressed the screwdriver into Helen's arms. 'Do you want this? Do you?'

'No, no. I'm sorry, I'm sorry,' Helen implored. The screwdriver stung her arm. Maud twisted it. 'No, I don't want it, I'm so sorry. I don't want it!' Helen bit down hard on her lip as Maud released it.

'No, of course you wouldn't want this.'

Helen closed her mouth and shakily sighed. The marks up Derek Leckie's arm filled her vision. She shuddered.

The screwdriver plunged into her forearm. Helen screamed. It plunged again and again then Maud stopped and shook her head and knelt down in front of Helen. Whatever tablets they'd given her were working because there was no pain. Helen looked at marks on her arm. It felt like she was looking down at an arm that didn't belong to her.

Maud tilted her head to the side. 'Do you know something?' she asked, as if it was the most natural thing in the world.

'What?' Helen responded through gritted teeth.

223

'He must've been laughing at us,' she muttered to herself. 'Laughing, behind our backs.'

'No one's laughing, Maud. I promise.'

'They were laughing but it doesn't matter. We got the last laugh though... we made him pay. You're right... we did make him pay.' She was nodding her head now, a strange smile spreading across her face. 'They deserve it.'

'Maud, listen to me, please!' Helen shouted.

Maud paused, her lips pursed. She was looking over her shoulder as if someone was standing behind her.

'Maud, please.'

Maud turned round and was pointing the screwdriver. 'I know that... I'm going to do that... I'll tell the bitch that.'

'Maud!' Helen broke into a sob.

Maud snapped her head around and screamed at Helen. 'Shut up! We can't bloody think with your horrible screechy voice.'

'What are the voices saying?' Helen asked, her arms and legs trembling.

'It's nothing to do with you.'

Helen carried on. 'I can investigate what happened to your family and get the case reopened. I can get justice for you. I can find out what really happened—'

'Find out what really happened? We were there, we know what happened!' Her eyes were wide and her pupils dilated.

'Please...' Helen pleaded with her. She looked around the room for any drugs. Was Maud psychotic or had she just taken something? What had they shoved down her throat?

Maud composed herself. 'I'll let you go, alright. I'll let you both go. *You'll* go six feet under.'

'No. Please!' Helen begged. She was trying to disguise the panic in her voice. 'What good will it do? Reg Leckie is dying. He's got months at the most.' Her heart hammered in her chest and she fought back a wave of nausea. 'Reg Leckie's riddled with cancer, did you know that?' Helen sighed.

'Yes, I know that and he will live out what little life he's got left in agony.'

'Think of your brother. You need to look after him. Stop this and I can help you get out of trouble.'

Helen pulled at the ropes behind her back feeling more give in them than before. She twisted her arm and pulled her arm. *It wasn't enough.*

'No, Reg Leckie got what he deserved,' Maud stated. Her voice was shriller than when she'd spoken to Helen at the office. It was as though it belonged to a different person.

Stanley shook his head. 'Helen, don't bother trying to reason with them. You're wasting your time.' He turned to Maud. 'Do whatever you're going to do, you're not going to get us to beg if that's what y're wanting.' Stanley scrambled up so that he was sitting in front of them. 'I was just starting out in the police and I was only doing ma job.'

'Don't you dare speak to my sister like that!' Maud's brother appeared out of nowhere and levelled a boot a Stanley's head, knocking him back down to the ground.

Reeling from the kick, Stanley wiped the blood from his mouth with the shoulder of his shirt.

Helen knew it was best to keep the conversation going and try to tire Maud out.

'Maud, have you taken your medication?' she asked, frantically trying to think of something to distract her.

Tyres crunched over gravel. They froze. Relief washed over Helen. Craven must have figured it all out. 'I told you that the police knew where I was. You need to let us go.'

'Shut up.' Maud spat at her. Her face had gone white. She started to shake.

'You've had it now, Maud,' Helen said, gasping for breath. 'You'll spend the rest of your life in jail unless you do the right thing and untie me now.' Helen twisted and pulled her hand back and forth in the rope. She managed to get half her hand up. 'Maud – you can make this better.'

'I can't.' Maud shook her head. 'I can't trust you.'

'Yes, you can.' Helen pulled her hand. The rope burning, squeezing her flesh as she did so. She twisted it again, wincing as she felt the skin tear but she managed to release her hand. She exchanged a look with Stanley and kept it hidden behind her back.

'Right now, you can make things better. You wouldn't get away with murdering us. The police will be on their way looking for me but if you let us go now you'll be in a lot less trouble.'

Stanley mouthed the words, '*If you can, run*' to Helen.

The sound of a car door opening filled the silence between them.

Maud ran over to the window. 'Larry, it's those builders. I told *you* to cancel them.'

'I did cancel them!' Larry rushed over to the window. 'I d-did.'

'Why have I got to do everything? All you had to do was phone them when I asked. Get rid of them now. You can't let them come near the house, do you understand?'

Larry nodded and stormed out of the room.

A sob escaped Helen at the thought of Craven and the rest of the team finding her body, and Ted and her mum planning her funeral. Mum would be left alone. She'd never cope.

The front door slammed. Maud stared out the window.

Anger rose inside Helen. 'The police will be here soon. Let us go. Where is your medication? Have you been taking it?' Helen pulled her hand. Her shoulder popped. It moved. Her other hand was free.

'Fuck off!' Maud rushed towards her, Helen swung her elbow back wildly, but it must have connected because Maud screamed, and cupped her nose.

'You've broken my nose!' she shouted, raining punches down on the back and side of Helen's head. Pain ripped through Helen's skull. She wrapped her arms around her head to try and protect herself. A bell echoed in her ears: another blow. The room spun around. Gathering her senses, she managed to block a punch and kick out. Maud gasped and clutched her stomach.

'Just run, Helen. Get out of here!' Stanley shouted.

Helen staggered to her feet and ran towards the door. Her thighs throbbed. Swaying and dragging her feet, she made it

226

out onto the landing. Maud ran towards her, grabbed Helen by the scruff of the neck and was pulling her back into the room. Helen's shirt tore and her legs gave way. She crumpled to the ground. Maud lashed out, losing her balance. Helen kicked. Maud tripped forward and crashed through the bannister. She let out a bloodcurdling scream. The sound of flesh smacking against concrete echoed in Helen's ears.

'Oh, God!' Helen stared at the gap in the bannister. The wood smelt of wet rot. She couldn't look down. No way could Maud still be alive after falling down three floors. Helen swallowed the bile in her throat. She knew exactly what a fall from that height did to the body. She forced the image of Maud's mangled corpse from her mind.

A car engine turned over and the tyres churned up the gravel. Not much time.

'Helen, untie me.' Stanley was fighting against the rope tied around his wrists and trying to pull them apart.

'Okay,' her voice croaked. Tears streamed down her cheeks. She scrambled onto all fours, her fingers fumbling as she attempted to undo the rope. Out on the landing, she heard him gasping for breath.

'Can you get down the stairs?'

'Aye.' Stanley nodded, lumbering up to a standing position and swaying like a drunk.

'I've got to try and get help. There's a phone box down the road.' Helen drifted down the stairs, not feeling in control of her body. Every step creaked and groaned. She tripped over the bottom step. Her knees crashed into the concrete with a slap. Her face contorted in agony. Stanley's breath was on the back of her neck. He slipped an arm around her waist and dragged her back up. Her knees felt wet and blood trickled down her shins.

Maud was lying in the hallway, her right leg at an unnatural angle. Eyes wide-open. Blood pooled underneath her head. Helen clamped her eyes shut as Stanley dragged her out the house.

The van was parked, doors wide open. Larry was in front

of it. He was on top of the van driver, with both hands around his throat. Squeezing. She picked up a half-brick from the grass verge, ran over to Larry and cracked him of the back of the head with it. He yelped and slumped on his side, clamping his hand to his head. She felt in his pockets for the bottle of pills and pulled out a bottle of Valium tablets. The driver began to cough and shake. Larry's eyelids fluttered. Helen looked back at Stanley who was still lying on the grass verge. She shoved them in her pocket and started towards the phone box. Everything around her was spinning and her skull felt as if it were about to crack.

\*\*\*

The Cortina turned into the road, followed by a police van, sirens blaring. Helen was sitting at the side of the road outside the entrance to the garden. She hugged her knees into her chest for warmth. A crystal frosting covered the leaves next to her but she felt warm even though her whole body shivered. The car looked like it was going to drive straight past but it stopped, brakes squealing, a few feet ahead of her. It screeched and reversed. The police van pulled out and raced ahead into the garden.

Craven wound down the window and stared at her. His jaw dropped and his face looked ashen, so it must've been bad. 'What the hell happened? Helen, are you alright?'

'I thought I was going to die.' She stared ahead. The wet grass had soaked through her clothes. 'They were going to kill me.' Her feet and fingers were numb. She looked down at them; they were red. 'Maud's dead. Stanley's still…'

McKinley jumped out of the passenger side and heaved her up. He lost his balance and ended up with a knee in the ice next to her.

'Are you okay?' He cupped a hand around the cut on her forehead. 'That looks bad. Your lips are blue.'

'Are they? I feel fine. I…' She put her hand to her mouth. 'I didn't think I'd get out of there.'

McKinley swallowed hard and his voice shook. 'I'm

228

sorry... I'm so sorry, Helen. I shouldn't have let you go to see Stanley.'

'It's my fault...'

'Are you alright to stand?'

Helen nodded.

He put a supporting arm around her. Taking a step forward felt like a punch to the stomach. Her knees collapsed underneath her but McKinley kept her up. He bundled her into the back of the car. 'You're safe now, Helen.'

'What happened?' Craven asked. He was looking at her in the rear-view mirror.

She shook her head. 'Maud fell from the landing... she's dead.'

'Is it just her?'

'No, there's a male knocked out in the garden – her brother Larry.' She rubbed her blurry eyes. 'I had to leave Stanley on the grass, he wasn't in a good way, and there's a builder Larry attacked too.' Gingerly, she felt the back of her head; a hard goose egg had formed. All the nerves in her face tingled, even her teeth ached. 'She fell through a rotting bannister... she was trying to... she fell.'

An ambulance followed them into the garden. The siren screeched in her ears.

They drove up the path. A uniformed officer was leaning over Stanley and trying to feel for a pulse. There was blood on his hands and white shirt.

As soon as Craven wrenched up the handbrake, Helen climbed out of the car. She managed a few steps before Craven grabbed her arm.

'Helen, you're not going back in there.'

Helen tried to twist her arm free but it was too sore.

'You're not going anywhere, except in an ambulance.'

'Jack, I want to help.'

Craven scrunched his face. 'You've done enough.'

'If she hadn't fallen through the railings I'd probably be dead. She let out a shaky laugh, blinking back tears and pulled her arm away, flinching as she did so. 'I tried to find common ground with her, like I was taught at university but she wasn't having any of it.'

'If it's anyone's fault, it's them that orchestrated the robbery of Clifton's. The ones that killed her parents. Stanley—'

'I should've been able to talk some kind of sense into her.'

Helen watched the paramedics carry Maud's lifeless body away on a stretcher. She put her head in her hands. 'I tried…'

'You can't save everyone.' He pulled her towards him. 'I'm serious.'

'Hot tears stung her eyes. 'Stanley, is he…? '

'He helped with the robbery in 1957. He was the getaway driver, that's why he wasn't being helpful with our initial enquires.'

'No.' She slumped down onto the grass. Everything spun around her. The sound of Maud falling. The smack. She kept hearing it. Again and Again. She turned to Craven. 'If I hadn't tried to run…' She looked over at Stanley, ambulance men were lifting him onto a stretcher.

Craven followed her gaze and sucked air through his teeth. 'They're going to get him to hospital. If he survives. He won't get away with what he did, though.'

'There's another…' Before she could finish, two uniformed constables dragged a sobbing Larry from the house. His hands were cuffed behind him and he looked at her with pleading eyes.

'You were lucky you got away when you did.' Craven sat down beside her. 'We're going to get you in an ambulance and straight to hospital.'

'Thanks.' Helen nodded, wincing as she did so. Pain wormed its way deep in her head and her mouth tasted of metal. Her jaw ached. It was hard and felt tender.

# Chapter Fifty-Five

It was just after eight in the evening, and Helen was sitting under a poster about waiting times in the accident and emergency department of the Royal Infirmary. The blanket was still draped around her. A grey-looking woman was hunched over opposite her, clutching her stomach. They both looked up as Ted approached.

'Look at the state of you.' Ted held out his arms. 'I knew something like this would happen. It was only a matter of time.' He hugged her tight and kissed her forehead.

'Careful.' She flinched and pulled away. 'I've got a bruise on my head, I think. I've not looked in a mirror yet.' She gently pulled away a few hairs which had stuck to the cut on the side of her head. They felt sticky and a little blood came away on her fingers.

Craven had gone to get her some water and to find out more about Stanley's condition. From what she had seen earlier, it didn't look promising. Ted's stubble scratched her cheek. 'I was so scared, Helen. When you called me…'

Ted took a step back and cradled her head in his hands. He peered at it over his glasses. 'It looks a bit bruised but it's hard to see properly in this light.'

There wouldn't be much the doctors could do for her and she just wanted to go home. Ted sat down next to her. He put his head in his hands. 'The doctors should be out here treating you.' He made a move to stand up.

'Don't,' she replied. 'I'm waiting for the doctor to come back. They've already examined me.' She tenderly touched her jaw, wincing. The hard lump was even bigger.

'You're one of the lucky ones. You could have died.' He shook his head and raised his voice 'You should be getting priority treatment.'

Lucky? A smile tugged at her lip. She didn't feel it. She looked ahead but could feel his stare on her. 'It wasn't that dramatic.' She closed her eyes and could feel the water drowning her again and the smell of wet rot hung on her clothes. Gasping for air.

Ted said something but she didn't hear what.

'What did you say?'

'I said. Do you know when they're going to let you get away?'

'Nope.' Helen held a half-drunk cup of tea, and a biscuit that she couldn't face eating. She put them down on the empty seat next to her.

A matron rushed past them. Her shoes clattered on the hard floor. Helen watched her disappear around the corner and listened until the sound of her shoes died away.

'I've always hated hospitals.' Ted slumped back in the seat and crossed his legs. 'I can't even watch *General Hospital*.'

'I know.' She smiled.

'I think this is it, Helen. Take the job in London with me. I can't do this anymore.'

'Ted, I—'

'This is not the way I wanted to do it but…' He tilted his head to the side, fished in the pockets of his rain jacket and produced a purple velvet ring box. 'I've got plane tickets in my pocket for Majorca.'

'I've been wanting to go to Majorca for years.'

'I know.'

\*\*\*

Craven turned the corner, glass of water in hand. He froze. Ted was down on one knee in front of Helen, smiling, then slipping a big diamond ring onto her finger. His pulse raced. Helen looked down at the sparkly ring and wiggled her finger.

She looked happy. What the hell did she see in him? The lanky idiot clambered back to his feet and sat back down beside her. Helen looked up and saw him watching. Her lips pursed as though she was going to say something, but Craven doubled back before she could and put the glass down beside the vending machine. He was half-tempted to go over and interrupt but it had winded him.

Instead, he followed the corridor down to the ward reception. A dumpy-looking matron looked up from the station.

'Which bed is George Stanley in?'

'He's not accepting visitors at the moment.' She frowned and looked back down at her folder.

'Aye, he is.' Craven held out his warrant card. 'I'll be quick.'

There were at least ten beds in a row – all filled with grey-faced zombies. Orange curtains hung limply at the sides of their beds. Nursing students were moving around them with tea trollies. The hospital smell was even stronger through here.

The nurse eyed him warily for a second. 'Right.' She pointed to a bed with the curtain closed around it. 'He's over there, but make it quick. He needs his rest.'

Craven nodded.

'Well, well, well, they sorted you out didn't they?' Craven said, slipping through the curtain.

Stanley peered through bulging purple eyelids. Craven wouldn't have believed it was him but his name was written on the board above the bed. Stanley let out a moan; his face was swollen and covered in angry bluish bruises and there were grazes on his forehead. His left leg was elevated and in plaster and his left arm bandaged across his chest. Craven sat down in the plastic chair. He picked up Stanley's medical notes, whistling as he flicked through them. 'Can you talk?'

'Yes.' Stanley's voice was barely a whisper.

'I want to know everything.'

# Chapter Fifty-Six

Helen closed her eyes and tried to think happy thoughts. Beethoven's Symphony No. 6 swirled around her from the record player; one of Ted's old records. She smiled to herself. He'd never believe that she'd actually listen to it. The music softened and she sunk deeper into the water, feeling it creep up around her neck. The record was enjoyable but it wouldn't convert her from rock and pop anytime soon.

The bath was hotter than Helen would normally have it and gritty from the bath salts but the doctor had said this would ease her aching muscles. A salty bead of sweat trickled down into her eye and her head pounded. She took a long deep breath, then heaved herself up. Some of the soapy water sloshed out and landed with a slap on the lino. She bit down on her lip hard and her face twisted as a bolt of pain jabbed her in the ribs. 'Ahh,' she gasped and put her hand over them, waiting for it to ease enough for her move. Her heartbeat quickened. The sharpness suffocating her, pulling her back into the room and into the darkness. 'No.' She took short breaths and focussed on the record listening to every subtlety. She traced a finger over the star-like scars on her arm.

When the pain eased, she climbed out the bath using the handrail on the wall for support. The flat had previously been adapted for an older tenant and Helen couldn't have been more grateful. She pulled the plug, the water slowly gurgled and drained away. She tenderly stretched out her shoulders; the bath and muscle soak salts had done little to ease the stiffness. She caught sight of her left shoulder in the bathroom cabinet mirror, it was covered with a yellow and brown bruise.

*Damn*. Her slippers were in the middle of the puddle of water. She slipped a foot inside one, water squelched in between her toes. Yuck. She wiped her foot on the bathmat and carefully slipped on her robe. Her pills were in the living room and she was just about due for a couple more.

The intercom buzzed. *Can't I be left alone?* She had just managed to lift the needle from the record when it sounded again, this time one continuous sound, broken by two short ones. If it was another stupid parcel for the neighbour across the landing, she was going to lose it. She clicked on the television. She couldn't face speaking to anyone.

A few seconds later, there was a forceful knock on the front door. She knew exactly who it was.

'What do you want, Jack? I was in the bath.' She sighed, not opening the door fully.

'I want to talk and I've tried to call you.' He held up a bottle of whisky in front of him.

'It's off the hook and it's late.'

She tightened her dressing gown.

A roll-up dangled on the edge of his lip as he spoke. 'I had stopped for a few drinks with a pal that lives no' far away and I wanted to make sure you were alright.'

'You can see I'm fine.'

He looked at his watch. 'It's not late. It's only gone eight.' He smiled. 'I can stay for a wee while.'

The netting twitched in the glass-panelled door of the opposite flat. Why did she have to pick a flat where none of her neighbours seemed able to mind their own business?

'You better let me in or the neighbours will talk.' Craven half-smiled and slipped the bottle into his pocket. 'I'm no' going anywhere and I heard you had something to celebrate.'

Helen rolled her eyes. 'I just want to be left alone. I'm tired.'

'Ah, c'mon, I've got a good bottle here; I don't want to waste it.'

She let Craven in and he followed her through to the living room of her flat. A tinge of pink coloured her cheeks.

Her slippers clapped off the bare floorboards in the hall and the robe was riding up her thigh. *Steptoe and Son* flickered on the TV in the living room, Harold was shouting, 'You dirty old man.' She switched off the TV.

She hadn't bothered unpacking most of her books and records except for her favourites. Her dinner plate with the remnants of a chicken Kiev was on the floor in front of the sofa and boxes were stacked against the empty shelves. She would need to either unpack soon or take the decision to leave, as it didn't feel like home any more. She pulled her robe tightly around herself. Her hair was damp and stuck in clumps to her cheeks.

The tan leather sofa was covered with the frilly cushions she had been sleeping on. Craven put a couple to the side as he sat down. She didn't like inviting him into her flat. It was her own private world away from work and he was invading it. He brushed a finger along the couple of battered paperbacks that were on the shelf.

'I don't get time to read them.'

He nodded but said nothing.

'I'll go get changed and get us some glasses.'

'Is Ted not here?' he called after her.

She returned a few minutes later wearing a knitted cardigan and jeans, and with two glasses in her hand. Craven looked up when she walked through the door. He was freshly shaven and the top button of his lilac floral-patterned shirt was open.

'Have you been out somewhere?' she asked putting the glasses down on the coffee table. She slipped her bottle of tablets into her pocket.

'No.' Craven poured the drinks then downed his in one. He immediately poured himself another. 'I was meant to see the kids but Liz wouldn't let me.'

'I'm sorry.'

'No, don't be. She gets like this, she'll calm down.'

Helen took a sip of her whisky; she tried to savour it before swallowing but it burned her throat. 'I'm not really much of a drinker.' She rubbed her lips with the back of her hand and sat down on the sofa. The smell of his Old Spice tickled the back of her throat. She took another sip then looked down at the purple bruise that covered her left knuckles, flexing her fingers to ease the pain. Her heart beat faster in her chest, thinking of the question she was dreading to ask, 'Did Stanley mention anything about my father?'

'Aye, he says he had nothing to do with it.'

Helen closed her eyes and tilted her head back. Why would he lie for her? She thought about telling Craven everything but took a sip of her drink instead.

'There's something else I wanted to explain…' He hesitated. 'I first met George Stanley about twenty years ago. We both joined the police at the same time. He was flash, took backhanders, anything to get him a bit of easy cash and it didnae matter who got hurt in the process.'

'Ah,' was all she managed.

'For all my faults, I'm no' like that. I've always done what I thought I needed to do, to get the job done.' He gave her a look – a sideways glance as if expecting her to say something.

*He must know about her dad surely, so why wasn't he saying it?* 'I wish you would have just told me that before.' Helen sighed.

'I know.' He drained the glass and wiped his mouth with the back of his hand. 'Sometimes we don't tell everything, do we? The investigation into the robbery will be re-opened.'

'That's good.'

'There's more. Strathclyde went to talk to Reg Leckie this morning, but he had already died in hospital.'

A short silence followed. She wasn't surprised.

'Cheers.' He held up his empty glass. 'Anyway, we shouldn't be talking about this. I should be congratulating you.'

'I don't know about that.' She poured him another.

'Aye.' he swallowed. 'I saw him propose to you at the hospital,'

'I know.' She held up her ringless left hand and wiggled her fingers. 'I thought you might have noticed something was missing?'

'Is he?' He managed a thin smile.

She shrugged her shoulders. 'I just couldn't go through with it in the end. I didn't know what to do at the hospital when he proposed. My mind was all over the place.'

Craven was nodding.

'He wanted me to leave the police and move in with him... I just couldn't do it. Part of me wanted to though. I work twice as hard as some of them in that office just to be ridiculed but this is something I've wanted to do my whole life. I can't just chuck that away.'

'I thought he was a bit of an idiot. You're better off without him.'

'He went away to Majorca, this morning. I very nearly went with him.' She flicked a glance over to her full holdall. 'I was all packed and everything. I got as far as the airport.' She took another sip. This time it didn't taste that bad. 'It was never going to work. I was never going to be that person he wanted.'

'It's better finding out earlier.' Craven shuffled forward in his seat putting his glass down on the table. 'I took too long to learn that lesson and ended up with nothing.' His knee grazed hers. 'Helen, I wanted you to work in the department. I've always...' He touched her hand.

'Let's just work through the bottle,' Helen said, pulling away. She poured some more into both glasses.

Helen noticed him look down at the sheet of paper on the table. It was a draft of her resignation letter and she'd written out most of it. She snatched it off the table before he could pick it up. 'That's just some rubbish for the bin,' she said, crumpling it into a ball.

'That's good, because I've got another big case.'

\*\*\*

When Craven left. Helen's head felt foggy from the drink. She poured herself a glass of icy tap water, looking out the window as she lifted the glass to her lips. It was dark but it was a clear night outside. A couple of boys in school uniform were kicking a football about on the grass.

They'd all probably be in the pub drinking tonight. She could almost hear them laughing, and taste the smoke in the air. Ted would be at that five-star hotel now. No doubt enjoying himself. He wasn't that bothered when she told him she wasn't going; just more exasperated. Anxiety started to creep inside her and spread its icy fingers over her chest.

She grabbed her jacket off the door and eased her arm into it. She might not be able to run at the moment but at least she could go for a walk. It was colder outside than it looked up in the flat and the pavement was shiny from ice. She gingerly stepped over it.

'I was just coming up to see you.'

Helen looked up and saw McKinley crossing the road towards her. She wrapped her jacket tight and forced a smile. The wind blew some of her hair into her mouth. 'I'm not really in the mood for visitors, Terry.'

'I'm sorry, I just thought you could use the company.' He stuck his hands in his pockets and awkwardly bounced on the spot for warmth.

'That's sweet but…'

He swallowed hard and took a step backwards, pulling out a rolled-up newspaper from his pocket. 'I had thought about the flicks.' He looked down at the ground, his cheeks flushed with pink. 'If you fancy it?'

'What's out?' Helen couldn't even remember the last film she'd seen in the cinema.

He half-smiled and unfolded the paper. '*Close Encounters of the Third Kind,*' he replied.

'I'm just going to go for a walk,' she sighed. 'I need the exercise.'

'Well, I guess I'll see you around. I hope you're back at work soon.' He gave her a small smile and a wave. 'Maybe another time.'

'Sure.'

Helen watched him walk up the street.

'Wait, Terry.' She broke into a jog to catch up with him. 'Do you want to go get some food instead?'

# Fantastic Books
# Great Authors

CROOKED
CAT

Meet our authors and discover our exciting range:

- Gripping Thrillers
- Cosy Mysteries
- Romantic Chick-Lit
- Fascinating Historicals
- Exciting Fantasy
- Young Adult and Children's Adventures

CPSIA information can be obtained
at www.ICGtesting.com
Printed in the USA
LVHW08s2056230718
584662LV00001B/235/P